PE

FORBI

Paula Morris (Ngāti Wai) was born in Auckland. She is the author of three novels: *Queen of Beauty*, *Hibiscus Coast*, and *Trendy But Casual*. She lives in New Orleans.

FORBIDDEN CITIES

PAULA MORRIS

PENGUIN BOOKS

PENGUIN BOOKS

Published by the Penguin Group

Penguin Group (NZ), 67 Apollo Drive, Rosedale,
North Shore 0632, New Zealand (a division of Pearson New Zealand Ltd)
Penguin Group (USA) Inc., 375 Hudson Street,
New York, New York 10014, USA
Penguin Group (Canada), 90 Eglinton Avenue East, Suite 700, Toronto,
Ontario, M4P 2Y3, Canada (a division of Pearson Penguin Canada Inc.)
Penguin Books Ltd, 80 Strand, London, WC2R 0RL, England
Penguin Ireland, 25 St Stephen's Green,
Dublin 2, Ireland (a division of Penguin Books Ltd)
Penguin Group (Australia), 250 Camberwell Road, Camberwell,
Victoria 3124, Australia (a division of Pearson Australia Group Pty Ltd)
Penguin Books India Pvt Ltd, 11, Community Centre,
Panchsheel Park, New Delhi – 110 017, India
Penguin Books (South Africa) (Pty) Ltd, 24 Sturdee Avenue,
Rosebank, Johannesburg 2196, South Africa

Penguin Books Ltd, Registered Offices: 80 Strand, London, WC2R 0RL, England

First published by Penguin Group (NZ), 2008

1 3 5 7 9 10 8 6 4 2

Designed by Mary Egan
Typeset by Pindar New Zealand
Printed in Australia by McPherson's Printing Group

ISBN 978 0 14300 914 6

A catalogue record for this book is available
from the National Library of New Zealand.

www.penguin.co.nz

The assistance of Creative New Zealand towards the production of this book
is gratefully acknowledged by the Publisher.

Contents

Author's note:

Various incarnations of some stories in this collection have appeared in *Barrelhouse* ('Like a Mexican'); *Best New Zealand Fiction* Vol II ('Rangatira'); *Best New Zealand Fiction* Vol IV ('Red Christmas'); *Get on the Waka! Best Recent Contemporary Māori Fiction* ('Rangatira'); Hayden's *Ferry Review* ('Bright'); *Huia Short Stories 4* ('Many Mansions'); *Landfall* ('Mon Desir', 'Rangatira'); *New Zealand Listener* ('Like a Mexican', 'The Argyle'); *Metro* ('The Party'); and *Witness* ('Red Christmas'). Versions of 'Bright' have been broadcast on Radio New Zealand and Iowa Public Radio.

Like a Mexican

You meet him in the bar of the SoHo Grand. It's late summer, early evening. You're there lolling on a low banquette, drinking with your colleagues. He walks in with Rico, and Rico introduces him. When Rico says his name – Carlos – it rumbles out, stately and purring, like an expensive vintage car. When you repeat the name in your too-bright English accent, it sounds tinny and cobbled together, like the brand name of a mystery pharmaceutical.

Your name is Nina. He repeats it, smiling. In Spanish your name means something, you think – a girl, a storm – but your parents didn't know that. They named you for a woman in a novel by Evelyn Waugh. This is too much to explain, especially to someone busy pulling up a chair and ordering a drink.

You've met Rico a few times: he's an A&R scout working in the Mexico City branch, and he often comes up to New

York to play demos for you and your boss, Mitchell, and to talk about the state of things. Tonight he's wearing the usual record company uniform of T-shirt and jeans. Carlos wears a dark suit and tie. He's in his mid-forties, maybe, older than everyone else there. He has olive skin, short dark hair. There's a squareness to his head that makes him look adult, upright. Rico tells him you work in International. Carlos, he says, is an old friend from Mexico City. He's a vice-president at a bank here in New York.

You barely speak to him at all. One of your colleagues has important gossip to tell you, information on lawsuits, cutbacks, falling sales. The business is changing, going bad, and you all need to talk about it night after night. You and everyone you work with are Scheherazade, staving off death with your endless evenings of talk.

Rico and Carlos murmur together in Spanish. They have to leave after one drink because they're meeting some other people for dinner and then going to hear a band. Carlos asks if everyone would like to come along.

'Maybe I'll see you later,' you tell him, but you don't mean it. You've been living in New York for almost two years: you know about keeping your social options open. So you drink three martinis, eat some sticky marinated olives and a few shrimp popovers, and go home in a cab around nine o'clock. This is a typical Monday night for you. This is a typical dinner. You don't think about Carlos again because you don't care about banks or Mexico or Mexican banks. He's not part of your world. The doors of this chattering harem are closed.

• • •

A few weeks pass: it's a late-summer Friday night, and you're out with a larger group of people at El Teddy's. None of you have been there for years, but everyone's saying El Teddy's is going to close soon, so Mitchell insists on going there one last time. You've all just been to hear a singer-songwriter from Cleveland at Arlene's Grocery and then a *mizik raisin* band from Haiti at the Mercury Lounge. The night is warm, and the Mercury Lounge was too stuffy, the floor varnished with spilled beer. At El Teddy's you all drink, and eat chips, and talk in loud voices. The music's loud too, but strangely muffled, so you can't make out the words to any song. The echoing noise and the blue mosaic tiles on the ceiling turn the room into an upside-down swimming pool.

There's hardly anyone else in the place, but the food takes a long time to arrive. Veronica Clark from Corporate Communications sits to your right, stroking her slick blonde hair as though it's a harp. Even though he's on expense-account probation, Mitchell – on your left, his bald head bright with sweat – calls other people on his cell phone and urges them to come along.

'We're going down fighting,' he shouts. 'Me and El Teddy both!'

After his fourth call, he whispers to you that you may need to put some of the drinks, maybe all of the drinks, on your credit card.

A tall, blonde woman who is too old for her black bustier turns up, pushing between your chair and Mitchell's. He stands up so she can kiss him three times. She wants to know everybody's name and job title. A chubby boy in a baseball cap shuffles in behind her. The blonde woman pushes him into Mitchell's empty seat.

'This,' she says, staring down at you with wide, crazy eyes, 'is DJ Jeffy.'

'Hey,' says DJ Jeffy. He has a look on his face – something between blank and smug – that reminds you of the intern who's been wandering your floor all the summer, the one who knows about Napster's rise and fall the way kids used to know about the last days of Kurt Cobain.

'He's a protégé of the Neptunes,' the blonde woman tells the table. DJ Jeffy reaches straight for the chips.

'Is it OK if I just call you Jeff?' you ask him, and he looks puzzled. The blonde woman frowns at you.

'Order DJ Jeffy a margarita,' she instructs, walking off to the bathroom, arm-in-arm with Mitchell. There's no time to tell her you're not Mitchell's assistant. You are an A&R manager. You find artists. You find songwriters. You put the two together. Two years ago, when you transferred from London, you went to clubs to hear live music four nights a week, but now you spend most of your time online – searching, listening, downloading. Your iPod is more important than your cell phone. Mitchell's boss describes your office as a lean, mean machine, and he's right, in a way: the already skimpy department is losing a lot of weight. Nobody is replaced. Nobody is promoted. Mitchell, according to Veronica Clark, may be too expensive to last much longer. She mutters this behind his back. When he leans over her to grab his drink, she strokes Mitchell's sleeve and blows him a pouting kiss.

More people show up. By the time your food arrives, the party has spread to another two tables. Mitchell circles the groups, clapping people's shoulders, taking calls, making introductions. You're squeezed between Veronica Clark and DJ Jeffy, so you have to push back your chair to say hello to Rico, who's just arrived. Carlos stands behind him. He's not wearing a tie tonight.

Rico wanders away to talk to Mitchell, but Carlos crouches next to your chair. You stop eating your soggy burrito.

'Would you like to meet DJ Jeffy?' The blonde woman is shouting at Carlos, who ignores her. She's sitting at the next table, the back of her seat almost touching DJ Jeffy's. When she blows smoke rings, they float like miniature haloes over his head. She has been warned twice already by the waiter about smoking in the restaurant, but she keeps saying she's from Colorado and the rules of a fascist state don't apply, and what's the City going to do anyway? Close the place down? This makes everyone laugh, except the waiter.

'I was hoping you'd be here tonight,' Carlos tells you. He speaks quickly, clearly, almost impatiently. His tie is stuffed into the breast pocket of his jacket; a striped roll of silk bubbles out. 'I was hoping I'd see you again.'

His skin is lighter than Rico's, and his accent is more American, or maybe more European. You've been to Spain; you've seen men like Carlos before. You walked past them each evening in the streets of Seville, where they stood around outside bars with big windows and tiled floors, expensive jackets flung over their arms, laughing and drinking and smoking. They were sturdy and well-fed. They seemed to know the order of things in life, the way things were done. They weren't like English men, who stood outside pubs, pint glasses balanced on window sills, or crammed themselves

11

into aluminium café chairs on a wind-blown pavement, shouting over the roars of passing buses.

'Yes,' you say, because there's a pause, though he hasn't asked you a question.

'I can't stay right now. Would you have lunch with me? Perhaps next week?' When you say nothing he smiles at you. His teeth are small and white. 'It's just lunch, OK?'

'OK,' you say. You wish Veronica Clark wasn't listening to every word of the conversation, observing the exchange of business cards. You wish she couldn't hear where you're meeting – the Café de Lune on East 56th Street – or when.

After Carlos and Rico leave, Veronica Clark pretends to be shocked, the way you pretended to sound reluctant.

'You know, I think he's married,' she tells you.

'Really?' You turn to the left. 'Are you married, DJ Jeffy?'

DJ Jeffy can't speak. His mouth is stuffed full of food.

'I meant the Mexican,' she says, scowling. The waiter tells everyone they have to smoke outside or agree to pay the thousand-dollar fine.

You don't know if Carlos is married or not, and in this moment – faced with chipped mirrored tiles, stubbed-out cigarettes, the sight of Mitchell stroking his flush face over and over again, the coagulating remains of dinner, a bill longer than your forearm – you decide not to care.

On Wednesday you catch a cab to Café de Lune, even though it would be almost as quick to walk. It's a sultry day, and you don't want to arrive looking damp and out of breath. For some reason, you want to impress Carlos. He's a banker who wears a suit to work and eats lunch in the East 50s. Everyone else you know works on the other side of Fifth Avenue. They got into the record business because they wanted to wear jeans to work, hang out in the studio with Daniel Lanois or Dr Dre, and get free tickets to Bob Dylan tributes at the Garden. They complain that Norah Jones has sold too many records and won too many Grammys, and demand that you find the next Norah Jones, the next Coldplay, the next OutKast. They spend all day talking about units and scans and shipping and adds and hits and ringtones. Compared with them, Carlos is an international man of mystery.

Normally you wear Capri pants and a tank top to work, but today you've chosen a shiny, low-cut blouse, a pencil skirt, and mules. Everyone's been asking all morning if you have a job interview at another company. You think you're dressed up, but you're the only person in the restaurant, male or female, not wearing a suit.

Carlos sits waiting for you at a table near the back, thrumming the rim of his glass. He's more attractive than you remember. As soon as you sit down, he's waving over the waiter, ordering you a glass of wine, the sea bass. The last guy who took you out for a meal worked in production at another label: he explained to you that O-cards added six cents cost per CD. Carlos doesn't talk about his job. He wants to know about you.

'You're English and you're beautiful, that's all I know,' he says. 'Tell me everything.'

Your face flushes, because you're drinking red wine and talking about yourself at lunchtime. After a while you're not even talking about work: you're telling Carlos about Stroud, the town where you grew up, and Cheltenham, where you

13

went to school, and Durham, where you went to university. When he repeats the place names, they sound elegant and mysterious. Ladbroke Grove, your neighbourhood in London, is suddenly a wooded glen: you see trees and a meadow, a fountain. You hear pan pipes.

Carlos is from Mexico City, and the bank he works for is a Mexican bank. He was transferred here a few months ago. He's known Rico all his life.

'You don't look like a Mexican,' you tell him. 'Not that I really know what Mexicans look like, apart from Rico. And Benicio Del Toro, I guess.'

'He's from Puerto Rico.' Carlos smiles at you. 'And I'm not really a Mexican, you know. Both my parents were born in Spain. So I'm Euro-trash, really. I hope you don't mind.'

You don't mind. There's a second glass of wine, and crème caramel, which Carlos calls *flan*. He's not square and stocky at all, you realise. He's a cartoon of a man, thick and muscular. For the first time you understand words like 'virile' and 'rugged'.

Something has to be wrong with him. Men like this don't exist in New York, or if they do, they live on the East Side and work in the Financial District and you never get to meet them. Sometimes you glimpse them hurrying out of Brooks Brothers, but they're never in the places you think they might be, like eating oysters at Grand Central, or at the theatre, where at least you could sit next to them. They're hidden away out of reach, in member-only lounges at airports, in town cars, in first class.

'You're married,' you say.

'Yes.' He doesn't seem surprised that you know.

'What does your wife think about you asking other women out to lunch?' You hope you look stern and unimpressed.

'Look,' he says, brushing one hand over yours, as though he's sweeping away crumbs. 'My wife and I are separating. She's already back in Mexico.'

'I'm sorry.'

'Everyone is sorry. It's a bad situation.' He swirls the dark puddle of wine in his glass.

'I'm sure it's complicated,' you blurt, because you've been talking too much today and can't stop. 'You don't have to talk about it.'

'It's not complicated, really,' he says. 'She wants to have a child, and I don't. But you're right – we don't have to talk about it today. Please don't think I'm always asking women out to lunch. It's just – when I met you, I couldn't think about anything else. I kept asking Rico about you and wanting to see you again.'

You have nothing to say to this. All you can do – and this is another word you understand for the first time – is simper.

You leave the restaurant and he offers to walk west with you, although you know his office is in the opposite direction. Near a side door of the Plaza Hotel, he grabs your hand and hauls you up the steps.

'Come here,' he says. He pins you against the wall and kisses you hard on the mouth. Around the mouth, in the mouth – a hungry, invasive kiss. One minute you're both walking along the street, not touching; the next you're suctioned to each other in a doorway. The kiss overwhelms you, but you don't shrink from it. Instead you lean into Carlos, arching your body up into his, trying to forget things

15

like doorway and public place and married man.

When the kiss – this rude, flagrant kiss – ends, you're still in the doorway, clutching each others' elbows. People walk along the street not looking at you, as though nothing's happened. Carlos grins and says goodbye, and you teeter down the stairs, leaving him there, not looking back.

Alone in your office, you're giddy and hot. You shut the door and sit in the low armchair in the corner, trying to steady your breathing. Your skin prickles. A headache's beginning, and a stomach-ache as well. Your legs tingle; your heart seems to be beating in your pelvis.

Mitchell barges in without knocking. He's wearing a Hawaiian shirt and waving a stubby cigar around, even though this is a non-smoking building. He wants to know if you were over at Sony. Veronica Clark saw you walking in that direction.

Veronica Clark is jumping to conclusions, you tell him: you had an appointment at the gynaecologist's on Central Park South. There's no reason why you can't tell Mitchell about your lunch, but this is the first thing that enters your head. All you can think about right now are your sexual organs.

Several days and many telephone calls later, you meet Carlos for dinner at Gotham. He's waiting in the bar, and you sit on high stools pulled close together, facing each other. Other people are close by as well, but Carlos does not seem to notice them. He strokes your arm and the back of your neck. He tells you how desperate he is to see you. He says he thinks about you all the time.

After two drinks, you're making out. Perhaps other people

are looking: you don't know. You can't see anybody but Carlos. You pause to sip your drinks, and the waiter bobs up; perhaps he's been waiting a while to tell you your table is ready. You look at Carlos and Carlos asks if you can eat at the bar.

You're wearing a wrap-around dress that falls open a little when you sit down. You bought it at lunchtime in Saks. Usually when you buy new clothes you model them back in the office for the assistants, but Jennie left last Friday and this is JJ's last week: she spends all day at her desk, scowling and working on her résumé.

Carlos draws his fingers up and down your inner thigh.

'The first night I met you, I could see your underwear every time you crossed your legs,' he tells you. 'It was driving me crazy. I remember, there were these little flowers over your panties. Grey flowers, maybe, or purple.'

'I don't have any floral underwear,' you say, but he doesn't believe you. 'All my underwear is either black or white.'

'I remember it exactly,' he says, frowning. 'Little flowers. Or maybe they were numbers?'

'You must be thinking of someone else.' You gulp down the dregs of a vodka martini, the twisting sliver of lemon tickling your lips.

'There's no one else,' says Carlos. He sounds hurt. 'There's only you.'

His face splits into a smile, and you slump towards him, your tongue mashing into his. He tastes like salt and cigarettes, and tonight this is the most delicious taste in the world. You want to lick his tongue dry. You want to eat the mouth off his face.

At the end of the evening, you can't go to his place because, he tells you, his wife is there. She's back from Mexico to collect her things. And he can't go back to your place, because his wife will get hysterical if he stays out all night. She won't accept that the marriage is over. She wants Carlos to move back to Mexico City with her and have a family. Her name is Valeria.

'So you're not really separated,' you say, slurry with drink. You're both standing on the sidewalk, ignoring the lurking cabs. Reflected in the restaurant window, your face is pale, the lipstick sanded off your mouth.

'It's complicated,' he says, and you want to point out that this is exactly the opposite of what he said in the Café de Lune. You want to stalk away from him without any goodbye embraces. You want to ignore his calls from now on. But instead you let him kiss you again, let him help you into a cab. At home you go to sleep thinking of the way his accent adds extra syllables to the word 'complicated.' Although you're annoyed with Carlos, thinking of the sound of his voice makes you smile.

You can't ignore his calls. You meet up with him every few days. You travel all over the city to find bars – Dip, Milk & Honey, Flute – where you won't bump into your colleagues or his. After three weeks, you've been out together eight times. You've had sex at your apartment and – just once – standing up in Mitchell's kitchen; he's away in Paris, and he'd given you the key so you could feed his cat. Carlos can't spend the whole night with you because Valeria is still here. She wants him to visit a therapist – a marriage counsellor – on East

57th Street; you're not sure why he tells you the address. She wants him to talk to someone.

He says he has no intention of going. Carlos doesn't need someone to talk to. He talks to you. Every time you're out together, neither of you can shut up. You dissect every conversation you've ever had, what you were feeling on a particular day, exactly what you were thinking at the SoHo Grand, at El Teddy's, at Café de Lune. You have so much to tell each other. You agree on so much. You both like the Marx Brothers and anchovies. You both dislike Pernod and the Dutch. You discuss movies and books, and tell each other childhood stories: yours involve damp picnics, sandcastles on North Devon beaches, the ferry to Boulogne; his are about ski trips to Colorado and a ranch in the country. He describes Mexico City and says he wants to take you there. He's already been to London, but the pieces of your life there – the Market Bar, the Hammersmith Apollo, the Number 52 bus – are new to him.

You sit close together, knees touching, and announce things: I miss you, I need you, I love you. Somehow you've skipped the tentative stage of a relationship, when no one wants to give too much away. Too much is what you and Carlos are all about: you both say too much, feel too much. He's not like the American guys you've been out with, who always seem to be looking out for what they can get, what they can get away with. And he's not like an English guy, either, pasty and diffident. It feels as though you've invented him, as though you've invented each other. It feels as though you've never been in love before.

It feels as though you're having an affair, but neither of

you will call it that. Carlos is separating; he tells you this over and over. He hasn't separated yet: he is separating. And the larger part of him is already yours.

Although he doesn't want to, Carlos agrees to talk to the therapist. He and his wife go together but, at the end of the session, the therapist says she wants to see Carlos alone.

'She asked me to stay behind for a minute,' he says. He's calling you from his office, as usual. He calls at least three times a day. 'She asked me if I was having an affair.'

'What did you say?'

'I told her I was in love with an English woman, and she said she could tell.'

'She could tell I was English?'

'She could tell I was in love with another woman.'

He says he's decided to keep going to marriage counselling, even though he thinks it's a waste of time. He's not in love with his wife anymore, but he thinks that he owes her this much. He owes his family, too. When he married Valeria, the wedding was huge. Everyone rich and important in Mexico City was invited. Eight hundred people, six different bands. They even had fireworks. His wife is the one with the money, he tells you. He doesn't usually talk about money, though you know he didn't grow up poor. His parents have maids and a cook, who still call him Master Carlitos; there's the ranch in the country. Everyone in Mexico has a maid, he insists, but his family seem to have a lot of them.

'The wedding was a big deal,' he says. 'It's going to be an even bigger deal if we get divorced. Everyone will be angry with me again.'

You want to ask him what 'if' means, what 'again' means, but Mitchell fills your doorway, screaming something about getting your ass to the conference room. International has made a video for an act you're taking to the big conference in London; it's important you sell them around the world. Mitchell hates the video. It looks cheap. The main dancer is too fat. This is what happens when nobody will spend any money, he screeches; you get fat dancers and a no-name director.

'I wanted Sophie Muller,' he complains. 'Who do we get? Kenny Ortega's nephew. The dancer's probably his niece. She's probably his slut illegitimate daughter!'

'Can't they stretch her?' you ask.

'If we stretched her from here to Acapulco, she'd still look fat.' Mitchell's face is so red it looks sunburned. 'I don't want all of Kenny Ortega's fat fucking Mexican relations in the video!'

'I think Kenny Ortega's from Palo Alto,' you say, and tell Carlos you'll call him back later.

When you do, that afternoon, he's been speaking to Rico. He's sworn Rico to secrecy and told him about your relationship. Rico disapproves.

One evening, after you and Carlos make love at your apartment, Carlos finishes getting dressed in the bathroom. He needs to look in the mirror to make sure his tie is straight. He's supposed to be at a business dinner.

'Remember when we had lunch together that first time?' he calls. You're still lying in bed, the sheet taut around your waist. 'I was so excited to see you again.'

'So was I,' you tell him. You've had this conversation

before. 'Though I didn't really know what to expect. Not that kiss in the street, anyway.'

'You looked so beautiful,' he says. 'Though I was disappointed when you walked in. I thought you would have dressed up more. I thought it meant you weren't interested in me.'

'What are you talking about? I was dressed up!'

'I thought you would have worn something really special.' He sounds petulant, as though you betrayed him, somehow, with your choice of outfit.

'I don't live in your world, you know,' you tell him. This is as annoying as the underpants conversation. Obviously your clothes are a language he misreads, can't translate. 'I don't work in bloody international finance. I can wear shorts and a bikini top to the office if I feel like it.'

Carlos blows you a kiss from the bathroom door.

When he's gone, you run a hot bath and lie there with your eyes shut until the water turns tepid. Carlos exhausts you. You've never had such ferocious, athletic sex before. Each time you see each other, it's a round in a boxing match: brief and intense. Your tongue is tired. Your stomach muscles hurt. Everything – eyes, teeth, fingernails – feels gritty, except the pulverised stickiness between your legs.

Every week, Carlos and his wife go to see the therapist. You thought that Valeria was back in the city just to pack her things: she must have a lot of things. Carlos still talks about separating, and perhaps, in his head, he and Valeria have separated. But most of the time – when he's not with you – his body is still married and living on 71st Street.

• • •

You discover that Carlos's apartment is not only on 71st Street: it's just off Fifth Avenue. The only person you know who lives that close to the park is Mitchell, and he lives on the West Side.

He calls you with good news: his wife is going back to Mexico City on Thursday, and he wants you to come over and see his place. There's bad news as well. She's only going away for the weekend, and he's going too, on Friday. They have family to see, talks to conduct. Nothing good can come of this trip, you decide. In your imagination, the eight hundred wedding guests are lined up outside his parents' stucco mansion, waiting to knock some sense into Carlos's head. They gave gifts; they saw fireworks; they are Catholic. Like Rico, they will disapprove of a relationship with another woman. They will not hear of a separation.

The building on 71st Street looks as though it used to be some kind of grand residence or embassy. The floor in the lobby is marble; the curving staircase is ostentatiously wide. Carlos's apartment isn't especially big or especially light, but there's a subdued elegance to it. Everything's muted: books, paintings, furniture. The only strong colour is the green of the park, visible through the bay window in the living room.

After you and Carlos make love – which you do almost immediately, because you can't waste a second of this night sitting on the sofa or chatting in the kitchen – you lie twisted together in bed, singing snatches of old standards. Carlos seems excited that you know so many old songs. When he sings 'If I Loved You', you tell him he looks like Gordon MacRae. He's very pleased by this, smacking little-boy kisses all over your face.

He's not looking forward to going to Mexico City in the morning. The trip is Valeria's idea.

'She says she hates it here,' he says. 'She says we were happier at home.'

He worries about tell-tale stains on the pale green bed linen, but when you suggest he change the sheets, he shakes his head.

'That would make her suspicious,' he says. 'She would see the sheets in the laundry hamper and ask questions.'

'Why don't you just wash the sheets yourself?'

'I would never wash sheets. It would never enter my head that sheets need washing. She knows that. The housekeeper comes once a week – *she* washes the sheets.'

'Well, what day does the housekeeper come?'

Carlos has no idea.

You step into the small bathroom off the bedroom and close the door. The room looks bare, as though it's been stripped of all its soaps and bottles and lotions. But drooped over the towel rail is a silky, mushroom-coloured bra. Valeria's bra.

Smaller and flimsier than anything you would wear, it's as transfixing as a giant billboard on the side of a highway. *I still live here,* it shrieks. *This is my home.* Whether she intended to or not, Valeria has marked her territory. When you draw one finger down the skinny strap, you see her as a real person for the first time. She's small, you decide, as delicate and wispy as her mushroom-coloured bra. She's dark-haired and petite, gentle in her gestures. She has slender, expressive hands.

Maybe she looks slightly nervous or worried, which wouldn't be surprising: her husband has persuaded her to move to New York, and she doesn't like it here. He won't agree to have children; he tells her he wants to separate. She begs him to go to a marriage counsellor and even though he agrees, he's reluctant. Four years after their huge, expensive wedding, he thinks that trying to save their marriage is a waste of time.

She doesn't even know the worst of it: that there's another woman in their home, having sex with her husband. A stranger standing naked in her bathroom, stroking her silky, mushroom-coloured bra.

You tell Carlos that you don't want to stay the night, that you have a big meeting first thing tomorrow. He doesn't seem to mind; he has to get up at five to catch his flight to Mexico City. You both need some sleep. You've worn each other out.

Mitchell announces that he's tired of being out of the office all the time, because he's getting nervous about the way all the haters conspire against him every time he's out of town. It's not his fault that business is bad; it's the fault of the business, he says, and the businessmen who run it have to work out a way to fix this mess. He's a just a records guy from way back, he says. He used to be the hottest DJ in the city. This is true: everyone in the London office used to talk about him as though he was some kind of god. But even a minor deity can't make people go into record stores, or stop them from downloading things for free.

You have to pick up some of the slack, he tells you. This means you have to go to Vancouver and Los Angeles. Mitchell only gets tired of travelling when it doesn't involve Europe or Bangkok.

In Los Angeles, at the House of Blues, you meet up with Rico. You're both there to hear a Mexican ska band, and afterwards you go backstage together to tell the band they were great. The band members are sweaty teenage boys, slouching in armchairs. They struggle up to shake your hand. They can tell by the way their manager is behaving – jumpy, almost panting – that they need to make a good impression.

Rico comes back to your hotel and the two of you sit outside by the pool. Los Angeles is all around you, sparkling and stretching. In New York it's beginning to feel like fall, but here it's still warm, the way it was the night at El Teddy's.

You both order vodka martinis. Rico shows you pictures of his two children. You tell him you're in love with Carlos.

'No,' he groans. 'No, no, no. It's just an affair.'

'A love affair.' You want this to sound better, and it *would* sound better, you know, if Carlos were here, and it was some other era. The 1950s, perhaps.

'You have to stop.'

'I agree.' You don't know why you're saying this. Perhaps you want it to be true; perhaps you just want Rico to like you again. 'I think we should stop seeing each other for a while. We can start again – you know, when he and his wife separate.'

'If,' says Rico. He lights a cigarette and flicks the match on-to the ground. 'Look, forget Carlos. He's no good for you.'

'You don't really believe that.' You roll your eyes. 'He's your friend.'

'That's right. I know him better than anyone, so you should listen to me. He's a fool.'

'And I'm a fool, too. I miss him terribly.'

'Don't miss him,' he says. 'Forget him. He's a fool and he's a Mexican.'

'What's wrong with being a Mexican? You're a Mexican.'

'Listen to me.' Rico shakes his head. 'You know what Mexicans are like? Mexicans work in McDonald's.'

You choke back a laugh and inhale a mouthful of vodka.

'I'm serious. Every time you think you miss Carlos, remember that. He's a Mexican. Mexicans work at McDonald's. Mexicans bus tables at restaurants. Mexicans clean hotel rooms. Mexicans sell oranges on the street. Keep away from them.'

'You're ridiculous.'

'Listen to what I'm telling you. You don't want to fall in love with a Mexican.'

'Why not?'

'You're not from here. You don't understand. He's not for you.'

'Whatever you say.' Rico is right: you don't understand. But you both clink glasses, drinking to not falling in love with Mexicans. It's too late, of course. You have fallen in love with a Mexican. The weekend Carlos spent in Mexico City, you were miserable. The day you flew to Los Angeles, you had your first argument with him, over the phone. You told him you were tired of all the sneaking around. You said you were tired of waking up in bed alone. He told you he loved you, and then you were both quiet for a long time.

The day after you return from LA, you get sick. You feel too miserable to leave the house. Carlos is desperate to see you, he says, so after work he comes down to Chelsea, to your apartment.

You answer the door wearing your robe, a flaking tissue pressed to your nose. Carlos is standing in the hallway looking boyish and concerned, clutching a towering bunch of red and pink roses.

Everything's overwhelming: the flowers, the sight of him, the aching in your joints. You leave the roses to soak in the kitchen sink and go back to bed. He strips off, climbs into bed alongside you. Propped against the ridged board of his body, you're not too weak for sex. The two of you stick together with sweat and saliva.

You don't talk about your conversation with Rico in Los Angeles. Carlos is as ardent and desperate as ever. He tells you how much he loves you, right before he glances at the clock on the nightstand and says he has to go. Valeria has invited people over to dinner, and he's going to be late.

His visit lasts barely over an hour.

The roses are beautiful. Their stems are two feet long. Nobody's ever given you this many roses before, not even Mitchell. He sent you two dozen after you procured a prostitute for Big Daddy V at the conference in Rome. Really, it was the concierge who got the prostitute, but you deserved the roses: Big Daddy V kept following you around for the rest of the conference, wanting you to find out if he could get AIDS from a blow job.

When Carlos's roses begin to wither, you pluck off a few handfuls of petals and save them in a glass dish. You don't like pot pourri, but you're reluctant to let these roses go.

• • •

Carlos asks to meet you at the Oak Bar for a drink after work. You both have other places to go tonight, so you're drinking quickly, hurrying through the vodka and the conversation.

He says you have to stop seeing each other for a while. Rico and his therapist are badgering him. He has to give his marriage another chance. He has to make an effort.

'I really have to,' he says, moving coasters around the table with one finger. 'I don't want to, but I have to try.'

You nod, as though you were expecting this. You don't allow your face to crumple. You don't throw your drink in his face. In truth, you are not surprised. The separation was taking too long. It needed to be quick and brutal, like hot wax stripping away hair. Maybe you should have refused to sleep with him, the way Anne Boleyn strung along Henry VIII. But how could you say no? Not after that kiss in the Plaza doorway, the one that melted your brain away to nothing. Now you're back at the Plaza – on the inside now, in a bar where no kissing will take place.

Carlos has a story to tell you. Ten years ago he was seeing a girl called Julieta. They'd been going out together for years. Her family knew his family, and everyone thought they'd get married. But Julieta was killed in a car accident. He didn't hear the news for almost two days, because nobody could find him. He was away, on the Pacific coast, with another woman.

'Everyone found out about it. Everyone knew,' he says. 'They were all angry with me. They were trying to arrange the funeral, but they couldn't find me. I didn't have a cell phone, and I hadn't told anyone where we were going. My maid let Rico into my apartment, and he found some notes

I'd made about places in Puerto Vallarta. He managed to track me down and tell me what had happened.'

Valeria, he explains, was Julieta's best friend.

'She was more angry than anyone else,' he says. 'She didn't want to forgive me. But eventually, we became friends again. And then we became more than friends. I think she felt sorry for me, in a way. Nobody could forget this bad thing I'd done. Nobody would forgive me.'

'And that's why you got married?'

'People expected it. Our families, I mean. And I was getting older; it was time. We were good together, good friends. I thought I'd grown out of all this. Being in love. Passion. Romance.' The word 'romance' rolls out, sweet and unironic. He gives you a rueful smile.

'Is that what it means to grow up? Giving up passion and romance?'

'I don't know.' He peers into his glass, tilting the dregs from left to right. 'I thought I'd settled down. Become a man, not Master Carlitos any more. But instead I feel guilty about Julieta and guilty about Valeria and guilty about you . . .'

'Don't feel guilty about me.' You're number three now, you realise, in the line of wounded women. The first one died, the second one was betrayed by her husband. You can't compete with them. You're in bronze-medal position, a distant third – tied, perhaps, with the girl on his dirty weekend in Puerto Vallarta.

'I feel guilty all the time. There's something wrong with me – I'm not happy being married, and I'm not happy being in love. She's not happy, I'm not happy, you're not happy.'

'You've made me happy,' you tell him; your voice is shrill

with sadness, disappointment. He leans forwards and grips your hands between his.

'Tell me you'll wait,' he says. 'I want to have children with you. Tell me you won't have children with anyone else. Promise me.'

It's a ridiculous thing to promise, but he won't let you leave until you do. You're both crying when you make the promise. In the street, you kiss him, climb into a cab; you're already late for the showcase at CBGB tonight, and then you have to make it to Don Hill's by nine. As the cab jerks away, you twist your head to stare through the streaky back window at Carlos. He's standing there, watching you go, his eyes as dark as the evening. Even when you can't see him or the Plaza anymore, you're still looking, trying to fix the moment in your mind.

Several times over the next week, late at night, you call Carlos's office number just to hear the sound of his voice. You cry and mope. You sniff the pot pourri. You even write a bad poem, one with lines like 'streets littered with oblivious kisses' and 'a summer scored with goodbyes', and tuck it into *The Rough Guide to Mexico*: this you buy to torment yourself, and because you want to see Puerto Vallarta on a map. A month later, Veronica Clark tells you she's going to Tulum over Thanksgiving and you present her with the book – the poem removed, shredded, and flushed down the toilet.

The fall and winter trudge by. Your life returns to normal: emails and meetings, drinking, picking up the dry-cleaning. Carlos doesn't get in touch and you stop calling his voicemail at night. You try to avoid anything to do with Mexico, but

Mexico is everywhere. Travel ads in magazines, *Once Upon a Time in Mexico* at the video store. A new Mexican restaurant in the East Village. An article in the *Times Magazine* about sex trafficking across the border. Bottles of tequila and Mexican flags everywhere you look. Mexicans working in McDonald's, Mexicans busing tables at restaurants.

Early in the new year, work changes. Rico argues with his boss and leaves the company. Mitchell gets fired. For months, you discover, he's been carrying on an S&M relationship at the office – that is, in his office and on the conference room table – with his boss's executive assistant. This isn't why he's fired: it's because she complained to HR that he was harassing her, refusing to accept the end of their relationship. Mitchell tells you it's because he earns way too much. He says you have to get out of the business while you're still young enough to change careers. He's going to sell his apartment and move to Berlin and do something that involves art and smoking.

You decide to take his advice and go back to London, where you can work for a friend who's a concert promoter. You're tired of the record business and you're tired of New York. In London, there are almost no Mexicans. All the low-paid restaurant workers are European teenagers who need money for nightclubbing and drugs.

The Friday night before you leave the States, you're up late packing the last few boxes. You're still padding around the apartment, brushing your teeth and looking for a magazine to read in bed, when the telephone rings. It's Carlos.

He says your name, and he sounds breathless, a little upset. You pull the toothbrush from your mouth.

'I just wanted to know that you're all right,' he says.

'I'm all right.' A rope of anxiety coils in your belly. You feel sick, excited.

'I just wanted to know.'

'I'm moving back to London.' You speak quickly, sensing that he's about to hang up. 'Next week.'

'Good, good.'

'And you're all right?' You want him to keep talking. You want to hear his voice. You want to hear his breathing, heavy and steady, at the other end of the line. He sounds like he's been drinking.

'Me? Yes. You're moving back to London, we're moving back to Mexico City.'

'Oh.' A glob of toothpaste drips from your mouth, and you rub it into the rug with your toe. You're leaving the rug here. You may roll it up and leave it on the street corner for someone to take. When you carried out a box of coat hangers and the broken DVD player, they'd disappeared by the morning.

'So, you're all right,' he says. 'Every day I want to speak to you. So many times I've wanted to pick up the phone, just to hear your voice and know you're OK.'

'I call you all the time,' you confess, but there's a click at the other end of the line. The conversation is over.

In the bathroom, you sit on the edge of the tub, feeling dizzy. You could call him back and tell him you still want to have his children, still want to wait.

But you don't call him back, because he's married to someone else. You're moving back to London, the place you belong, and he's moving back to Mexico City, the place he belongs, the place where he was married in front of hundreds of people, hundreds of witnesses, hundreds of affluent, well-dressed, well-spoken Mexicans. Carlos did something bad, but everyone forgave him and he married his dead girlfriend's best friend. There were six different bands. There were fireworks. Maybe there was a stucco mansion; you're not sure. He never described his family's house. That part you made up.

The day you leave New York, you tip the dusty rose-petal pot-pourri into the trash. In London, at Smythson's on Bond Street, you buy a new address book and decide not to copy Carlos's telephone number into it.

Your life changes. You work at the concert promoter's office, then take a new media job at the BBC. London is expensive, so you move to Shepherd's Bush, drink fewer cocktails, buy an Oyster card. You don't work so late in the office anymore, or eat bar snacks for dinner. People invite you over for supper. Your friends have names like Emma and Kate, not DJ Jeffy. You only go out with single men.

Late in the summer you meet a man named James at a barbecue. He's a tall, good-looking barrister, and all your female friends are envious. He takes you out to dinner and to the theatre; you go away for weekends to Brighton. After six months, you're a real couple, hosting dinner parties together at your flat, watching films together on the big-screen TV at his place. Going out gives way to staying in. You have sex the way some people eat dessert: occasionally and furtively, as a special treat. You hardly think of Carlos at all. One day you realise you can't remember his last name.

After a year, James suggests moving in together. He says it will save time and money. You'll merge your books and

DVDs and measuring jugs and appliances. At some hazy point in the future, he hints, you may get married, perhaps in a marquee on your aunt's lawn. She lives in Somerset; he's seen the lawn. It's broad and picturesque, sloping down to the river's edge. Very Merchant Ivory, he said at the time.

You can see this wedding: the trays of burnished-gold Pimms, the hazy summer evening, the pyramid of profiteroles. Girls dangling their slingbacks in one hand, paddling in the river. Your strapless dress, the bag packed for a honeymoon in Croatia, Turkey, Marrakesh. There won't be fireworks, of course: this is an English wedding, and it'll be light until late in the evening, anyway. No fireworks, no Mexicans.

So you say no. You're very fond of James, but you don't want to live with him or marry him or merge with him in any way. You don't want a big wedding to feel guilty about when you sit there in marriage counselling four years later, in love with someone else.

When you tell him this – or some of this, at least – he looks both sad and relieved. There isn't a scene of any sort, because James isn't one for scenes. James is English. He takes things on the chin. He cares deeply about some things, but women are not high on that list. He doesn't have to care, anyway: London is full of women like you – a thirty-something living in a one-bedroom flat who buys tea towels from the Tate Modern and lamps at the Conran Shop sale. The New York thing made you different, but you hardly talk about the New York thing anymore. You don't tell people about flying to Los Angeles, or going to the Grammy's, or getting Big Daddy V a blow job in Rome. It sounds like boasting. It sounds like a lie.

The evening you and James break up, he kisses you on the cheek and wishes you all the best. He says he'll be back at some point for his things. You can't even think of what those things are, apart from a spare toothbrush that needs to be thrown out, and a half-drunk bottle of gin. It takes him several goes to manoeuvre out of his parking space. You stand in the doorway of your flat, wondering if you should wave or not. You decide not to wave. He appears not to notice.

On a drizzly day, two years after you move back to London, you're in the back of a taxi driving along the Hammersmith flyover.

The last time you saw Carlos, you were saying goodbye in the street. You think you remember a tree twisted with fairy lights, but you can't be sure about this detail anymore. You remember clinging to him. When he kissed you, the sensation of his mouth on yours, his face so close, made you feel intensely happy and desperate at the same time. Your last kiss was soft and slow. You'd had three months of afternoons and evenings, love and talk, and this was where it ended – in the street, Carlos standing on the sidewalk and watching your taxi drive away.

The sky that evening was the deepest blue and empty, unfurling like a long ribbon above your heads. When you gazed back at him through the grubby back window of the cab, he was standing, still and rumpled, on the curb. Your faces were turned towards the place you last stood together.

Now you're just looking out the window at nothing in particular, watching the rain dribble down the glass. Traffic is heavy, and the taxi crawls. You're passing a huge billboard advertising tequila. A grinning man wears a sombrero and holds a giant bottle, its label painted the colours of the Mexican flag. A bubble as big as a swimming pool reads: 'The real taste of Mexico.'

The brown-skinned man on the billboard looks happy. He's probably just been to a big wedding, and heard a lot of music, and seen a lot of fireworks. Perhaps he knows that some day a reckless, love-drunk foreigner will sit with him in a bar and promise to bear his children.

Thinking of the sound of his voice still makes you happy, even though you haven't heard it for years, and may never hear it again. You hope that wherever he is, whatever he's doing, he's happy as well. So you smile up at him and blow him a kiss. Rico was right. He looks like he works in McDonald's. He looks like he sells oranges on the street.

Bright

The dog is from Puerto Rico, the girl tells Mrs Gunderson, and Mrs Gunderson asks how did the dog come to be in New York City, because surely that's illegal? Puerto Rico is part of America, the girl says, stroking the wriggling dirty white dog. The dog looks two ways at once, swinging its pointed head from side to side. Mrs Gunderson hears the dog's jawbone crack against the girl's brown elbow. She wants to be free, says the girl. Smiling, she lets the dog drop to the tiled kitchen floor. Mrs Gunderson flinches at the sound of the dog's sharp nails on the smooth terracotta. Our dog's dead now, says Mrs Gunderson. I'm sure Billy told you all about him, old Crocket; he was a beautiful golden Labrador; he liked to sleep in the sun.

The girl laughs, and her mouth drops wide open. Inside it is pink and wet. Mrs Gunderson can see it all, raw and unfinished, like uncooked meat. This one's not much for sleeping, the girl tells her. That's why we call her Bright. She's got those bright, wide-awake eyes. But it's your dog, isn't it, says Mrs Gunderson, frowning.

The dog jumps up against Mrs Gunderson's leg again and again and then scrambles across the room, slamming into the taut screen of the door. White hairs drift like dust through the air. It's not Billy's dog, is it? asks Mrs Gunderson. It's really your dog, isn't it? Someone gave her to me in New Jersey, the girl says, if that makes her mine. Mrs Gunderson is nodding yes, yes, yes, she thought so, bending over to wipe the paw prints from the floor with a dish cloth. I'll clean that up later, says Billy, walking in through the screen door. Shall I put our bags in the guest room or are we sleeping upstairs?

Mr Gunderson arrives back from the big Kmart off the highway with a tether, a long, thick chain attached to a shiny green metal contraption that winds it in and out, just like the one for the hose. He stakes it under the tree and waits for Billy to catch the dog. It was worrying the ponies, last time, he says. Look, it can still run around. I've put the stake under the tree, for the shade. Last time it got into the neighbour's garage and there were complaints. It's not cruelty, you know. The dog can still run the length of the garden. Can still reach its water. And this way it can't get in the house. Everyone's happy.

Billy carries the dog over, holding her at arm's length. Her underbelly is green with shit from the donkey pasture down the road. She's just not used to the country, Billy says. No wonder she gets excited. This is like paradise for her. She's locked up in a small apartment every day in the city. Well, that's no life for a dog, says Mr Gunderson. You'll have to wash it before you go home. Make the car stink. Lucky the donkeys didn't kick it to death. Small dog's no match for a donkey. Tell your girlfriend this is for its own good. It's not a punishment.

I know that, says Billy, it just looks like one. The dog whimpers and strains at the collar. It's only for a while, Bright, Billy tells her. We're just over here. This is for its own good, says Mr Gunderson. Billy stands up, rubbing khaki-coloured shit stains down the legs of his shorts. Jesus Dad, he says, you don't have to keep saying that. It just makes everything worse.

I keep forgetting how to say her name, Mrs Gunderson calls from the flower bed where she's bent double, pruning, hacking out a weed. For the hundredth time it's Eugenie, Billy says in a loud voice. Don't worry, she can't hear. She's inside having a nap. Lovely day like this, Mrs Gunderson says, maybe the last time this summer. Billy lies back on the lawn and pretends he can't hear the dog yelping at him from the other end of the garden. You know, Billy, says Mrs Gunderson, we've offered to pay. Pay for what, he asks, feeling guilty about the tone of his voice and the sound the dog makes and for saying they would come that weekend after how terrible it was last month and the month before. For obedience training, says Mrs Gunderson, rising from the sunflowers red-cheeked, her pruning shears ajar. They say there's no such thing as a bad dog, just a bad owner.

It's not up to me, says Billy, his eyes shut tight. And anyway, Eugenie took her to obedience training once. I don't know

41

why she didn't want to go back. I can't make her. I know, I know, Mrs Gunderson says, it's not your dog. But it's not fair on anyone and I can't look Mrs Graves in the eye anymore because of that business with the hamster last time. What do you want me to do, Mother, asks Billy. His eyes are shut and Mrs Gunderson hears herself saying something and she can't believe she's saying it but there it is, coming out of her mouth, and suddenly it's said and there's no going back: I just think, sometimes, that it would be better for everybody if the dog was put down, or if something just happened to it.

Billy sits up and looks at her. You want me to kill the dog? Mrs Gunderson swats a fly away and says nothing. Billy stands up and brings his face close to hers. Some of his spittle flies into her mouth. She is frightened by the look on his face. He is shouting at her in a whisper. That dog is the only thing she has in the world. She's never had a real home or a big car or a swimming pool or all these acres of land. She loves that dog more than anything. I don't know what your problem is. You're just prejudiced against it for no reason. Billy stomps off towards the house and slams the screen door shut behind him. That's not right, says Mrs Gunderson in a voice too soft for him to hear. I'm not prejudiced against anybody.

The girl sits under the tree on a bed of fallen leaves, petting the dog and watching Mr Gunderson pacing the lawn. This is where we're putting the tent, he tells her. The one for Billy's sister's wedding. We're expecting over two hundred people. Better be a big tent, she says. Oh it will be, he says, with a dance floor and a bar and another bar over there next to the pool house. What happens if it rains, she asks and he tells her it better not and they laugh together but he stops laughing first and goes back to counting. I've never been to a wedding in a garden before, she says, and he asks what will you do with the dog that weekend? Can your friends take care of it? Not really, she says, scrunching the leaves with her free hand. I don't go anywhere without Bright. Maybe the wedding can be an exception, says Mr Gunderson. All these people, not to mention cars.

She's used to cars, says the girl. The silver glint of her bracelet hits Mr Gunderson in the eye. It's these paddocks that make her crazy. Well, says Mr Gunderson. Don't want a dog underfoot when everyone's carrying round trays of champagne. Don't want a dog jumping up on the bride's dress. Wedding's not really a place for a dog, is it? Maybe, she says, not looking up. Going to get cleaned up now, says Mr Gunderson, slapping his hands together. Plenty of time for a shower before dinner.

The girl watches him leaving and slips the dog's collar off. Good dog Bright, she whispers. You run around for a while. You have a good time. The dog rolls over, legs dangling in the air like broken stalks, and the girl scratches the dog's stomach. Billy jogs into the garden, a towel round his neck, calling how are my girls this lovely evening? He drops down next to them on the grass, spreadeagled. We're tired of this garden, says the girl. We're both going out tonight.

All ready nice and early, I see, says Mrs Gunderson, smiling at everyone. Which car are we taking? Ours is covered with dog hair, says Billy. Ours then, smiles Mrs Gunderson. Mr Gunderson is opening doors, asking if Billy is going to drive.

43

Eugenie can drive, says Billy. He looks hard at his mother. You don't mind, do you? No, says Mrs Gunderson. Why would I mind? If you think it's a good idea, says Mr Gunderson. I do, says Billy.

My ex-boyfriend had a car like this, the girl says, grinning. Really? says Mrs Gunderson and Mr Gunderson says we've got plenty of time, so take it slow on the bends and remember, you're not in the city now. Everyone pretends to laugh. Everyone climbs into the car.

Eugenie likes the feel of the steering wheel leather, warm in the last of the light. Her foot goes down hard on the gas and Mrs Gunderson gives a little shriek from the back seat. Easy does it, says Mr Gunderson behind her, but Billy says nothing and she wonders if he's still annoyed because the dog got loose and ran off, because she said don't worry and don't tell your parents and for god's sake don't keep going on about it.

The road twists down the hill. It's narrow and the turns are more sharp than she remembers. We've got plenty of time, says Mrs Gunderson, her voice high and nervous, and this makes Eugenie speed up more until Billy shouts watch out! and she sees the dog streaking across the road in front of them. She pushes the brakes to the floor, kicking up dust all around the car. Billy's left hand stretches over to grab the wheel, keep it steady. He's leaning back, braced for the thump of the dog under the car, but Eugenie says no in a quiet voice, no, no, no, and swings the wheel away and they're all falling into each other. The car mashes into the tree at the side of the road, crumpling like corrugated cardboard. It rolls into the ditch, and inside the car everything is upside down and squashed and contorted. The wheels spin and there is no sound except for the car wheezing as it settles. It hisses into the pink evening air like a steaming pile of fresh dung.

The dog sees a rabbit in the tall grass across the road and tears away after it. Then something skitters beyond the fence, and she runs towards it until a bird, swooping low, draws her away to the far side of the field. She keeps running and running until she comes to a road she doesn't know and everything is quiet. She looks from left to right to left to right from left to right, listening to the cicadas. A red truck drives by and stops further down the road. She runs up to it, wagging her stump. A man gets out and bends over her. She jumps up at his legs over and over. What's your name, girl? he asks. What's your name? He picks her up and she licks his face until he laughs and drops her through the open window into the front seat. They drive away from the field to his house in Connecticut where there's a small backyard. Inside, the television's been on all day. The children fight over whose bed the dog will sleep on that night.

Lonelyville

Every second Friday that summer, Robert Anderson tidied his desk an hour early and walked to the train station, carrying a small backpack and a plastic bag bulging with supplies.

Lydia always told him what to bring. Every second Thursday afternoon she dialled his extension to issue her orders, even though their cubicles were separated only by a thin wall of grey wool. All day long he could hear the clatter of her fingers on the keyboard, the sound of her chair rolling away from the desk. The low hum of her voice on the telephone when she talked to other people was like the purr of his computer monitor, constant and insinuating.

Lydia had pinned the train and ferry schedules directly above her telephone, along with a list of the names and numbers of the other four people in the half-share on Fire Island. Throughout the week she would update him on their plans. Someone had a wedding to attend and couldn't make it, so her sister's boyfriend's cousin was coming instead. Someone else was inviting two friends from her book club, both of whom were vegetarians. At the beginning of the summer, Robert had not met any of the other people sharing the house. Lydia and her old college friend, Nicole, had gathered the group together: Robert was just Lydia's colleague, brought in to make up the numbers. She told him – smirking, eyebrows raised – that he would be the only man in the house.

The first weekend at the house on Fire Island, Lydia had introduced Robert as 'a friend' to the four girls sharing the house with them. It was an introduction that would be repeated every second Saturday morning when the flotilla of everyone else's acquaintances, laden with magazines, bottles of wine, and extra bedding, drifted in from the dock. This excess of other people was something Robert hadn't expected: six people in a three-bedroom, two-bathroom house was enough of a crowd without adding guests and relatives and recently acquired lovers. Someone was always sleeping on the sofa, or on the carpeted floor between bedroom number two's twin beds, or even on the back deck. Lydia did not approve of the parade of non-paying guests. She complained about them in advance at lunch in the cafeteria, all weekend long when the door was closed on the small twin bedroom she shared with Robert, and during the train ride back to the city.

Robert was twenty-nine, a year younger than Lydia. They'd worked at the magazine together for over a year, eating their lunch together most days in the staff cafeteria; because they lived within three blocks of each other on the Upper West Side, they often rode the subway home together, or went to a movie on weekends. Lydia was short, with the tense athletic build of a runner. Her dark, frizzy hair overwhelmed the pinched features of her face like an overgrown hedge, and sometimes, sitting in his cubicle, Robert would fixate on the sound on the other side of the partition – Lydia's barrette, snapping open and closed, open and closed, open and closed, as she tried to tame the bushy clumps of her hairstyle.

They were both promotion managers, organizing events for clients of the sales team and making sure material in the media kit was up-to-date. Most of the other promotion managers were women. There was a man in his late fifties who used to be a sales rep but, it was rumoured, couldn't cope with targets and rankings; the only other guy was just out of college, filling in time in the city – he said – until he got into B-school. Their boss and their boss's boss were both women, and they treated all the men in the department – graphic designers, freelance copywriters, marketing managers, interns, Robert and his colleagues in promotion – with a kind of benevolent indifference, as though the male employees were only there to fill a quota, or to keep a seat warm until a more dynamic, organised, ambitious, and creative female employee could be found to take their place.

Although Robert had lived in New York for six years, he'd never rented a house for the summer before. The cheque made out to Lydia – two thousand dollars, several years of savings – was his first-ever extravagance. Their route sounded exotic: Jamaica, Babylon, Bay Shore, Fair Harbor, Lonelyville. But the trip turned out to be hot and too long, punctuated by the slams of sliding doors and bursts of other people's conversations. They had to scramble to get a seat as soon as the platform number was announced at Penn Station and sometimes, when they weren't quick enough changing trains at Jamaica, they would have to stand the rest of the way in rattling, crowded corridors.

On Friday nights, everyone else on the crowded ferry seemed irritable, as though they were being forced to go away for the weekend against their will. By the time he and Lydia reached the wharf at Fair Harbor, it was already evening, usually hazy and cool. They trudged towards the rented place in Lonelyville past crowded rows of plain grey houses set in thickets of pines. Robert followed Lydia's short, slapping steps along the narrow boardwalk, watching her overnight bag bounce against her high, firm backside. The walk to the southern side of the island was long, and they rarely spoke until they reached the board pathway to their house. Lydia always had a few last things to whisper to Robert while he unlocked the front door: that it was their turn to cook dinner tomorrow; or that it was Nicole's turn to replenish the kitchen supplies; or, most often, that hopefully that awful, tacky Chloe would not be arriving until the next day.

The small house they rented was scruffy, and it looked scruffier every weekend. All the furniture was cheap and mismatched. A bleached poster of the South of France hung askew on the kitchen wall, but otherwise there was little decoration. The fridge was crowded with food belonging to the six people who had rented the other half-share, each bottle and container marked with an unfamiliar name.

Every weekend he spent at the house that summer, Robert followed the same routine. He would open the windows when they arrived and empty the dryers before they left. He lit the grill when required, and walked to the shop at the dock on Sunday morning to buy the newspaper. He set the table and made the salad, and occasionally, when he seemed to be in the way, he sat out on the porch with his back to the kitchen window, waiting to be called in to dinner. He carried Lydia's folding chair to the beach while she complained that Chloe, yet again, had annexed the only recliner.

'He's so good,' Nicole said to him. 'Aren't you, Robert? Lydia has you very well trained.'

Nicole worked as a copy-editor at an entertainment magazine. It was smaller and less venerable than their magazine, but Lydia deferred to Nicole anyway: editorial trumped sales and marketing, even if editorial in this case only meant (as Lydia muttered one night across the dead space in the stuffy twin bedroom) glorified proofreading. Nicole's air of perpetual anxiety seemed to generate its own slight breeze; she was always in motion, slapping at insects, jumping up to grab a forgotten item, dashing off to the store. Lydia sat stately and rigid in her high-backed beach chair while Nicole fluttered around her, fidgeting and commenting, constantly re-twisting her top knot of dark hair.

Lydia had told Robert a great deal about Nicole – her college bulimia, her rent-stabilised apartment, her twice-married boyfriend – over their daily sandwiches, but the other girls in the house were just names on the list until the first weekend on the island. Serena and Miriam were both associate editors at Nicole's magazine. They were not really friends with Nicole – editing trumped copy-editing – and Serena told Robert that they had rented the house with one aim only: to get killer tans. He was impressed by their diligence. They spent most Saturdays prone, often silent, rolling over on their towels at the same time, as if on cue. Late afternoons they paced the beach together, looking brown and crisp in their white T-shirts. During these walks they appeared to be bursting with things to say to each other, gesturing and laughing, Serena grabbing Miriam's arm to emphasise a point.

The fifth girl in the house, Chloe, didn't work for a magazine. She was a shop assistant at a designer boutique on Madison Avenue. She sold seven-hundred dollar belts to rich Spaniards and Italians who wanted to know how much things cost in Euros. The money she made in commission, she announced, was paying for her house share that summer.

Chloe was tall, with long yellow-blonde hair she wore pulled back into a ponytail. She walked in loping strides to the beach each morning, the ponytail swinging between her shoulder blades. There was something about the way she moved, fluid and elegant, that made Robert feel short of breath. Next to Chloe, all the other girls seemed ordinary, interchangeable. Lydia, in particular, looked more short and squat whenever Chloe was in the room.

The very first weekend in the house, Lydia told Robert she did not like Chloe. She didn't like the way Chloe left her cigarette stubs, bloody with lipstick, in a stunted line along the back porch railings. She didn't like the way Chloe referred to her boyfriend, allegedly working in Zurich all summer, as The Man I Fuck. She didn't like the way Chloe talked about the money she made on every item she sold – her transactions, Chloe called them.

'She sounds like a prostitute,' Lydia muttered to Robert, who was carrying plates and cutlery to the dinner table. Chloe had a good week – *molti* transactions, she said – and she'd celebrated by buying crab cakes and ready-made Caesar salad for dinner. 'Looks like one, too.'

'Did you buy the crab cakes here?' Robert asked Chloe, trying to talk over Lydia. Chloe looked up at him, her brown eyes dark as mud, as though she was seeing him for the first time. 'On the island, I mean.'

'Duh!' She rolled her eyes but smiled at him, not unkindly. 'They'd be stinking before we were out of Queens. Plus, you know – this is the sea. This is where you buy seafood.'

'Everything costs twice as much in the store here,' Lydia said, tight-lipped, glaring at the bowl of salad Nicole was tossing. She held out her plate reluctantly, as though the salad was somehow tainted, and pulled it away after Nicole dispensed a drooping spoonful. As the summer went on, and the girls got used to his presence, or forgot he was there, Robert noticed that bowls were filled to the brim, that plates were scraped clean. But this first weekend, everyone toyed with their food.

'Money's no object,' sighed Chloe. 'Not this week, anyway. Two weeks' time may be a different story.'

'I wish we had this place every weekend,' said Serena. 'Even though the trip is *so* long.'

'Overcrowded.' Nicole tapped her chin with her fork, smearing her face with creamy dressing. 'Worse than the subway.'

'Like riding the bus to summer camp,' said Miriam.

'Like getting shipped off to the gas chambers,' said Chloe.

'I think that's in very poor taste,' said Lydia, frowning.

'Oh, please,' said Chloe. 'What do you think, Robert?'

Robert wasn't sure what she was asking him: how he'd describe the trip, or whether he thought her comment was in poor taste. His mouth felt stuck together with salad, too heavy to move. He gripped the stem of his empty wineglass and stared at Nicole's hands. She was twirling the fork like a baton between her fingers.

'We like the journey.' Lydia was speaking for him. 'We used the time to read and unwind. Our jobs are pretty demanding you know.'

'Is that right,' said Chloe. She mashed up a crab cake, covering up the floral motif on her plate. 'I had no idea that typing emails was so strenuous. Or do you have to, like, print out labels and stick them on envelopes as well?'

Lydia's face flushed. She sat perfectly still, a piece of crab cake skewered on her fork. Robert thought for a moment that she was going to throw it at Chloe.

'I'll have you know I organised two wine tastings, a business breakfast, and a colloquium on personal finance this week.'

Chloe snorted.

'And Robert,' Lydia said, addressing the salad bowl, 'he's been really busy as well. Haven't you, Robert?'

'More wine tastings?' Chloe's mouth trembled with laughter. 'A business brunch or two? A business tapas? A business dessert tasting?'

A lot of meals, he wanted to say. Stupid meals, boring meetings, pointless events for disloyal clients and ungrateful reps. A waste of everyone's time and money. All this he wanted to say. Smiling, laughing – he should be laughing when he said it. But he knew he'd never be able to pull it off.

'I don't . . . I don't really like talking about work,' he said.

'A man of few words,' Chloe said. She winked at him. 'My favourite kind! Nic, is there any more salad?'

'Another bag, I think,' said Nicole, bustling out of her chair, and the conversation shifted abruptly, like a rip tide. Lydia got up too, walking stiff-shouldered into the kitchen, holding her plate as though it contained toxic residue.

Chloe was Nicole's cousin; they shared the biggest and most expensive bedroom, which housed the only double bed. At night Robert could hear them laughing while they brushed their teeth and jammed the bedroom window open. Late on Sunday afternoons, Robert stood at their door while Chloe retrieved dirty towels from the floor of their small en suite bathroom and tossed them out to him. Their room smelled like a department store.

Robert and Lydia shared the tiny front bedroom. At night Robert lay in his narrow bed, hands folded on his chest, and listened for the sound of the sea, three blocks away. But all he could hear was Lydia, three feet away in the other single bed, breathing in and out, in and out, in steady, wheezing beats. He closed his eyes, and imagined Chloe clicking open the door, beckoning him out into the hallway. *Let's smoke out on the deck*, she'd mouth. *Let's take a blanket down to the beach*. Her presence, golden and aromatic, filled the room, her soft hair draping his face, her sleek limbs pressed against his. The compass of his erection pointed to the window, where the moonlight dirtied the cheap beige curtains. Then the small bedroom constricted and expanded like a blood vessel, until Robert had to grip the edges of the bed to stop it exploding. He could say nothing, do nothing; he just had to wait for the long moment to pass, hoping that Lydia would not wake up and see him in this state somewhere between terror and desire, or – even worse – think the hard lines of his body were leading her way.

The housemates spent all their Saturdays on the beach. There was nothing else to do in Lonelyville, as Chloe often pointed out. Throughout the morning, they wandered in pairs towards the same patch of sand, ending up marooned together on a raft of towels encircled by an ad hoc reef of faded deck chairs. None of the girls ever chose to sit further away, out of earshot. Even Chloe always stretched out in their encampment, her long legs stretched out, the ice-cream mounds of her breasts in their white bikini top perfect and unmelting.

There was always talk: talk of work, mostly, and other people – girls who thought they were *so all that*, men who were clueless or controlling or commitment-phobic – and how annoying it was that the beach was so busy that weekend. It was almost impossible for Robert to join in with these conversations. Topics were taken up and discarded at speed, and most of them seemed to involve people he didn't know, their every word, gesture, and action chewed over and derided.

'Remember that guy I was telling you about?' said Nicole, throwing the newspaper aside after a cursory glance at the first section. It was the fifth week of the summer, and Robert had long lost track of the guys in Nicole's stories. 'Here's the latest.'

'You know who he reminds me of?' said Lydia. 'That guy you were talking about, Serena.'

'FYI, I have an update.'

'Do tell.'

'Close your ears, Robert.'

Miriam was always telling him to close his ears, as though he was a child or elderly invalid who might be shocked, offended, or corrupted. Robert grinned in what he hoped looked like a good-natured, long-suffering way. Miriam needn't worry: even when he was listening, nothing made much sense. Robert might work in an office of women, but he had no sisters, and the two girls he'd slept with in college were both fleeting hook-ups, one catatonically shy, the other catatonically drunk.

The girls in the house were fluent in a foreign language, glib and explosive. It wasn't always clear when they were talking about someone at the office or someone on a television show. They were all pundits, intimate with the world, eager to give instant expert commentaries on other people's lives. Serena and Miriam were breathy and confidential; everything they had to say was an exciting secret. Certain topics – stupid colleagues, say, or celebrities who wore leggings instead of pants – animated Nicole even more than usual, and Lydia, whatever the subject, presented herself as close to the source and sure of her information.

In these conversations, Lydia's voice was always the loudest – more strident, more assertive. Robert came to think of it as her beach voice. Perhaps she was excited to be free of the muted cloister of her cubicle, or maybe she was afraid the wind might carry her words away. Perhaps she just wanted to make sure that Chloe, to whom her back was always turned, would hear what she was saying.

He liked it best when the girls all fell silent, dozy with lunch or sun. Sometimes he'd lie on his stomach, one elbow propped in the sand, pretending to read: that way he could sneak glances at the gentle dune of Chloe's backside, the sliver of her white bikini pants a reverse tan line, her taut brown butt cheeks and thighs powdered with sugary sand. When the view of Chloe was impossibly obscured by the others and their endless chairs and hats and umbrellas, he lay on his back, face sweating beneath an open book, and tried to think of things to say. He could recite the ad insertion deadlines for every special issue through next Valentine's Day, but that was hardly conversation. Sometimes he pretended he'd seen a TV show that everyone else was talking about, because agreeing gave him something to say.

If only someone would ask him a question occasionally, something he could answer with ease and authority – perhaps a query about his position on a social issue, or a request for statistics. He imagined Chloe asking him these questions, her long, expressive face turned towards his. *What do you know about the island, Robert?* Fire Island is thirty-one miles long, and its permanent population is just 310, ten people per mile. Thousands more stay here between Memorial Day and Labor Day, of course: there are more than 300 people on each ferry to Fair Harbor alone every Friday night in the summer. The first house in Lonelyville was built in 1905. Anne Bancroft and Mel Brooks used to spend their summers here. Frank O'Hara, the poet, wrote about Fire Island and was killed here, mowed down on the beach late at night by a dune buggy. *Really, Robert?* Not here – not in Lonelyville. Further east, up near the Pines. July, 1966 . . .

Maybe Frank O'Hara wasn't a good subject: nobody wanted to think about freak beach accidents when they were tanning. And Frank O'Hara was gay; the Pines, then as now, was a gay colony. When Robert told some of the women at work that he was renting a summer place on Fire Island, he saw a knowing, unsurprised look flit across their faces. He didn't want Chloe to think this as well.

But Chloe didn't ask him any questions. Usually at the beach she spoke very little, unless she was telling a story about selling luxury goods to ostentatious Brazilians, reporting on a gift sent by her absentee boyfriend, or making sarcastic asides about other people's anecdotes. Today she was interested, Robert noticed, even though the conversation was much the same as usual: work, stars, shows, reluctant men, minor medical scares, other people's failed relationships. She'd even put her magazine down.

'This guy – is he the one you were seeing in May?' she asked Serena.

'A different one. Same kind of thing, though.'

'It's a pattern. A behavioural pattern,' said Lydia, in her loud voice. Was Serena the culprit here, the person with the bad behavioural pattern? Of course not, Robert realised: it was the usual suspect, the nameless man who was doing the same kind of thing the last nameless man had done to her, which – it seemed – was not fall in love with her. When a woman failed to fall in love with a man, he'd learned, it

59

was because the man in question was lame, stupid, and/or unattractive. When a man failed to fall in love with a woman, it was not the woman's fault in any way. She was never lame; she was always intelligent and attractive. The man who rejected her was immature, unfaithful, unreliable, unable to commit, unwilling to grow up. In the secret world of women, men were seen as problems to fix, puzzles to solve. Men were children with lessons to learn. The girls were not interested in hearing about a man unless he was a case study of poor behaviour and attitude. When a man behaved well – like Chloe's boyfriend, who was flying her to Rome for a week in September, after his assignment in Zurich finished ('I think she's lying,' Lydia muttered) – there was nothing to tell. That was fine with Robert: he didn't want to hear about Chloe's boyfriend either.

'Malcolm Gladwell wrote an article about exactly this subject three issues ago in the *New Yorker*.' Lydia was still talking.

'I saw Malcolm Gladwell last week at the Royalton,' said Nicole, flapping sand out of a towel. 'His hair is out of control.'

'I'm so over that place,' said Miriam's muffled voice; she was lying face down again. 'It was better before they changed it.'

'I don't like hotel bars at all,' said Serena. 'They're so *pre-theatre*.'

'Either two or three issues ago. I can check when I get home.'

'At least I think it was Malcolm Gladwell,' said Nicole. 'Is Malcolm Gladwell black?'

Swimming was the only way to escape the whirring conversations. The girls rarely went swimming. They occasionally wandered to the water's edge to examine the tidemark and sift through the debris, and sometimes they posed in the shallows, picking at their damp bikini bottoms and flinching whenever a wave splashed up at their bellies.

Robert swam three or four times a day. After Serena and Miriam returned from a late afternoon odyssey to other parts of the island, full of chatter about the horrors of elsewhere (too many gay men, too many families), Robert stood up, tipping his book upside down into the sand. There was no one else in the water at this time of day. He walked into the waves, hands on his hips, striding through the shallows in an almost-straight line. Once he was waist deep in water, he dived sideways into a crumbling wave.

He loved the sensation of tumbling through the surf, pushed down and sideways by the force of the water. Waves broke around his ears, and he swooped down again, kicking away from shore. He couldn't hear or feel anything but the gluey rush of water. Swimming was the only time he really felt alone. Even sitting in his small, blank apartment, the sounds of the city – its horns and sirens and strident voices – intruded. He ducked through another wave, and then another, bobbing up only to shake the water out of his ears.

After a while, when he was far enough from shore, he floated on his back in the warm water at the surface, cradled by waves. The sky was streaked pale blue and tangerine. Around this time in the afternoon, the girls usually packed up and headed back to the little house. They all spent their evenings squashed into its stunted awkward rooms, their faces red with sun and wine. Perhaps later tonight he'd go for a swim. He'd slip away after dinner and make his way along the straight line of the boardwalk, through the spindly fences lacing the dunes. Perhaps, at the tide line, he'd drop his jeans and boxer shorts, let the sea seduce him. Chloe would follow him, her footsteps silent in the cool soft sand, and they would writhe in the shallows like Burt Lancaster and Deborah Kerr.

Back on shore, someone was calling his name. Lydia. They could probably hear her in Virginia Beach. He rolled onto his front, plunging deep into the cold water again to punish his erection, making sure it was sufficiently chastened and cowering by the time he swamp-walked out of the waves. Lydia had returned to their encampment: she was sitting in her chair, folding up a newspaper. When he approached, bending down to grab his towel, she and Nicole shrank away from him, as though he were a dog about to shake himself dry. Robert sat down on a low folding chair and lay the towel across his knees. Out in the distance, the sea flattened into dull grey and disappeared into the horizon. Water trickled down the back of his neck; he shivered. How far would he have to swim before losing sight of the land?

'Robert,' said Chloe's voice, somewhere behind his head. 'Is that, like, your tenth swim of the day?'

'Well,' he said. He wasn't sure whether to say it was his fifth. Counting suddenly seemed childish.

'I was watching you out there. You're a seal. Very impressive.'

'Thanks.' He glanced back at Chloe. Her head was bent, and she was biting her lip, tying up her hair with a speckled bandana. Her bikini top had slipped a little. One of her breasts, brown and round and smooth, was about to slide out.

'Robert.' Lydia leaned towards him, drumming on his arm with her fingertips. He jerked his head around, flicking her with water. 'We should go in now.'

'OK.' He was thinking about Chloe's bubbling breast, her long slender fingers, the way her toenails, painted a sparkling blue, lay half-hidden in the sand like exotic shells.

'It's our turn to do dinner. I'm thinking spaghetti with red sauce.'

Chloe sniffed.

'We're all on a budget,' said Lydia quickly, frowning at the seagulls picking around the high tide line. She shuffled sections of newspaper into her beach bag.

'Sounds good to me.' Nicole brushed at the sand islands clinging to her legs. 'Red sauce to go with my red shoulders.'

'It's a good budget meal,' said Lydia. Her mouth was set in a straight line.

'Budgets are good,' said Chloe. 'I mean, with the extra therapy I need after a weekend here, this summer is getting very expensive.'

'Better sell a few more belts, then,' said Lydia.

'Excuse me?' said Chloe.

Nicole scrambled to her feet, dusting off her backside.

'Come on, Lydia,' she said. 'I'll walk to the store with you. Give Robert a break.'

'Why would he need a break?' said Lydia. She stood up, tucking her towel around her like a sarong. 'He doesn't need a break.'

'Do you, Robert?' Chloe appeared in front of him suddenly, stretching her arms in the air. She'd pulled a T-shirt on, but the white triangles of her bikini top beamed through the thin fabric. '*Do* you need a break?'

'Or shall we make a list first, back at the house?' Nicole asked Lydia. 'Let's do that.'

'Robert?' said Lydia.

He wanted to sit for a while, looking out at the sea. Chloe might walk down to the water. She did that sometimes, towards the end of the day, standing with her hands on her hips, swizzling her feet into the sand. But there was something plaintive in Lydia's voice he couldn't ignore, and she looked squashed and pink, like she'd been squeezed too hard.

'Coming,' he said.

He picked up his book and gathered the newspaper together, placing his things one by one in Lydia's canvas beach bag. Nicole and Lydia set out towards the boardwalk stairs, walking as briskly as the floury sand allowed.

'She's a piece of work,' Chloe said, shaking her head.

Robert twisted his towel around his neck and slipped one arm through the curved legs of the folded chair.

'See you,' he said. Nobody replied. He stood there for a moment or two longer, suddenly uncertain if he'd spoken at all, then set off along the slurred trail of footsteps. He wondered where it was, exactly, the point at which the land disappeared, the point at which he could tread water and turn his head and see nothing but the horizon, every way he looked.

• • •

He didn't go for a midnight swim that night, or on any other weekend. And because of changes in the cooking roster, initiated and enforced by Lydia – it wasn't fair, she said, for her and Robert to be making dinner all the time for everyone else's friends – they didn't have to prepare another meal until the last Saturday of the summer.

Although it was their final weekend in the house, nobody had invited any guests. Usually there was quite a crowd at dinner on Saturday night. Robert would have to drag in plastic chairs from the yard to seat everyone around the table, because they only had four dining chairs and a kitchen stool. Some weekends, the little house felt as stuffed and frenetic as the train station, a place of transit for dozens of strangers. Of course, they weren't strangers to Miriam or Chloe or whoever had invited them, but Robert never learned more than a name or two. Most of them seemed to treat the house like a youth hostel, and they treated him like he was a sad, slightly sinister long-term resident, or possibly the caretaker.

But tonight even the girls seemed worn out, at last, with other people. They lolled around the living room, drinking wine and watching TV. Chloe lay across the sofa, which was as lumpy and brown as oatmeal, her long legs stretched over Miriam's lap, a cushion tucked behind her head. When she got up to fill her wine glass, light filaments of hair stuck to the cushion. The house smelled of fried onions and garlic. Lydia stood in the kitchen, stirring the contents of a large, battered pot. Robert sat on a hard-backed chair close to the ancient television set, adjusting the volume and changing the station as requested.

'Robert, you are our very own remote control,' said Chloe.

She shouted with laughter, and then everyone was laughing – Nicole, Serena, Miriam. They'd already finished a bottle of wine, and now they couldn't stop laughing. Nicole choked on a cashew nut and had to be thumped on the back: this made everyone laugh more. Chloe looked at Robert with a rueful half-smile. The television buzzed in the background, loud and bright. Robert's face prickled red, but he tried to smile back at her, as though he was laughing too. There was nothing else to do, at this point, but pretend.

At dinner, Robert sat on the same side of the table as Chloe. Serena sat between them. He preferred it this way: the same side, with someone else between them. There was something about the way Chloe looked, and the way she looked at him, that made him acutely self-conscious. Cutting his food, lifting his glass, even swallowing was difficult under her scrutiny. The briefest of glances made him nervous about the ugly shapes and sounds of his mouth.

Nicole appeared in the kitchen door with another bottle of wine and some good news: the freezer, which had been growing a bulbous inner coating of hard ice all summer, wouldn't close. They would have to eat all the frozen berries and leftover ice cream.

'We'll leave a note and some money for the others,' said Lydia. 'I'll price it out at the store.'

'You do that,' said Chloe.

'Someone has to,' said Lydia.

'Good for you,' said Chloe.

'Good that somebody's doing it.'

'You should get a medal.'

'You know, the others can't complain,' said Nicole,

rummaging in a drawer for the ice cream scoop. 'They got Labor Day weekend, after all.'

'Bitches,' said Chloe. 'Bastards. Which are they, anyway? Bitches or bastards?'

'Bitches like us, probably,' said Nicole. She threw the scoop onto the table; it hit the metal candlestick with a clang. 'Sorry, Robert. You're an honorary bitch.'

'What an honour!' Chloe leaned back in her chair to look at him. 'What do you think, Rob – are the other half of this share bitches or bastards?'

'Well,' he said. He glanced at her and then back at his hands, his fingertips resting on the edge of the table. 'A combination, I think. Judging by the names on the food in the fridge.'

'You'd know that, Chloe, if you ever cooked dinner,' said Lydia.

'Let's drink to them,' said Nicole. 'The bitches and bastards who got Labor Day weekend.'

'And us,' said Serena, shaking defrosting blueberries and their pink ink over the last of her ice cream. 'Let's drink to us, too.'

'To us.' Chloe raised her glass. 'The bitches – and bastard – who got stuck with this shit-hole every other weekend.'

'You think this is bad?' said Serena. 'You should see my apartment.'

'Well, I'm sorry the summer's over,' said Nicole. 'I'll miss the beach.'

'I'll miss the beach,' said Miriam, her mouth full. 'But I won't miss the mosquitoes.'

'I'm not sure what I won't miss,' said Serena. 'Maybe the

weird guy at the store?'

'I know *exactly* who I won't miss.' Chloe tapped Robert with her spoon. 'Can you guess who it is?'

He grinned up at her, his cheeks sizzling again, but this time the sensation wasn't unpleasant. They were having a moment, he and Chloe – a private moment.

Lydia's chair was pushed back with a screech; she stomped into the kitchen, her hands scrunching damp berry packets. Miriam asked if anyone thought it would rain that night; Serena said they should bring the deckchairs in, and wondered if Robert would take the empty wine bottles out to the recycling bin on the back porch. As he stood up, Chloe reached out and grabbed his arm.

'Don't worry,' she told him, her voice low. His arm pulsed where her fingers touched his bare skin. 'You'll never have to see any of us bitches again after tomorrow. Except Lydia, of course.'

Outside, the evening tingled with rain. He dumped the bottles into the plastic tub, and stood looking out over the small sandy yard. One of Chloe's cigarette butts lay on the wooden deck, toppled from its perch on the railings by the wind. She'd been out here before dinner, smoking, tapping ash onto the parched boards of the deck. He crouched, gingerly picking up the butt with this thumb and forefinger. Just forty minutes or so ago, Chloe's mouth had touched this. Her lips, moist with gloss, had puckered around this rusty husk.

He held it to his mouth and sucked. It was dry and papery; it didn't taste succulent, as Chloe would. He could sense no residue from her lips, no hint of her scent or saliva, no tang of the night or the sea or the summer, but Robert sucked it anyway, as though he was ingesting the tiny stab of nectar from a plucked sprig of jasmine.

The screen door banged open, and Robert tried to spit out the cigarette butt; it stuck to his lips, hanging like a shred of skin. Chloe stepped outside, carrying another empty bottle.

'Lydia said I should give you this . . .'

He stood up, still trying to swat the butt from his mouth. Chloe gazed at him, mouth open, her face already contorting into amazement, laughter. She said nothing. Robert's tongue felt thick and dry in his mouth. The sea was in his ears: he was spinning head over heels, clogged with salt and sand, to the bottom of the ocean. On the ground between them, tacky with his spittle, lay the cigarette butt. He'd sucked out and swallowed its venom. Now his throat was thick with bile.

Still silent, Chloe held out the empty bottle and he took it. The green glass was dark as seaweed, reflecting nothing. He was still looking at it when the screen door slammed again, closing behind her. When he looked up, the kitchen window framed Lydia's face, looking out at him. She was almost smiling. Her eyes were as hard as rocks.

Sunday was sticky and hot. Lydia went wading, her cotton wrap tucked into her swimsuit, the backs of her thighs patterned with the thatch of the deck chair. Serena and Miriam, sleek and burnished, decided to take a swim. It was a strange kind of swim, Robert thought, if you didn't get your hair wet, but they seemed to enjoy it.

Nicole suggested they all stay one final night and catch the early ferry in the morning. Everyone agreed but Chloe. The guy from Zurich was flying in that night. She was desperate, she said, for good Mexican food and some male company.

Robert was swimming when Chloe got up and said her goodbyes. She and Nicole were almost at the boardwalk by the time he returned. Chloe held her chair over her head, and Nicole was laughing, stooping to pick up a dropped bottle of suntan lotion and then scrambling to catch up.

'Bye!' he shouted. They didn't turn around. He stood watching the chair bob and disappear over the dunes, until Miriam complained he was dripping on her.

Robert rubbed his back and face with a towel, and lay flat on the ground. Sandy water dribbled into the grooves of his ears. His hair felt caked with salt. An indolent conversation was going on around him: Serena wanted to know if the tide was coming in; Miriam read something aloud from a magazine. And then there was Lydia, rustling one of her lists, telling everyone how much they owed her for dinner the night before.

Robert held the newspaper over his face and closed his eyes. Newsprint words melted into his skin, the ink seeping into the cracks in his lips. He imagined himself swimming with long, steady strokes out to sea. He crested wave after wave, soaring towards the horizon. Finally, he broke through the ring of surf. He couldn't see any part of the island from here. Beyond the breakers: that was the place. Nothing but saltwater and sky and silence.

That night, he lay awake in his narrow bed. Across the room, Lydia was fast asleep, flat on her back with her mouth open. Her breathing seemed more coarse than usual. Each exhalation mimicked the swish of the sea. Suck and swish, suck and swish. And now there was a variation: a small popping noise every few seconds.

It was the most unbearable sound Robert had ever heard.

He found himself standing up, holding his pillow with both hands. Asleep, Lydia's face was as bland and unremarkable as the island. She twitched suddenly, wrinkling her nose, and relaxed again. Another breath, another pop. And now there was something different about her face – just the suggestion of a smile, petty and smug. That was the way her face looked last night, framed by the kitchen window. Robert fingered the empty edges of his pillow case. He wasn't sure what was worse, the sound or the smile.

He sat down gently on the edge of Lydia's bed, the pillow clutched in his lap, and leaned towards her. All he had to do was raise the pillow, move it in a slow arc towards her face. One simple movement, from him to her. But his hands were quivering, as though he'd been in the water too long. He clung to the pillow, trying to steady his breath and his hands.

Lydia snuffled and shook her head. She opened her eyes a little, blinking at Robert's frozen form. He sat as still as he could, waiting for her eyes to close again.

But Lydia was awake now, he could see that; she was pushing away her sheets, stretching her hands up to touch his face.

'Oh, Robert,' she said, in a soft voice he'd never heard before. Then she was pulling him towards her, his mouth towards her mouth, her tongue reaching for his, and the look on her face said she'd been expecting him all along.

The Party
(After Chekhov)

Whatever anyone said, it was not perfect weather at all. The expansive white tent wilted in the heat like a damp handkerchief. The pond was murky green, and the slice of beach visible from the back yard was crunchy and brown, as though the sky – gloomy, heavy, close enough to touch – had vomited it up.

Every time Olivia Sanford saw the caterer, he was mopping the back of his neck with a dish towel. All she could think of was how unhygienic that looked. She wanted to say something to him, in a disapproving tone, to make sure that the towel didn't end up being used to wipe glasses or the backs of chairs, but she couldn't find quite the right moment. There was too much coming and going, and people asking her questions, and children multiplying around her like tadpoles.

'I'll take them to the beach and get them out of your hair,' called Selly, her sister-in-law, as if she were doing

Olivia a favour, when they were Selly's children and Selly's children's friends, just unnecessary uninvited appendages of Selly's hauled out from the city like so many extra pieces of luggage.

Paul, of course, was nowhere to be found. Olivia was tired of signing for everything and ordering things and being asked where tea candles in small brown paper bags needed to go. It was all the same as last year, surely, and the year before that.

'Just decide everything yourself,' she told the housekeeper, who sniffed. Olivia didn't know if the sniffing was an allergic thing or an attitude thing; she suspected the latter. That was the thing about life up here, something Olivia would never get used to: everyone did what they were paid to do, and not an iota more. 'I don't care where the candles go as long as they don't burn the house down.'

Olivia swung open the kitchen's screen door and decided to go looking for her husband. It was ridiculous to throw big parties like this late in August, she thought, even at the beach. Where she was from, parties where you expected guests to dress up and eat several courses took place in the winter, and everything was set-up with much less fuss. Every January at her parents' house in New Orleans, white tents appeared first thing in the morning, clipped into place in the front and side yards; one was centred over the front pillars, and the other stretched over the cobbled driveway. They looked as elegant as a pair of white evening gloves. Her parents wouldn't dream of throwing a party in August, not even at the place in Pass Christian. August was hot; August was hurricane season. August was for lying around sucking on pieces of ice and dreaming of a breeze.

Here on Long Island it was hot and it was hurricane season, but lying around wasn't permitted. Everyone in the Sanford's beach club was bustling and self-important, organising play dates and tennis lessons for their children, making deals, talking on their cell phones. The Sanford's annual party was just more of the same – New York City transplanted to the edge of Georgica Pond, except with more sunburn, more mosquitoes, more young girls drifting about in flimsy dresses, and a photographer from *Hampton Style*.

Paul Sanford was on the croquet lawn setting up lights. Olivia could hear him laughing before she saw him, on tiptoes, waving at her from a stepladder. The ladder leaned against one of the hedges, notching its sheer green side. For some reason, the tennis instructor from the Association's private club was there as well, measuring the space between hoops, grinning at her inanely from underneath his red cap.

'You go in and rest,' Paul called in an over-loud voice. Who was he trying to impress? The tennis instructor? 'Everything's under control.'

'I don't need to rest,' Olivia told him. She knew she sounded petulant, and that this was her normal way of speaking these days – a bleat, one waver away from sobbing. 'I'm not an invalid.'

The tennis instructor smiled at her like a contestant in some kind of demented pageant. Olivia wanted to tell Paul to come down right now, this minute, and stop trying to electrocute himself, and to attend to something more important like the impending parking fiasco, or the way the housekeeper's sniffing was becoming louder and more impertinent. But there was no way she could say any of this in front of that beaming, freckle-faced tennis instructor. That was probably why Paul had him there, as a buffer. He was certainly not invited to the party.

'Well, you could start getting ready,' Paul said at last. He wrapped a plastic rope spiky with lights around one hand, and then lowered his voice, as though he was addressing the hedge. 'I know how long it takes.'

Olivia swivelled on her heels and walked away. She wouldn't give him the satisfaction of responding to such a comment. *The favor of a reply is requested.* Isn't that what it said on the invitations? She wouldn't favour Paul with a reply. She hoped it would start raining soon, and that the party would be a washout.

Inside, the old house was no cooler than the garden. Even after a shower, Olivia's skin still felt warm and moist with sweat. She put her hair up and took it down again; the clips gouged her scalp. On the bed lay the dress she had chosen to wear, a long beige linen shift. Off its hanger it looked like a sack recently emptied of its cargo of coffee beans or grain. It was not a particularly flattering dress and it wasn't very pretty, but it was loose enough to hide the slight roundness of her belly.

Olivia was almost three months pregnant. She and Paul had discussed it, and decided not to tell anyone this time until she was out of the woods. No point in getting everyone excited again, he said, just in case. Olivia didn't remember anyone being actually excited the last time she was having a baby – earlier this year, unbelievably enough. They were relieved, perhaps. She was thirty, and she and Paul had been married for four years. Paul's family, and their New York friends, seemed pleased that she would have something to do at last. She was pleased, too, after four years of pretending she was about to do something – go back to work in Paul's office, go back to work in the gallery on 61st Street, open her own gallery. There was no shame in not working, Paul had always insisted, especially when she didn't need to.

But the foetus didn't give her much of a chance to do anything: it surfed out on a rip tide of blood and washed away down the plughole of the bath on Easter Sunday. One minute it had been there, floating inside her, and the next it was just so much dirty water. These things happen all the time, everyone said, especially when you're – *you know* – stressed, and went back to talking about hedge funds and real estate. Best to get right back on the horse, according to their doctor, and that's what they'd done, though it wasn't really a plan. To be pregnant with two different children in one year – in one six-month span, even – seemed heartless to Olivia, almost promiscuous. Paul was right about keeping this brash new foetus, with its unknown intentions, its unreliable and slippery smallness, a secret.

It would have been different, perhaps, if her parents were still alive; someone would have cared enough to console her last time and cheer her on now. But they'd washed away as well – her father in a boating accident off Pensacola, the year she turned twenty-one; her mother just six months ago. It was during Carnival, and her mother had been to see Proteus and Orpheus ride; unlocking her own front door on Camp Street, she'd been felled by an aneurism. That was the official explanation. But everyone knew it was the hurricane that killed her – the storm and its angry roar of storm surge that splintered the old house in Pass Christian and swept it out to sea like so much driftwood. Everything gone, her mother said, standing there last September, an empty plastic bottle in her hand, the sea placid and smug now on the other side of the crumpled road. The plastic bottle, probably dropped by a utility worker or news crew the day before, was the only whole thing her mother could find to pick up; they drove back to their cousin's house in Jackson that afternoon with the bottle inside her mother's purse, wrapped in a paper napkin, as though it were a piece of salvaged family china.

The place was called the March House, named for Olivia's great-great-great grandfather. He built the house with sugarcane money, before the Civil War. Every summer the family came here on the steamer from New Orleans; in those days they had their own jetty. Hurricanes in 1915 and 1947 knocked the place around, and Hurricane Camille, in '69, flattened and stripped it. By the time Olivia was born, the house had been patched together and reconstructed, more or less; the sugarcane money was long gone. In the place she knew, growing up, nothing much was original aside from its name. Nothing was very old in Pass Christian anymore: that was what Paul said, what he dared to say, after Katrina rampaged through. He couldn't even pronounce the name of the town correctly. He knew nothing.

The March House might have been a replica, but it was Olivia's mother's house, and her grandmother's; it was going to be Olivia's. Instead, when her mother died, Olivia's brother got the place on Camp Street and Olivia got a piece of land scarred with foundation stumps and the relics of trees. There would be money, too, eventually, once the court case against the insurance company came to trial, but the Sanfords might not use it to rebuild. Not yet, Paul said. He wasn't having such a good year either, and it took a lot of money to rent the summer place on Georgica Pond. Money to pay for the membership in the Association. Money to throw a big party.

It was still too early to get dressed, but Olivia didn't know what else to do. She stood in front of the bathroom mirror dabbing on lipstick with a moulting brush. A damp tidal line curved across her dress where it brushed against the basin rim. Stumping footsteps on the staircase announced the return of Selly and the children from the beach.

'Everyone! In the bath! Now!' Selly called. 'Olivia?'

Olivia reached out a foot to kick her door shut but Selly was too quick for her.

'You're ready early,' said Selly, scattering sand from the grooves of her sunhat onto the bathroom floor. 'Is that what you're wearing?' She lingered, waiting for a reply. Selly was always looking at her, sizing her up and apparently finding her lacking. In Selly's face, Olivia read a persistent, bemused disapproval: Olivia was somehow not vivacious and strenuous and vital enough to be a Sanford. Usually Olivia didn't care what Selly thought. Everyone knew the Sanfords had nothing to show for themselves but loud voices and expensive tastes and too many divorces.

'This is what I'm wearing.' Olivia brushed on another sticky layer of lipstick. Her mouth looked clownish now, too red for her pale face.

'You should have come with us. You missed Caroline Kennedy,' said Selly, smacking her lips, and padded off to her room without waiting for a reply.

• • •

Olivia and Paul had rented the house on the pond every summer of their married life, after Paul's uncle sponsored their application to the Association. They started having the party when Paul's agency went from boutique to mid-size, and had its first eight-figure year.

Each year it was the same. People started arriving around seven, and the last guests finally drifted off at two or three. For the first hour everyone kissed and talked and drank and ate, the back lawn a patchwork of tan lines and boat shoes and spaghetti straps. After that there was dinner in the tent, and a band playing cover songs; some drunk people danced, some very drunk people swam. However large the tent or mild the night, many guests seemed determined to spend as much of the party as possible inside the house. They were always looking through things – flicking through books, opening up the roll-top desk. No matter how many waiters were circulating with drinks, the liquor cabinet was thoroughly plundered. No matter how many portable toilets were set up along the driveway, and suitably accessorised with scented candles and Turkish cotton hand towels, women still trooped upstairs to the bathrooms and ended up lying on beds in companionable gaggles, picking at coverlets and chatting. Olivia had found people watching television in guestrooms; she'd found people in the kitchen, making themselves a midnight sandwich. Somewhere in the house, at any given time, someone would be playing a guitar, someone would be throwing up in the housekeeper's bathroom, and someone else would be pulling framed photographs off the wall to scrutinise the owner's friends and relatives.

The Sanfords' guests, swarming around the house and invading the grounds, reminded Olivia of the flying termites that descended on New Orleans every May, when you couldn't risk leaving on a porch light, or turning on a bedside lamp without making sure the drapes were tightly drawn. The termites followed the light to every crack in the house, and then whirred about inside, brazen and fluttering. Maybe if Olivia turned off all the power, the party would be over. She stood on the back lawn laughing to herself: she'd been wrong to long for a little rain. What they really needed was an electrical storm.

'Nice to see you smiling,' Uncle Ned said, brushing her face with his damp lips, his wiry beard. He was a big man in real estate on the South Shore; he knew everybody. He'd always been kind to Olivia, unlike most of Paul's family, who'd always thought she was too young and prissy and Southern for Paul. She'd gone to college in Charleston, for God's sake. Instead of a junior year abroad, she'd flown back and forth to New Orleans to attend parties and luncheons and balls, and to make her debut. To them she was quaint, outmoded, and perhaps a little simple.

A young waiter carrying a tray of champagne inserted himself between them, the tray denting Olivia's left breast.

'There's so much to be thankful for,' she said, but the look that flickered across his face made her regret the sarcasm. He was growing bored with her unhappiness, perhaps. God knows she was tired of it herself, so it must be unbearable to other people.

'I'm sitting at your table, I hope?'

'Of course.' Maybe later she'd whisper to him about

the baby. It would explain things.

'Is Anthony Conti here yet?' Uncle Ned had lowered his voice. Anthony Conti was Paul's biggest client; Uncle Ned had introduced them at this very party two years ago. Conti owned a long chain of small expensive hotels: the smaller the hotel, Olivia learned, the more it cost to stay there. Paul's agency won Conti's worldwide business, which meant Paul could take Olivia to stay in chic Conti hotels in Istanbul and Sydney and Madrid. But now the agency was down to the North American business and that, Paul had told Olivia, might not last much longer: Conti's people were rumbling about going to a bigger agency, about tapping into fresh creative ideas elsewhere.

'I haven't seen him.' Olivia gazed around, pretending to look for Conti. He wasn't here; he wasn't coming. Paul hadn't told her this, but she was sure of it, somehow, just as she was sure this would not be an eight-figure year. Paul's agency had lost three important accounts since March. He wouldn't admit that losing another would jeopardise the business, of course, but earlier this month, at a dinner party in the city, she'd heard him talking openly about the case against State Farm, talking about the money they were expecting from the wreckage of Pass Christian. 'Thank God for Katrina,' she'd heard him say, though later, on the way home, he denied it. This made Olivia so sick she could barely speak to him.

Uncle Ned wandered off to find Paul, but Olivia stood in the same place, holding a flute of orange juice she pretended was a mimosa, allowing people to kiss her and tell her untrue things about the weather, her dress, and the lovely, lovely party. Her heels dug welts into the lawn. Tomorrow, the garden would look flayed and exposed, its usually serene expanse scarred with hundreds of dirty rivets. On Monday, when all the tents and tables and Port-A-Potties were gone, someone would arrive to roll and primp the lawn back into shape. Nobody would know the party had ever taken place.

There were more people than usual, she decided. But there were fewer she knew, or remembered meeting. And they all seemed to be talking more loudly than usual, and demanding more. She would never use this caterer again, that was certain. He asked her another question every ten minutes, as if she cared at this point about extra vegetarians and the suddenly glucose-intolerant, as if she had the power to prevent the flower arrangements from shedding chalky yellow pollen onto tablecloths.

When dinner was ready, everyone crowded into the tent, drawing up rented chairs to dozens of moon-like tables. There were ten people at their table. The place cards for Anthony Conti and his wife had been whipped away and replaced, on Olivia's orders, just before everyone sat down. Teen waiters in white shirts and black Bermuda shorts set down arugula salads; later there was poached salmon. One of Olivia's new potatoes didn't feel very new. The green beans squeaked against her teeth. She had to resist the urge to eat every bread roll on the table.

'This is the new Gilded Age,' Paul was saying to the table at large, in the strident voice he had started assuming every time they had guests. 'Luxury and excess. No taste, no authority.'

'It's strange that you're this dismissive of what you call the new Gilded Age,' Frank Grange said. He was one of Conti's management team, a tall, intense man; his wife was Isabel, Olivia silently recited, trying to remember everyone's names, and she was from Uruguay. She looked very austere. Paul had told her once that the Uruguayans were even snobbier than the Venezuelans. Olivia didn't know one way or the other: they'd never taken any trips to Conti Hotels in South America. 'So many of your clients rely on the desire of their customers for exclusivity and luxury. Our businesses – our brands – are built on this demand for personalised service. I'd argue that expectations and taste levels are high right now.'

Paul started ranting again about how slutty 'it' girls and socialites with drug problems were role models, how people were bombarded with information and yet still underinformed. Someone started arguing with him about advertising's role in all this. Didn't advertising bombard and misinform? Didn't the industry rely on celebrities to launch and promote brands?

A familiar sense of panic rose in Olivia. It seemed that dinner would be ruined, yet again, by Paul's arguments. When they were first married, she thought of Paul as gregarious, but now he just seemed like a bully. Uncle Ned was obviously irritated: he'd told her before that Paul had to learn to tell the difference between friends and business acquaintances. Agencies opened and closed every year. Past success meant nothing if you couldn't pay your bills and couldn't keep your clients.

'You can't be saying that now is worse than the eighties,' Jamie Fuller was chiding Paul. Jamie owned DiveDeep.com, a big online travel company. He wore chic narrow glasses, and looked European, but he wasn't. Paul's agency had devised the national television campaign. The ads featured a talking otter which dived into pools and rivers and oceans and surfaced in another country. There'd been talk of making DiveDeep.com otter dolls, modelled on the Pets.com sock puppet. Olivia had asked Paul who would buy such a thing, and he lectured her for ten minutes on how the Pets.com puppet became a collector's item after Pets.com closed down. When she asked him how soon DiveDeep.com would be closing, he marched out of the room, telling her he was sick of her negativity.

The woman sitting to Jamie's left was glamorous and fifty-something, her dark hair pulled back into a tight, shining bun. Her long earrings were silver – platinum, probably – and looked like three spears, or perhaps three feathers, or three miniature surfboards, hanging from each elegant lobe. Olivia couldn't bear wearing earrings at the moment. Her ears felt itchy and dry, rebelling every time she inserted a stud.

'You probably don't remember the eighties,' the woman said to her, smiling. She was Jan Jacobson, and she was a senior executive for a digital camera company. Sitting next to her was her nephew, who was an investment banker with a place in Southampton – he was Olivia's main competition for the bread rolls – and her nephew's wife, who talked about tennis.

'I grew up in the eighties,' Olivia told her. 'That was my childhood, so I have a lot of fond memories.'

'That's right,' Paul interjected. His face was red. 'Fond memories of the Redneck Riviera. Really, that's what they call it down there – the Gulf Coast.'

'I thought you were from Atlanta?'

'New Orleans. But he's talking our summer place in Mississippi. Pass Christian.'

'They've never heard of it,' Paul told her. He leaned forward to address Jan. 'It got wiped out by Katrina. The whole town.'

'Oh, I'm so sorry! Did you lose everything?'

Olivia had come to hate this question and its breezy fake concern, but one of them had to pretend to be polite to their guests.

'Yes, but we hope to rebuild soon.'

'There's no point, really, is there?' This was Jim Halpern from the cell phone company, one of Uncle Ned's old friends, and one of Paul's first clients when he broke away from the big agency and started his own place. 'It'll just flood again. It's like all those people in the Carolinas who build those houses on sticks in the sand, and then cry like babies when the storms wash everything away.'

'What about Southampton?' Uncle Ned shrugged. 'It's just as bad up there. But everyone wants to be on the beach. You can't tell anyone anything.'

'Did you say you haven't rebuilt yet?' The investment banker was between bites. 'Taking your time, aren't you? The hurricane was years ago.'

'Last year,' Olivia corrected him. She was still trying to smile, but her lips felt stuck together with orange pith and the last of her lipstick. 'Hurricane Katrina hit a year ago. A year ago on Monday, actually.'

'Really? It seems much, much longer ago, doesn't it?' He looked at his tennis wife; she nodded.

'Not like September eleventh,' Olivia muttered, disguising

the heresy by dabbing at her mouth with a napkin.

'Well, at least it was just your summer house that got the damage,' said Jan Jacobson, smiling at her in a it's-not-that-bad way that Olivia associated with OB-GYN nurses and elementary school teachers. 'It was only a second home.'

'Didn't Trent Lott have a vacation place down there?' asked Jamie Fuller.

'In Pascagoula,' Paul told him. 'You probably haven't heard of that either.'

'I mean,' Jan continued, still smiling at Olivia, 'at least you're not like one of those people who lost their actual homes. That was the real tragedy. I saw them on TV – it was terrible. I said to Alex, I said, can you believe this is America? You should consider yourself lucky you're not one of them.'

'So many of them have better lives now,' Jim Halpern explained to everyone, looking around the table. 'They're living in Houston or Dallas now. Some of them are up here even. They've all got better jobs and apartments. Turns out they couldn't wait to get out of New Orleans. That city was going nowhere. The hurricane was the best thing that ever happened to them.'

'You sound like Barbara Bush,' said Isabel of Uruguay. Her accent was American. She'd been to Yale, Olivia remembered. She'd been to boarding school in Massachusetts.

'It's not a racist thing,' Jim protested. 'God knows I'm no Republican. I'm just saying that it was a very unequal society down here, and a lot of people are way better off.'

'Olivia grew up with black servants,' Paul said. Nausea gripped her stomach: he was just being malicious now. Why was this conversation about her now? 'She grew up with black maids and cooks and gardeners.'

'Don't people in New York have black staff?' she asked, trying to keep her voice light. Her mother's housekeeper, Shirlee, was black, and Claude, who trimmed the hedges and put up the lights for Christmas, was black. Of course they were black: everyone in New Orleans was black, back then, anyway. Nobody wept as hard at her mother's funeral as Shirlee. She insisted on making crab cakes for the wake; she wouldn't budge from the stove. Shirlee was her mother's best friend. Olivia gave her all of her mother's clothes, all of her bags and shoes and church hats. Paul didn't know anything about love and home and loyalty. He didn't know anything about New Orleans.

'Our housekeeper is Chinese,' said Isabel of Uruguay.

'We had a black nanny,' Frank reminded her. 'For a while. Then we got the Swedish girl.'

'Let's not talk about the Swedish girl.'

'When you go to parties in New Orleans,' Paul shouted, as though everyone at the table were deaf, 'the only black people there are the ones serving you food and drink.'

'I don't see too many black people here tonight,' Olivia said. Nobody said anything. Jim Halpern looked around, perhaps hoping to spot a black person or two at another table. He'd be out of luck, she knew. There wasn't even a single black person on the wait staff.

Soon they were all talking again, careering from one subject to the next like a skittish school of fish. Olivia said as little as possible for the rest of the meal. She was tired of Paul shouting down their guests and ignoring whatever she said. Actually, nobody at the table seemed that interested in listening to her. Everyone just wanted to talk.

The tent seemed to inflate with all the noise of talking and clinking and music. The band played 'Moon River' and 'The Girl from Ipanema'. Olivia looked for Paul's business partners and their wives, all sitting at other tables nearby. Olivia had worked as an assistant to one of the partners, the senior art director, when she first moved to New York. She was just filling in while his PA went on maternity leave. That was how she'd met Paul. When she got a full-time job, of sorts, answering the phone in a small art gallery, he'd come after her, face pressed against the glass, pretending he was interested in buying sculpture.

They were married eighteen months later, because she wouldn't move in with him otherwise, and because – he said – Olivia was different from the other women he met in New York. She was softer, more ladylike. She was younger too, and not as strident and desperate as the gaunt harpies-in-black who assailed him, apparently, at every social event. By then he'd seen the house on Camp Street and the house in Pass Christian as well: Olivia didn't think about that at the time, but she did now. She thought about it a lot. Paul was from Bridgehampton. His parents were divorced. His mother taught high school. He spent his summers serving food and drinks at parties just like this one.

After dessert was served, and the band announced they were taking a break, Olivia slipped away. She hurried out of the tent as though she were on an important errand, walking with her head down towards the other side of the house. Maybe she'd sit by the pool for a while. It was too early for people to be drunk enough for swimming. She had to get away from her awful husband and his awful guests.

'Lovely party, Olivia dear!' someone called, sailing back to the tent from the bathroom, and Olivia smiled and bobbed her head. She felt like the little toy dogs she used to see in the back of cars: silly, decorative, pointless.

By the swimming pool it was quiet. Sometimes, in the garden, at this time of the evening, Olivia would go for a walk and focus on the baby forming within her, imagining its unfurling fingers, the curve of its head, its round sweet wholeness. She was protecting it, she whispered, from all the ferocious clatter of the world. Tonight it was hard to escape that clatter, especially once the band started playing again. She tried lying back on a sun lounger, but lying still made her feel sick. The humidity was a clamp around her head. Voices drew near and then ebbed. Every time Olivia thought someone was coming, she felt another bubbling of nausea, another panicky twist in her gut.

Oliva dipped her hands in the water, then ran them through her hair. She'd been pacing around the pool for twenty minutes at least, she decided, like a manic polar bear. Voices: she could hear voices again, growing louder. People walking up the path. They would want to talk to her, to tell her it was a lovely party.

The shed was close by: its door was unlocked. She stepped into its muggy darkness, stubbing her foot against something – filter equipment, sun umbrellas. The air inside was dead and dusty. It smelled of old swimsuits. With one trembling hand she held onto the handle of the door, waiting for the voices to pass.

It was Paul, with Lucy Lind, their neighbour's daughter. He'd abandoned their guests as well, and this irritated Olivia. Both of them couldn't run away. He could talk to Lucy any old time.

'I don't know if it was the right thing to do,' Lucy was saying in her clear, high voice. 'But I just had to get away. Sarah Lawrence just wasn't right for me, not now, anyway, and now the movie's taking off . . .'

'I know what you mean.' This wasn't the Paul of half an hour ago. This was warm, sympathetic Paul. Paul who loved women, loved listening to them. How dare he! The affront of it, Paul mocking his own wife, but happy to console a drop-out delinquent! Lucy was the very kind of celebutante-in-the-making Paul was criticising at dinner. He was the worse kind of hypocrite – the nearing-middle-age kind. 'It's so great that you're following your dreams. I totally loved the movie.'

Paul hadn't loved the movie at all. He'd told Olivia that it was sub-Tarantino schlock and that she shouldn't bother going: the hand-held camerawork would make her feel sick. She wished there was a window to peer through. Lucy was probably running her hand through her long black hair, over and over, an annoying habit that she'd learned from her mother. Davina Lind was a former starlet with an indeterminate accent. A family of starlets, thought Olivia, living right next door. A family of starlings, with their insistent cheeping and preening and thieving, spoiling every summer with their attention-seeking behaviour. She caught her breath, straining to hear the conversation.

'I don't know what I'm going to do myself,' Paul was saying. His tone was unrecognisable. Why did he never speak to her this way? 'Things aren't looking so great these days. Clients are bailing. The agency doesn't feel untouchable anymore. It's like we've lost our edge.'

'What about *your* edge?' asked Lucy, only a few feet away from the door, close enough to touch. Olivia wanted to step out of the shed and slap her. It sounded as though Lucy was reading lines from a script, something written by one of her over-entitled snooty sophomoric blogger friends. 'What do *you* really want from life?'

'I don't know.' Paul's voice was low and sad. 'I thought I wanted all this, but I'm not sure. It must sound stupid to you, someone who's nearly forty still not sure what he wants to do when he grows up.'

'It doesn't sound stupid at all.' Lucy giggled, and then Paul was laughing as well. It was pathetic. Olivia hated him for betraying her in this way. When he talked about 'all this', he meant more than the agency. He meant the house. He meant the party. And this was a lie: he was the one who wanted these things. She'd never wanted these things. They couldn't even afford these things anymore.

Or perhaps 'all this' meant their marriage. Perhaps Paul thought it was a good idea to marry Olivia, but now he was realising that he had many more years of playing the field left in him. The alternative to sweet, Southern Olivia wasn't the harpy-in-black; it was the girl next door who was going to Sundance and getting interviewed by Conan O'Brien.

'. . . these boring dinners,' he was saying, 'and the way everyone's obsessed with real estate and work.'

'God, I know! That's why I'm moving to the West Coast.'

More giggling. Olivia tensed her grip on the doorknob.

'Maybe I should think about somewhere else too. A fresh start. You know?'

'I do, I do,' agreed Lucy. As if she knew anything! As if she had done anything in her life but play games and pose for pictures and chatter at parties! The fact that Paul chose Lucy to confide in made Olivia sick with rage.

They were moving on now, towards the shouts of other voices beyond the hedge. When everything was quiet again, apart from the distant throb of the band, Olivia stepped out of the shed. Away from its suffocating heat, things seemed different. Paul wasn't telling the truth. He couldn't live anywhere but New York. He didn't know how to *be* anywhere else. At their wedding in New Orleans, he had a bemused smile on his face the whole time, as though they were getting married in a theme park rather than a real place.

Olivia sat on the edge of a chaise. She felt slightly dishevelled, and ashamed. Paul was stupid and conceited and blustering, but things were hard for him right now. He was worried about work, worried about the baby. And he wasn't in love with Lucy: she was just someone who was prepared to listen while he trotted out a few crazy ideas after dinner. The party was a strain on them; he wanted it over, Olivia suspected, as much as she did. She would find him and reassure him, the way she used to, the way a good wife should. She would squeeze his hand, and let him know, with a smile, that they were in this together.

Back at the house a group of men sat on the porch telling stories and drinking. Someone was talking on his cell phone: it was Frank Grange, probably reporting all Paul's indiscretions to Anthony Conti. Inside the living room, a young man played the piano to an audience of three, and she paused, pretending to listen.

'Very good,' she said to nobody in particular.

Paul was in the study, rummaging in the drawer for cigarettes. His shirt was too unbuttoned, Olivia thought. At dinner he'd left two buttons open; now half of his chest hair – a non-colour, something between brown and grey – was visible. It was not attractive, but she'd say nothing about it.

'I was looking for you,' she said. He glanced up, his face indifferent.

'What's the problem?' he said, looking past her, to the open door. 'Make it quick. We're going to start the croquet. You're not playing, I take it?'

She shook her head. Paul scooped up the cigarettes, and hurried towards the door. He couldn't bear to be around her, she thought. He wasn't interested in her smiles or sympathy.

'Sit down for a while.' He gripped her shoulder; it felt as though he was pushing her out of the way. 'Don't over-do it. You were all defensive and emotional at dinner. It's just the hormones, I know.'

Olivia said nothing. He left the room whistling the tune the pianist in the living room had been playing. Never before had she felt such antipathy towards her husband, such overwhelming disgust for everything about him.

The croquet tournament was going on in partial darkness. When Olivia passed by, half the lighting had collapsed, and the tennis instructor, who was not invited, was standing on a chair beaming a spotlight onto the players. She stopped for a moment to chat with some ladies – they wanted coffee, and she told them it was being served in the gazebo – and again in the kitchen garden, where the housekeeper seemed to be spearheading a raspberry-picking expedition. They would be sure to trample everything.

Olivia batted a cloud of midges away from her mouth, feeling both weak and cold, although the evening was still muggy. She wandered down to the water's edge in search of a breeze. Uncle Ned was there, showing off his new boat.

'Livvy.' He put his arm around her and lowered his voice. 'You must speak to Paul. He can't shoot his mouth off like this. It alienates people.'

'I don't think anyone's left yet,' replied Olivia, wanting it to sound like a joke; it didn't, she knew.

'Some of them didn't come at all. Where is Anthony Conti? I can see the lights on at his house.' Uncle Ned gestured at the compound on the far side of the pond. 'It's a very bad sign. Very bad indeed. Paul may think he's being amusing when he takes his extreme positions, but he has to remember that these people are clients, or potential clients. If they think he's a buffoon, they'll take their business elsewhere.'

'It's just a party,' Olivia said. She didn't want to defend Paul, but here she was, doing it anyway. 'People do stupid things at parties. They drink too much. They talk too much. It's a social event, not a business meeting.'

'Everything's business,' said Uncle Ned. 'Paul should know that.'

Something about this irritated her. It sounded as though Uncle Ned expected Paul to know things that Olivia didn't; that he saw Olivia as naïve, socially inept.

'Then it's up to him,' she said. 'I can't tell him what to do. He doesn't listen to me anyway. I'm sick and tired of parties like this full of people we barely know, pretending they're our friends when it's all about work.'

'Keep your voice down,' he said sternly, and Olivia thought she was going to cry. Why was she the one in trouble, when Paul was the one who'd been shouting all night?

Then Selly was there, pulling Olivia's elbow, telling her that Colin Brett had arrived and was asking for her.

Colin Brett was one of the few people Olivia knew in New York who was in her class at the College of Charleston. Paul didn't like him, of course, because he wasn't important enough. His MFA was from Columbia, which was the kind of credential that impressed Paul's set, but it hadn't turned into literary fame or riches of any kind. Now Colin taught at a community college in one of the outer boroughs, Olivia couldn't remember which, and slept on some friend's floor whenever he came out in the summer to this end of the island.

He'd been sidetracked on arrival by the croquet match. Quite an audience had gathered, Olivia was surprised to see, and Paul was enjoying all the attention, leaping over hoops and shouting advice to his team, which seemed to consist of Lucy Lind and the brainless De Vere twins. Colin was standing in the darkness, picking fruit salad and chunks of cold salmon off a plate with his fingers. He still looked as young and scruffy as he did in college. He hadn't even bothered to shave.

'You're very late,' she told him, and he laughed, spitting specks of melon onto her cheek.

'Not late enough,' he said, ruefully. 'I was hoping your husband would be too merry by now to object to my presence.'

Paul had given up coaching the more anaemic looking of the De Veres and was talking to a man on the other team. She heard him say 'on the Gulf Coast'.

'What is he saying?' she asked Colin.

'When I got here? He didn't say anything much.' Colin had misunderstood what she was asking. He eased a food fleck from between the gap in his teeth. 'The usual. I don't think he likes other men hanging around you, even if they're losers like me from south of the Mason–Dixon.'

'You don't hang around me,' said Olivia. 'I hardly ever see you. You're the one friend of mine who comes to this party.'

'I thought all these people were your friends.'

Olivia turned to face Colin. He was the only person who'd understand.

'They all despise me,' she whispered, but everyone was cheering and clapping some croquet manoeuvre. Colin leaned in, straining to hear.

'What?'

'They're not my friends,' she told him.

'Nobody's really friendly up here,' Colin said. He looked around for a place to leave his plate. 'But at least they leave you alone. That's why we moved north, remember?'

Olivia shook her head. She'd hoped that Colin would see things the way she did. Every time Paul talked about the South, it was an attack on her. Her husband would never forgive her, she saw that now. He would never forgive her for being the one with the money.

She wanted to tell Colin that she was having a baby, but that Paul was a monster, and this party was a mistake; everyone had to leave at once. Colin would have to make everyone leave. And first he would have to tell Selly to stop looking at Olivia in that endless, impertinent way, like a cat assessing its prey, from across the croquet lawn.

Colin brushed a hand against her arm. She hoped he was about to propose something illicit, something dirty. Maybe he wanted to do it standing up in the pool shed. He could whisk her away in that Toyota of his, except it was always breaking down. Why didn't he rescue her?

'Is that *the* Lucy Lind?' Colin asked. Lucy was running towards them. Her dress was completely, unbelievably see-through. 'That movie she's in isn't bad at all. Would you mind introducing me?'

'We've just had the best idea!' tweeted Lucy, so close that the wine on her breath made Olivia blink. 'Paul said we could if you're OK with it. We want to row to the beach and eat raspberries and ice cream! Can we do it? We'll take everything on the boats.'

'Whatever you want,' Olivia said. The party didn't belong to her; it was going on whether she wanted it or not. Let them all row to the beach and drop plates and glasses into the pond. Maybe the Association would ask the Sanfords to leave. It would be a blessing in disguise.

After the croquet was abandoned, everyone under twenty and over sixty seemed to be hurrying towards the dock, dropping things and shouting to each other. There was Colin, carrying a picnic basket, and Selly, carrying nothing as usual, and people Olivia didn't know who were drunk, and the tennis instructor, who now appeared to be in charge, and even Uncle Ned, good humour restored, loading women onto his boat with exaggerated care. Paul strolled by, smoking a cigar.

Olivia wanted to say something nasty and hurtful to him.

'I thought Anthony Conti was supposed to come,' she said, folding her arms tight across her chest. 'There are lights on at his house.'

Slowly, precisely, Paul blew a puff of smoke in the opposite direction.

'I'm glad he's not here,' he said.

'You're a liar,' Olivia told him, but he was already surrounded by twittering De Veres and was pretending not to hear.

Olivia did not cross the pond on one of the boats. It would have taken less time to walk to the beach. Rain began to fall, and the guests who stayed behind gathered in the tent or inside the house. She wandered from room to room, feeling breathless, wishing everyone would leave. Reports filtered in about the beach expedition: there'd been one near-capsize and a lot of broken glass. Making her way to the tent to thank the band, Olivia could hear a lot of idiotic shrieking. The rain was persistent; everyone was coming back.

The party was over. Uncle Ned left without saying goodbye while Olivia was attending to a disoriented child wandering the upstairs hallway. Colin Brett's car wouldn't start and, after various male huddles and conflicting mechanical opinions, he accepted a bed for the night next door at the Linds'. Olivia stood on the porch, tendrils of hair plastered to her forehead, waving goodbye.

When she went upstairs to go to bed, Paul was still down in the living room, holding court with Selly and her city friends. Olivia cleaned her face and brushed her teeth. Even after she shut the door and climbed into bed, the sound of Paul talking carried up from downstairs. His voice was louder than the rain, louder than the ocean.

Olivia had left her dress on the floor, a slick of dirt against the pale wood, and Paul skidded on it when he walked in.

'Still awake?' he asked, pulling his shirt over his head. She watched him struggling with his clothes like a little boy and felt a wave of pity for him.

'I wish you would tell me things,' she whispered.

'What?'

'Like the things you told Lucy tonight. I heard you. By the pool. I was in the shed.'

'What the hell are you talking about?'

Olivia started to cry. 'Those things you were saying to Lucy about work and your life. How you wanted to change everything and move somewhere else. How you didn't want the life you have.'

'Why were you hiding in the shed? What's wrong with you? Have you gone insane?'

'Why do you have to be so secretive?' she sobbed.

'I'm secretive?' he snapped. He threw his pants down on the bed. 'You're the one hiding and spying and eavesdropping, like a goddamned madwoman.'

Olivia couldn't breathe. She'd heard those words before –

when was it? When Selly was telling them some story once, about her husband leaving. He had told her she was mad, quite mad, insane, crazy, cuckoo. That was the reason he gave, just before he left.

'Though not so crazy I couldn't be left with all his damn children,' Selly had said, toasting her divorce with a mug of bourbon. It was right here, two summers ago, Olivia remembered. On the porch. Not long after the party.

Olivia stopped crying. She decided to get up that instant, get dressed and leave the house forever. This place was nothing to her. She wanted to go home. Except her brother had sold the house on Camp Street, and there was nothing in Pass Christian anymore, not even a mailbox. Paul stood in his boxer shorts, watching her.

'What are you doing, Olivia?'

'Going.' She picked up the T-shirt she'd been wearing earlier in the day and pulled it over her head. There was nowhere to go, but she had to leave. That much was clear.

'Get back into bed. We'll talk about it tomorrow.'

'I know why you married me,' she said, groping for something else to put on. She'd leave in her pyjamas if necessary. 'You wanted it all. You're just hanging on for the insurance money.'

'I don't know what you're talking about.'

'Of course you do. I hear you telling people.' Olivia reached for her flip-flops, flinching when she bent back a fingernail. 'I know you hate it there.'

'What are you saying?' Paul looked old and helpless now. He looked confused.

'I'm saying that I know you hate me.' She sat down hard

on the bed and burst into tears. 'You hate me, and I hate you.'

Paul didn't speak. He was bending over Olivia, stroking her hair. A clenched fist of pain hit her belly, and for a moment she thought he'd struck her. But then she realised that the clenching was internal, that Paul was gently lifting her feet onto the bed and sliding the flip-flops off.

'We don't hate each other,' he was saying. 'You know that's not true. This is just a hard time. We should never have had the party.'

He climbed onto the bed next to her, grasping her tight. Though she was trying to stay as still as possible, Paul was trembling; they both shook together.

'I'm so sorry,' she whispered.

'I don't care about the money. We'll rebuild the house. Next year, I promise you, we'll rebuild the house.'

'I don't care about the house,' Olivia said. Her father was gone; her mother was gone. There was nothing left of that life; it couldn't be assembled again. Her past had been washed clean. There was only the present now – lying with Paul on this bed, an intense pain wringing her insides. Paul was crying, shuddering against her back. She gasped, her sobs staccato.

'It'll be OK,' Paul said, his face in her hair, his voice muffled. 'Everything will be OK.'

He'd said this before, Olivia remembered. It was a year ago, the night after the party. The television was on in the bedroom; they were watching the angry red eye swirling up the Gulf. Her mother had left New Orleans late that morning, after the mayor declared evacuation mandatory. It had taken her ten hours to drive to Jackson, less than two hundred miles away. Camp Street was on high ground, near the river. A tree fell across the porch, half the roof blew off, and there was no electricity until after Thanksgiving, but Paul was right: it was OK. Further east at Pass Christian, the winds and the water bore everything away.

They were lying on the bed that night, too, but it wasn't so muggy. Tonight they were stuck together, damp; it felt as though it were raining inside the room. Olivia's thighs were warm and wet, liquid seeping down her legs. She placed a hand in her lap and felt the blood, sticky against her skin. She closed her eyes, breathing in its pungent sweetness. She was awash in blood; they both were, though Paul didn't realise it yet. He didn't know they were floating across the pond on a dark, determined tide. Olivia let him hold her. Soon he would stop shaking, go to sleep. The storm would pass.

Testing

On Mark's first day at the Center, his group leader introduced him to his group. Erma had been working there longer than anyone else, longer even than the group leader.

'It's Erma with an E,' she told Mark. 'Not Irma with an I.'

He had never heard of the name Erma with an E before, but Erma herself seemed strangely familiar. She wore glasses and a pink turtleneck. Her ears were slightly pointed. She could have been any age between thirty-five and sixty.

Next to Erma was Sarah. Like Mark, Sarah had spent the past couple of years at the university up on the hill. When she didn't work at the Center, she was finishing a PhD in Art History.

'I'm ABD,' she told Mark, and Erma explained that this meant All But Dissertation. Mark nodded politely. He knew what ABD meant.

'I'm sure Mark knows what ABD means,' said the group leader. 'He just finished his PhD.'

'Is that right?' said Erma. Sarah gave a strained smile. Mark couldn't tell if the spots on her face were freckles or acne. The lights in the Center were shrill and fluorescent.

'It was an MFA,' he told the table, and everyone looked relieved.

'We get a lot of those in here,' said Erma. 'They don't last long.'

Next to Sarah was Nathaniel, a big guy with bushy sideburns. He was a local, according to the group leader. He saluted Mark but said nothing. Next to Nathaniel was Jessica, who was small and slender, her fair hair wisping around her face. She looked miserable.

'Jessica just moved here from Florida last month,' said the group leader. 'Her husband works for the Co-op. She's having trouble getting used to our winters.'

'Brrrr,' said Jessica.

Outside it was twenty degrees. Everything was grey and brown, and snow was forecast for later on. But there were no windows in the workroom or the lunch room at the Center, and Mark realised he would not know if it was snowing or not until he went outside to the parking lot at the end of the day. Inside it was hot and bright. The walls were white.

Next to Jessica was Andy. Andy had recently retired from a long and successful career in accounting.

'Andy wants to keep his mind active,' the group leader explained. 'That's why he's here.'

'My wife wants to go on a cruise,' Andy explained. He had a hairstyle like the husband on *Bewitched*, flat and slick and old-fashioned. 'And we need the extra money. That's why I'm here.'

Next to Andy was Lan. He was probably the youngest person at the table. His black hair was gelled into spikes. Around his neck he wore a bone fish-hook.

'My girlfriend's in her first semester of the MFA,' he told Mark. 'She's a poet. I'm just hanging out.'

Erma bristled.

'Lan is from the Philippines,' said the group leader.

'I'm from California,' said Lan.

'And I'm Gil, of course, as you already know,' said the group leader. Mark had forgotten his name. 'It's easy to remember. G for group, L for leader.'

'His real name is Bill,' said Nathaniel, the big guy. 'They made him change it.'

'I should warn you, Mark,' said Gil. 'Nathaniel is our joker.'

'We get a lot of jokers in here,' said Erma. 'They don't last long either. The one before you, he was a joker.'

'Well, let's not dwell on the past,' Gil said quickly. 'We have a lot of work to get through this week. Mark, you're our eighth member. Welcome!'

He gestured at the empty chair next to Erma, and Mark sat down. He'd spent Friday at the Center, getting trained on the first floor. This morning he'd had two more hours of training and orientation. The digital clock on the wall read 10:12 AM. There were three minutes of break left. His group had given up their break so they could meet him. By 10:15 all the circular tables in the room would fill again. All talking would cease. Mark glanced around the room: twenty-five tables of eight. Two hundred people.

'We're still doing West Virginia,' Erma told him. 'Then it's Oklahoma.'

'And next week, Michigan!' Gil was smiling. He was no more than thirty, Mark decided. He looked and sounded like he smoked a lot.

'That means we grade on computers,' Sarah explained. 'We don't do it by hand. We don't have to sit around this table.'

'The computers are in the basement,' Erma said. Her fingers, flat against the table, were plump and white.

'Something to look forward to,' Gil told Mark. The doors to the stairs banged open and closed. The elevator door dinged. Everyone was coming back from the break room, where you could buy candy bars and drinks out of a machine; or the parking lot, where you could smoke out in the cold; or the bathroom. Bathroom breaks during work sessions were discouraged at the Center. Talking during work sessions was not permitted. Lunch was thirty minutes, unless your group won Top Group that week. For the following five work days, the Top Group got forty-five minutes for lunch, which meant there was enough time to drive home, use your own bathroom and kitchen, and drive back to the Center.

'It's nearly time,' said Andy, pointing to the clock. A supervisor's assistant, identifiable by the laminated badge around her neck, walked around the table, placing a thick stack of papers in front of each of them.

'Two a minute,' Gil told Mark. 'That's what you're aiming for. Remember, no marks on the paper – just check the ID number against the one on your sheet and fill in the bubble.

That's it there. Stack to the left when you're done. Any questions?'

'When's lunch again?' Mark didn't mean this as a joke, but several of the group laughed.

'Twelve-thirty.'

'It's time,' Erma said. The big room fell silent, apart from the scratching of pencils and the whisper of papers turning. Mark looked at the first paper on his stack. The handwriting of #75677, a seventh grader from West Virginia, was hard to read. He felt panicky and confused. He didn't know what he'd been expecting, exactly, but this wasn't it.

The job at the Center was not a permanent job. Mark just needed something to tide him over. Last May, when he finished his MFA, he decided to stick around in town. He wanted to spend the summer finishing up his novel. He couldn't face moving back to Tucson or trying his luck in New York just yet, and living here was much cheaper. He'd move to New York when he had an agent and maybe a deal.

But the summer was over, and the fall was over, and the holidays had come and gone. His novel was still unfinished. He'd done some teaching at summer school to pay his rent, but there was no teaching work for him once the new semester began because the new MFA students had priority. There were lots of bars and restaurants in town, but they preferred female employees. So Mark put his name down on the waiting list for jobs at the Center just outside town. It paid two dollars more an hour than the university library, where he'd been working part-time. One of the supervisors had called him last week and asked him if he could start right away. He was on two weeks' trial.

His girlfriend, Lisa, worked full-time at the university library. That's where they'd met. Lisa had moved here to do a graduate degree in child psychology, but she'd dropped out. Now she was applying to go to school somewhere else to begin a graduate degree in library science. Mark was considering going with her. He could write anywhere, though his novel would be finished, definitely, before next fall. Even working at the Center, he could write in the evenings and weekends.

Work days ended there at five. Lisa was on early shifts at the library, so she could pick him up. When he walked out of the building at the end of his first day, Mark gazed around the packed parking lot, looking for Lisa's car. He'd forgotten how cold it was outside. He'd forgotten it would be dark. His fellow employees pushed past him, racing to get away.

'Was it OK?' Lisa asked him. He kissed her. Her face was warm, flush from the car heater. She'd worn her dark hair in two long braids, like a hippie or a squaw, until a few weeks ago. Once she applied to library science school, she got her hair cut to chin-length and started wearing it pushed behind her ears.

'It's kind of a nightmare,' he told her. 'We're supposed to grade 120 papers an hour. I'm nowhere near that.'

'How it that even possible?'

'Everyone else in my group seems to manage it.'

'Why do they all wear pyjamas and carry flasks?' Lisa gestured towards the figures, lit up by head lights, scurrying to their cars.

In the lunch room, Mark had seen a number of people

with flasks. Erma had a tartan flask full of split pea soup. Andy said he always brought a flask with his own coffee – vanilla and almond roast – because he didn't like coffee out of the machine, and he only drove to the McDonald's on the other side of the highway to get coffee on Friday lunchtimes as a reward for getting through another week. Mark asked him how long he'd worked at the Center. Andy told him five weeks.

'Those are just sweatpants,' he told Lisa. 'A lot of people wear them.'

'Not to work,' she said, looking around the parking lot. 'If I didn't know better, I'd think this place was some kind of institution, and that everyone running out of the building was an escaping mental patient. I've never seen such a bunch of misfits and losers in my life.'

'It's OK,' he told her. He was too tired tonight to work on his novel. He couldn't face looking at any more words on a page. The seventh graders of West Virginia had defeated him. It was taking him two minutes to read and assess their essays, and this was way too long. He needed an evening off to recover. Tomorrow he had to speed up.

On the second day, he was a little quicker. Each essay was a page and a half long. He had to assign it a number grade. One was the lowest and five was the highest. He wasn't supposed to take poor spelling and grammar into account. It didn't matter if the essay was almost illegible, or if the student was almost illiterate. The grade was for the quality of the argument and the way the essay was constructed.

Some of the students wrote in tiny letters so their essays

were hard to read. Some students wrote dumb things in the middle of their third paragraph – like 'Katie Sitkins is a fox' or 'The Titans suck' or 'I bet you're not even reading this, are you?' One kid wrote every word backwards. 'Therefore' was 'Erofereht'. 'However' was 'Revewoh'. Mark saved the paper until break and talked to Gil about it. Gil said that he couldn't mark the student down for this. He had to read it and grade it, just like all the rest.

The backwards essay took Mark almost five minutes to decipher. While he was reading it, Erma glanced over at him three times, her face disapproving. He was taking too long, he knew. Their table would not make the quota for the hour.

Erma was wearing a white turtleneck that day, and a green-and-red brooch that read 'IRISH ROSE'. When they all got back to the table after lunch, Jessica asked her if she was Irish.

'No, I'm German,' said Erma. 'This is for St Patrick's Day.'

'St Patrick's Day is in March,' Nathaniel said. 'This is friggin' February.'

'It's just a few weeks away.'

'It's *five* weeks away. We haven't even had Valentine's Day yet.'

'This is for Valentine's Day *and* St Patrick's Day,' Erma said. The tips of her elf ears had turned pink.

'Why not make the petals egg-shaped? Then you could make it last until Easter.'

'It's nearly time, everyone,' said Gil, sitting down in the chair to Mark's right. He reeked of smoke. 'And bad news,

I'm afraid. We're behind on West Virginia. We won't be starting Oklahoma until Friday.'

Erma looked at Mark. This was his fault, he knew.

'What about Michigan on Monday?' Sarah asked. She looked desperate.

'We're off Michigan. Only the fastest groups get Michigan. After Oklahoma, we'll be getting Hawaii.'

'No!' This was Sarah, or maybe Erma. A supervisor's assistant plopped the third-session papers in front of Mark, even though he still hadn't finished his second-session papers from that morning. Gil whispered to him that missing out on Michigan meant missing out on the computers. Hawaii had to be done by hand.

'Can I transfer to another group?' Sarah asked.

'I've told you before, Sarah – no, you can't. The only way you can change groups is when you're promoted to group leader. That could happen, in time.'

'Hey, what's wrong with our group?' Lan was still cheerful. He was the only one at the table who hadn't spent lunchtime in the lunch room, apart from Gil, who had been summoned to a group leaders' meeting.

'We suck,' said Nathanial. He'd told Mark that Lan got high every lunchtime in his car. That's why he was so cheerful afterwards. That's why he ate three packets of chips at afternoon break.

'How much time?' Sarah asked.

'I've been here eight months,' Erma told her. 'I'm first in line.'

'She sure is,' said Gil. 'Now come on, everyone. We have a lot of catching up to do this afternoon. It's time.'

● ● ●

Time wasn't the only issue. This had been made very clear in Friday's training. Speed was one way each grader was assessed: this was called rate expectation. The other was accuracy, and this was called agreement expectation. Every paper had to be read and graded twice. If the graders disagreed, there was a problem. A third reader, usually a supervisor, had to read and grade the paper as well. This wasted time. It made state education boards nervous.

At regular intervals throughout the day, one or two of the supervisors would arrive on the floor. They always came by elevator, never by the stairs. Mark learned to fear the ding of the elevator, ever since Sarah explained to him at what it meant. Supervisors on the floor were there for one reason only: to pull out a reader who was not meeting agreement expectations. Someone who was slow might speed up or make up the time that day. Someone whose grades did not match the third reader's grades had to be removed at once for remedial training. If readers underwent remedial training and still couldn't meet agreement expectations, they were out. Sometimes people were led away and never seen again. Nathaniel told Mark they were put to death in the basement, but Erma explained they were simply asked to leave the building.

On the third day, not long after morning break, the elevator door dinged. One of the supervisors – they were all women – approached Mark's table. His innards flopped like a dying fish. This was it, he was sure. Not only was he slow, he was inaccurate. He awarded too many threes.

The supervisor bent over Gil and whispered something. She smelled the way Mark imagined tuna casserole would smell. He had never eaten tuna casserole, but he knew people in this part of the country ate it all the time.

Jessica was led away from the table. She was allowed to take her fleece jacket and small white purse with her. Andy caught Mark's eye and shook his head. Taking the jacket was a bad sign, Mark learned later. You didn't need the jacket down in remedial training. You only needed the jacket if you were leaving the building.

After lunch, Gil confirmed their fears. Jessica had been re-trained twice, but she was unable to meet agreement expectations. They would have to soldier on with seven. This meant no chance of Michigan, of course. Sarah looked like she was about to cry.

'Don't worry about Jessica – she's gone to a better place,' Nathaniel told Sarah. 'A place with windows.'

'It's just so much easier on the computers,' Sarah said. She scratched at the freckles that might be spots. 'The screens are big. I like reading things on a screen.'

'I hear at the other Center everyone uses computers,' said Lan. Gil and Erma looked outraged. At the Center, nobody ever talked about the other Center. Quietly in the lunch room, maybe. Openly in the workroom, never. The other Center was a rival testing corporation. It was housed in a long one-storey building on the east side of town. It had a cafeteria.

The next morning, Sarah didn't come in to work. Gil said she was sick, but she didn't come in on Friday either. Nathaniel said he'd seen her that morning, driving east.

Erma looked pleased.

'Don't cross the river if you can't swim the tide,' she said.

'What does that mean?' asked Nathaniel. He shifted around in his seat. Under his fleece-encased bulk it looked like a child's chair. There were fewer people in the room that day. Every table had one or two empty seats. 'Are we just quoting random song lyrics now?'

'We were strangers in the night,' Andy sang in a wavery voice.

'Goodbye, Ruby Tuesday,' sang Lan. Mark couldn't think of any appropriate songs. All he could think of was a line from a Kraftwerk song: 'I'm the operator of my pocket calculator.'

'It's time,' said Gil. His voice was sharp. He smelled like a bonfire that had been smouldering all night.

Monday was Oklahoma. The room was almost full again, but no new readers appeared at their table. At break, sharing some of Andy's vanilla-almond roast, Mark discovered this was another bad sign. Their group, Andy suspected, was being wound down. Soon Gil would be reassigned or promoted. They would be split up, scattered around strange new tables. Erma might be made a group leader.

'Why don't they just make her group leader of our table and add a few people?' Mark asked.

'They don't like to promote within a table,' Andy explained. 'It causes jealousy.'

Mark asked Andy if he'd like to be a group leader some day. Andy said he would not.

'Don't say anything to anyone, but tomorrow's my last day,' he told Mark. 'I need time to pack and go to the doctor for some shots. On Friday we fly to San Juan. It's a three-week cruise.'

'Will you come back?' Mark didn't particularly like Andy, but he didn't want him to leave. He didn't want to move to another table. Erma wasn't that bad. Before lunch on Friday, she'd had a little extra time: she'd read some of his papers for him.

'Maybe,' said Andy. He looked away, to the place where a window should be. Someone was kicking the pop machine and calling it a motherfucker.

The handwriting of eighth-graders in Oklahoma was terrible. They didn't seem trained at all in the art of stand-ardised testing. They appeared to have little commitment to academic success. A lot of the papers were ones and twos.

'Remind me not to send my kids to school in Oklahoma,' said Lan, scraping his chair back. His voice was hoarse and a ragged woollen scarf was wrapped tight around his neck.

'Do you have any children?' Erma asked him. Her turtle-neck that day was black. Nathaniel said she was in mourning for the group, because they would never win the forty-five minute lunch, and because they were dropping like flies.

'Not that I know of. Do you?'

Erma gave one of her sphinxy smiles. Mark wanted to ask her how old she was, but he didn't have the nerve.

Gil arrived, frazzled and out of breath.

'Big things going on right now,' he told them. 'All the Idaho people are here to check out the facility. They have a lot of special needs.'

Lan started giggling, and that turned into a coughing fit. He rested his head on the table.

'They don't allow half-point differences in evaluations,' Gil explained to Mark. 'Their rubric is predicated on total agreement. State law. OK, it's time.'

Mark was beginning to think he no longer understood English. Words shimmied in and out of his ears and in front of his eyes. He'd been working at the Center for a week and a half, and he knew nothing about half points. That night, when he lay in bed reading an article in the *New Yorker*, he wondered if he should give it a four or a five. His novel was terrible, he told Lisa. It was going nowhere. Nobody wanted to read another young-man's-coming-of-age story set in the Southwest. They wanted to read novels set in the Northeast written by Russian émigrés or disaffected Muslim youth or glamorous Indian girls who'd been to Ivy League schools.

'You need a platform,' Lisa told him. She was right. He needed to write a blog or start up a literary magazine. He needed to move in certain circles. Before he came to live here, he thought he'd find those circles at the university on the hill, but it had just been drinking and criticism.

He tried to tell Lisa about the circles.

'You mean crop circles?' Lisa asked. 'Very funny.' He dropped the magazine on the floor. Lisa didn't really listen anymore when he talked about his novel or his literary ambitions. All she seemed to be interested in was moving to Pennsylvania and becoming a Master of Library and Information Science.

'What about your circle at the Center?' she said. 'Don't you sit at a round table there, like at Camelot? That's your circle.'

On Wednesday, at the end of the work day, Andy shook Mark's hand and wished him well.

'I have to tell you, I won't miss Oklahoma,' he said. 'You

should have been here for North Carolina. The papers were shorter, and they weren't bad. Not bad at all.'

There were only four people left at their table. Oklahoma would stretch on into next week. Hawaii would have to be pushed back. Hawaii, Gil said, would not be happy.

The next day, a lot happened. Lan only lasted until morning break and then had to leave. His hacking cough was distracting everyone in the room. His nose was dripping onto test papers. Gil had to make an executive decision and send him home.

'He won't be back,' predicted Erma.

After break, the elevator door kept dinging. The sound reminded Mark of a microwave oven announcing that food was ready. Supervisors swarmed the floor, pulling people out for retraining.

Mark got the tap on his shoulder. A supervisor in orthopaedic shoes shepherded him downstairs for remedial training. The first papers that day had been control papers, and Mark's grades did not agree with the preordained grades established by the supervisors. He had to sit at a long table with the other retrainees, reading and grading more control papers, until the supervisors felt comfortable he could meet performance objectives. Lunch for retrainees was at one, for reasons that were unclear. He thought that maybe they didn't want despondent retrainees infecting the good readers with their defeatist attitudes and inability to meet rate and agreement expectations.

At two-thirty he was allowed to return to his table. Gil, Erma and Nathaniel were hard at work. Nobody even looked up from their papers. On the table in front of Erma stood a small toy troll. Its hair was pink and wild, and its moulded plastic chest was bare. Mark found it hard to concentrate on his papers with the troll staring at him.

When afternoon break began, Mark pointed to the new arrival.

'What is it?' he asked Erma.

'My mascot,' she told him, smiling.

'Are you going to do anything about this?' Nathaniel asked Gil. Gil was patting his pockets, not paying attention.

'It's not against the rules.' Erma stopped smiling.

'Well, I'm sure it is. I'm sure there's a 'no table crap' rule.'

'I know all the rules, and I can assure you –'

'What if we all just brought in stuff? What if Mark here brought in a giant stuffed panda and stuck it bang in the middle of the table? What if I brought in a goddamned pot plant and a ship in a bottle? What if Gil brought in a flat-screen TV?'

'Then you would be obstructing the table and disrupting the work of others.'

'I'm telling you this fucking troll is disrupting the work of others.'

'There's no need for that kind of language,' said Gil. He'd found his cigarettes and was fingering the packet, sliding the cellophane hood on and off. 'Mark, is the troll upsetting your work?'

'Disrupting your work,' Nathaniel corrected him.

Mark didn't know what to say. He didn't like the troll, but something told him this was a battle they could not win.

Erma said she knew all the rules and he believed her. She'd probably brought it in specifically to antagonise Nathaniel. The best thing to do would be to ignore it.

'I don't know,' he said at last. Nathaniel looked betrayed, his big face red with anger. Mark needed to say something so Nathaniel would know he wasn't on Erma's side. 'It may be a fire hazard.'

'That's ridiculous,' snorted Erma. 'All this *paper* is a fire hazard. *Cigarettes* are a fire hazard.'

The mention of cigarettes seemed to make Gil even more antsy.

'Right then. The troll stays. Let's keep everything in perspective here – OK, Nate? Let's keep our focus on education. On the kids, yeah?'

Erma sat beaming at her troll as though they were having a sexual relationship. Gil strode towards the stairs.

'It's either me or the troll!' Nathaniel shouted after him. Other people turned to look at him. Mark heard someone say how cute that little troll was, and what a good idea it was to have a table mascot.

'Dude, don't make me choose,' said Gil. He pushed the door open and disappeared down the stairs. When break was over and he returned, nothing more was said about the troll. At the end of the day, Erma packed it away in her bag. She stood up to put her coat on and winked at Mark.

'Trolly says bye-bye,' she said in a cloying baby voice. Mark pretended to smile. He wondered if F. Scott Fitzgerald ever had to work in a testing facility. He wondered if the *Saturday Evening Post* was still a national magazine, and if they still paid a living wage to fiction writers.

After Erma had gone, Nathaniel started complaining to Gil. Gil held up one hand. His fingernails were filthy.

'Not another word about the troll,' he said. 'When you're as fast and accurate as Erma, then you can complain. She's literally carrying the entire state of Oklahoma on her back.'

'This is why we went to college,' Nathaniel told Mark on the way down the stairs. 'This is why we took these very same tests at high school and worked hard to get a five – so we could go to college, and come to work at the Center, and give other loser jackasses a five. Soon *they'll* go to college and then they'll get a job here, and they'll have to sit here all day looking at Erma and her fucking troll, and listening to Gil spout his crap.'

'I mainly give threes,' Mark told him, but Nathaniel was already storming across the parking lot to the snowdrift where he'd parked his car.

Lisa flashed her lights so Mark could see her.

'You didn't tell me Hagrid worked here,' she said. He had to push trash off the front seat before he could sit down. 'This really is a place of myth and legend.'

'We had a troll at our table today,' Mark told her. 'It was a figure of controversy, but I think it may be back tomorrow.'

It was.

On Friday morning, Mark had only read three papers from his stack when he got the shoulder tap. His remedial training had not taken. This time he had to meet with a supervisor in her windowless inner office. Another supervisor joined them.

'We're going to do some papers right here,' the first supervisor told him. 'Ready? Go.'

Mark gave the paper a four. The first supervisor gave it a four. The second supervisor gave it a four. Mark was relieved.

'That's good,' said the first supervisor. 'But the thing is, when you graded this very same paper yesterday you gave it a three. Let's try another one.'

He hesitated over the next one, because it really seemed like a three. But then the two supervisors thought so as well.

'Yesterday you gave it a two,' the second supervisor explained.

'Maybe I'm being too hard on them,' Mark suggested. The next paper was another four, he decided. The two supervisors thought it was a three. Yesterday, they said, he'd given it a five.

'The thing is,' the first supervisor explained, 'states contract the Center for a reason. They expect consistency. They don't want lawsuits. They don't want frustrated students and confused educators.'

'It's the agreement that's important,' the second supervisor said. 'The state of Oklahoma, say, doesn't care if eighty per cent of its seventh graders score a three for their essays. All they care is that two qualified, trained people read each essay and agreed on the score.'

'Well, can't we just agree that whatever score I give a paper is the right score?' Mark asked. He didn't feel the supervisory conference was going well. He needed to construct a compelling argument.

'One of the things the Center offers state governments is integrity of process,' said the first supervisor. The second looked at Mark as though he was a dangerous subversive.

'These are children's lives we're talking about here,' she said. 'The future of our country.'

'But what if a paper could be either a three or a four, depending on your point of view? Neither score is wrong, exactly. It's just a subjective thing.'

The two supervisors exchanged glances.

'It's not a question of right and wrong,' the first supervisor said. 'It's not that one score is more right than the other. It's that there can only be one score. Do you understand?'

Mark nodded.

'Why don't we let you back onto the floor for a while?' suggested the second supervisor. 'We'll do a few more papers together, and then you can rejoin your group at the end of break.'

'They'll be glad to have me back,' he told the supervisors. He felt the need to say something that showed he belonged here. 'We're down to four at our table.'

But nobody seemed to notice he was back. The table was in an uproar. During break, Gil had gone outside for a cigarette and Erma had sped off to the bathroom as usual. While they were away from the table, someone had attacked the troll with what appeared to be a pair of nail scissors. The troll's plastic cheeks and rounded bare belly had been gouged and scarred. Hanks of his pink hair lay in fuzzy acrylic drifts around the table.

Erma was screaming at Nathaniel.

'Don't try to deny it! There are witnesses!'

'I'm not denying anything. That troll attacked me. It was self-defence.'

'Everyone, just calm down.' Gil was looking up at the clock. Mark felt kind of sorry for the troll. The attack had been quite savage. 'It's nearly time.'

The elevator dinged, and four supervisors arrived. The troll was removed. Nathaniel was removed. Erma started sobbing, and was led away. Gil told Mark he'd have to work alone for a while.

'Try to put all this out of your head,' he said. 'Just focus on Oklahoma.'

At lunchtime, rather than eat his sandwich alone, Mark walked across the road to the Sinclair gas station. Outside the wind was stiff, but inside the store it was warm and colourful. There were windows. He stood around looking out of one, drinking bitter black coffee and gnawing on some beef jerky. He thought about Andy on his cruise and Sarah at her computer at the other Center. Lan was probably in bed right now. Jessica might be at the mall, or at home watching a soap opera. He thought about his novel. He'd give it a three. The second reader would give it a two, probably. The third reader would agree with the second reader, and Mark would be overruled.

Back in the workroom, Gil and Erma were sitting at the table. Nathaniel and the troll had not returned. Erma looked wan, but otherwise calm.

'Let's just try and get through the afternoon,' said Gil, his face and voice tight. 'We have to try to make some progress with Oklahoma.'

'What's happened to Nathaniel?'

'I've decided not to file charges,' Erma said. 'But he won't be working at the Center anymore.'

'That's too bad,' said Mark. Erma glared at him. Her ears reminded him of the troll's ears. Erma and the troll could have been related. He turned to look at Gil. The three of them were sitting in a little row, in the seats they'd had for the last two weeks. All the other chairs were empty. 'Could we spread out a little, maybe?'

'No,' snapped Gil. He pointed up at the digital clock. 'It's time, OK?'

At five o'clock, as he was tugging on his coat, Mark saw the first supervisor walking towards him. It was noisy in the big room at the end of the day. He hadn't heard the elevator ding. She took his elbow and pulled him aside.

'I'm sorry, Mark, but we're going to have to let you go,' she said. 'We can't overcome the agreement issues, I'm afraid. We have to meet expectations. I hope you understand and don't take it personally. We have really high standards. Not everyone is cut out to work at the Center.'

Lisa drove him home past dormant corn fields and the big dairy, the one with the giant model cow in the yard. Up on the hill, the university glinted, lit up like the clear winter sky. Its doors were closed to him now. Mark didn't know why he'd hung around in this town so long. He didn't know what he'd been expecting, exactly, but this wasn't it.

Red Christmas

The evening before the inorganic rubbish collection, the three McGregor kids walked to Uncle Suli's and asked to borrow his van.

Ani didn't like asking Uncle Suli for things. It seemed like they were always there, crowded onto his peeling doorstep, waiting for the familiar dark shape to appear behind the frosted glass of the front door. He never said no to anything, not to requests for a loan of a sleeping bag when Tama had school camp, or for half a loaf of bread when they'd run out of everything at home except tomato sauce and there was no money left in the tin under the sink. He'd signed school reports for them, and handed over creased copies of Saturday's *Herald*.

Sometimes there'd be something extra, unasked for – a calendar he'd got free at work, the occasional dollar coin for Henry. Once he offered up a hapuku wrapped in damp newspaper: their mother had boiled it into soupy white chunks that made the house stink for days. They always arrived with nothing and left with something. It was embarrassing.

'Getting late for the kiddies to be out,' said Uncle Suli, scrabbling for the keys in his back pocket. He wore his usual summer weekend outfit: loose canvas shorts, and a polo shirt striped like a deck chair.

'We won't be long,' said Ani, the only one of the McGregor kids old enough to drive.

He told them to try the streets on the harbour side of Te Atatu Road: they'd find a better class of rubbish there, though they were leaving it late, in his opinion.

'The Islanders start cruising before lunch,' he said. 'Soon as church's over. They'll have picked through the lot by now.'

'I don't like going in daylight,' said Ani, staring down at Uncle Suli's feet: his toenails looked like pickled onions. 'It's embarrassing, going through other people's stuff.'

'They don't want it, do they?' said Uncle Suli. 'Nothing to them.'

'I guess.' Ani gripped the key ring tight, its feathery fuzz tickling her palm.

'Everything all right at home?'

She shrugged.

'Well, take care.' He nodded towards the driveway and the dusty green van, the two boys smudged against its scuffed flank. Tama's eyes were closed, and Henry was rolling his tongue around inside of his mouth. 'Don't want another accident.'

'I don't have accidents.'

'You don't have a licence. Here.' Uncle Suli leaned towards

her, pressing something crisp and papery into her hand: she glimpsed the blue corner of a ten-dollar note. 'Buy yourselves something to eat. And if you see anything like a toilet seat or a sink, chuck it in the back. I'm after a new bathroom.'

'Thanks, Uncle Suli,' said Ani, signalling the boys into the van with a jingle of the keys. They clambered into the passenger side, Tama hoisting Henry up by the shorts. Ani leaned against their door to close it. Uncle Suli stood in the doorway, gazing up at the streaky sky.

'Don't forget my Christmas present!' he called.

'Did he give you some money?' asked Tama, struggling with his seatbelt.

'Maybe.' Ani shoved the gearstick into reverse and backed out of the driveway in rapid jerks.

'Look,' said Henry, who sat squashed in the middle, one scrawny leg pressed against the gearstick, jandals sliding off his feet. Uncle Suli was staggering towards the stumpy bushes of the front garden, miming a heart attack.

'He was the one who taught me how to drive,' said Ani. She rammed the gearstick into first and drove away up the hill, eyes narrowed against the glare of the dipping sun.

Almost every house had a stack of rubbish, but Uncle Suli was right: most of it looked picked through, pieces of wood and machine parts and broken toasters separated from their original tidy piles and scattered across the mown grass verges. He was right, too, about the class of rubbish. The inorganic rubbish collection in their own neighbourhood, two weeks ago, had been a waste of time; much of the debris still leaned against letterboxes, unacceptable to the council's rubbish trucks, unwanted by anyone else. Next door to the McGregors' house, a hunk of concrete base from an uprooted washing line still lay on the verge, and a car door from an old Holden, rusty and dented, remained propped against the leaning letterbox.

On the quiet streets on the far side of Te Atatu Road, the stacks were higher and looked more inviting. People threw away whole appliances, not just broken parts; they carried corrugated iron and decking planks into the street, pushed out lawnmowers and old wheelbarrows. They dumped all sorts of useful things, like wire coat hangers and galvanised buckets and pieces of carpet. Last year, someone Tama knew at school had found a black bin bag filled with rolled-up socks, every pair perfect.

On a long curving street where the back gardens tumbled down to the mangroves of the creek, the McGregor kids passed another van, an elderly Asian man sitting behind the wheel. Two younger men angled a washing machine through the rear doors.

'Lucky,' said Tama.

'It's probably broken,' said Ani. 'Seen anything, Eagle Eyes?'

Henry knelt on the seat, one hand on Ani's shoulder, peering around her towards the footpath. He was the best at spotting useful objects obscured by tumbles of plastic and metal. So far this evening, he'd found them a rake with only one broken tine, a director's chair, and a bag of knitting needles.

Last December, he'd uncovered a ripped footstool and a box containing eighteen green glazed tiles. When they got home, their mother sat at the kitchen table fingering each tile as though it were a sea shell, arranging them into a perilous tower. They were too beautiful to use, she decided; she loved green, but they were too green. They reminded her of mussel shells, and of the sea at a place on the coast she visited as a child. They made her sad, she said, and Ani had to pack the tiles away and hide them in the carport.

'There's a lot of stuff there,' Henry said, pointing down the street.

'Quick,' said Tama. He looked over his shoulder, craning to see the other van. 'Before they catch up.'

Ani pulled up outside a dark brick house, its garden and driveway secured behind black wrought-iron gates, a dog yelping from somewhere inside the house. Tama tore the pile apart, but careful Henry crouched with his back to the van, picking through the contents of a cardboard box. The house's cobbled driveway led to a grey garage door, a striped basketball hoop fixed on the wall above. It looked like the kind of house that might have good rubbish, but you could never tell: often the shabbiest houses threw away the most. The poor were too lazy to fix things, according to Uncle Suli; that's why they were poor.

Henry raced up, panting with excitement.

'Here,' he said, shoving things at Ani through the open window. He'd found a power strip and a small metal box, the kind they used for money and raffle tickets at the school gala. Ani wriggled around in her seat to dump them in the back.

'Ani!' Tama slapped the side of the van. 'Open up the big doors.'

He sprang away, thudding off along the footpath to a house three doors down. By the time Ani swung the back doors open, Tama was weaving towards her like a drunkard to make her laugh, balancing a wooden stepladder on his head.

'I saw it,' Henry told her.

'Shut up,' said Tama. He slid the stepladder into the back of the van and pulled something out of his pocket. 'Look at this.'

Cradled in his hands was a bud vase, its narrow flute a mosaic of green glass.

'No chips or anything,' he said. 'Mum might like it.'

Their mother might be up when they got home, staring out the back window and dripping cigarette ash into the kitchen sink, or she might still be in bed, her face turned to the wall, one fingernail picking at a spot in the wallpaper where she said the pattern made an ugly face.

'Shut the doors.' Ani pulled herself up into the driver's seat.

'Move,' said Tama, pushing Henry over. The van crawled away again, and he cradled the vase in his puddled sweatshirt on the floor.

'I'm surprised they threw it away,' said Ani. 'Maybe they'll change their minds.'

'Too late.'

'Feels a bit bad, though, stealing it.'

'It's not stealing.' Tama lifted his feet onto the dashboard. 'And if we don't take it, the Chinks will.'

'I guess,' said Ani, slowing the van as they reached another half-toppled pile, pausing to see if Henry could make anything out in the mess.

• • •

The evening sky turned inky blue, splotched with stars. Ani drove the van down a long looping road, looking for the house they'd noticed last year. The rubbish wasn't great, but the boys liked looking at the front garden.

The house itself was small and expressionless, the kind of plain-faced brick house that looked like the owners were always away on holiday. Flower beds busy with marigolds edged a path twisting towards the terrace; a bridge humped over a tiny pond rosy with orange fish. A plaster gnome was seated, fishing line dangling, at the water's edge. In their street, the gnome wouldn't have lasted a week.

Any rubbish left out had already disappeared. The boys stood a footstep shy of the wall, surveying the garden as though they were prospective buyers. Tama planted his feet far apart: they seemed too big for his body. He was nearly as tall as Ani already, built on a larger scale. His father had lived with them for almost a year, off and on; he was the kind of man who filled a room, their mother said, and that's how Ani remembered him – bulky and towering, wide as a doorway. He was nothing like her own father, who appeared slight, almost ill, in the one photograph she'd seen.

Henry looked more like her in some ways, lean and small for his age. Ani wasn't sure about Henry's father: Uncle Suli referred to him once as a nasty piece of work, but that could have been any number of her mother's friends. Henry's skin was the darkest and Ani's was the lightest. She looked jaundiced, her mother said, like she'd been dipped in cat's piss. There was something of their mother in each of them, something around the eyes or the mouth that told strangers they were a family.

133

Behind the house, the harbour glinted beyond the dense mass of mangroves. The motorway was a string of lights, stretching across the water like a washing line leading to the city. Ani hadn't been to town in months, not since a school trip to the art gallery. Every trip she took was local – a bus to the mall, a walk to the dairy. Even these suburban streets in Te Atatu South, only minutes away from home in the van, felt like a foreign country.

If she drove away now, she could be downtown in fifteen minutes. Ani had never seen the open-air cafés of the Viaduct at night: there'd be candles on every table, wine glasses, white plates. Downtown was like television, brash and glamorous, humming with conversation and music. And beyond that was the rest of the country, a blur of green in her mind, indistinct and unknown. She could follow the snaking line of the Southern motorway to where the city dissolved into the Bombay Hills.

She'd have to leave the boys, of course – leave them right here, staring at the pond and the fishing gnome. Perhaps the old people who lived here would take them in. Tama was a hard worker: he could weed the garden, and fix things around the house, and they could send Henry out at night to crush snails, his favourite after-dinner activity.

But nobody would take them in; she knew that. The people who lived here wouldn't even invite them in for a mug of Milo; more likely they'd be calling the police to report two Māori kids messing up their neat front garden, trespassing on their front step. The boys wouldn't stick around, either. They'd chase the van up the street, calling her name; they wouldn't understand that they'd all be happier living somewhere else with new parents, a new school, a different name. They'd find their way back eventually to the scruffy blue house where the cracks in the driveway spewed weeds, where everything needed picking up or putting right, where their mother would be waiting.

And there was Uncle Suli's van, of course. He needed it because the buses, he said, were overpriced these days and, even worse, they were full of students, layabouts and foreigners.

Tama rapped on the glass and Ani wound down the window.

'Turn the van around quick,' he said. 'The big house back there, see? They're still putting stuff out.'

Ani jammed the van into reverse: it surged like an old sewing machine up to a big brick house they'd passed earlier. The boys ran alongside, Henry tripping out of his jandals, Tama racing ahead. They'd never got their hands on fresh rubbish before.

From the open garage, a grey-haired man in sweatpants and a young woman dragged rattling boxes onto the sloping driveway. A teenaged boy, jeans sliding off his backside, climbed out of a silver Pajero parked on the front lawn. It was hard to believe such a big car ever fit in such a cluttered space. Some people had more possessions crammed into their garage than the McGregor kids had in their whole house.

Tama and Henry lingered in the shadow of the van waiting to pounce. The woman struggled up the driveway with a rusty pair of shears and a garden hose, its tail dragging along the concrete.

'Damian, you carry the particle board,' she called back to the boy. 'It's too heavy for Dad.'

Her father dumped a box full of jangling parts on the verge. Tama and Henry conferred; Henry shook his head. Damian loped up with an armful of cork tiles, glancing up at the parked van and the huddling boys, flashing them a grin. Ani wound down her window.

'Get them,' she hissed to Tama, and he dashed to the verge, scooping up the tiles. Damian returned with a giant square of particle board, leaning it against the front wall and hitching up his jeans.

'It's too big,' Tama told her. 'We'll never get it through the doors.'

The boys made a few more quick raids, picking up a paint roller and tray, a tartan flask and a sagging shoebox packed with nuts and bolts. A car with a trailer had pulled up behind them and a man scuttled out, making for some lino off-cuts and the particle board. Tama scowled at him.

Damian lurched towards the verge, lowering a long folded screen with glass panels onto the ground.

'This is the last of it,' he said, to nobody in particular, and loped back down the driveway.

Henry sprang forward and dropped on top of the screen, his arms spread wide, guarding it with his entire body. The man jamming the particle board onto his trailer looked over, suspicious.

'The doors,' Tama told Ani. 'Quick.'

Ani slid from her seat and scampered to the back of the van, flinging the back doors wide open. Tama lugged the screen towards the van, Henry darting around him, protecting the flank. One of the panels swung free, revealing a brown plastic handle. It was a folding shower door.

'Well done,' whispered Ani, helping Tama to slide the shower door in, leaned over to unfold it: each section was perfect, ridged brown plastic with slender panels of nobbled amber glass.

'Sure you want that?' asked the man with the trailer, pointing an accusing finger towards the dusty back window.

'Bugger off,' said Tama, and they all scrambled back into the van.

'We got Uncle Suli's Christmas present,' said Henry, drumming his heels against the bottom of the seat. Ani drove away from the big house and its shining garage.

'It doesn't even look broken,' said Tama. Last winter, he'd borrowed Uncle Suli's saw and cut down a broken desk the Tongans across the street were throwing away: now they had a coffee table. Ani had thought about re-covering last year's plush stool, but a month ago her mother got upset with Henry walking in front of the television when *Shortland Street* was on, and the stool had been slung through a window. One of the legs snapped when it hit the window frame. Henry got five stitches that night: Ani hurried him up to the Emergency Clinic on Lincoln Road, a pyjama jacket wrapped tight around his punctures. When Uncle Suli knocked on the door later that week, wanting to know about the shattered window and Henry's bandaged arm, she told him that Tama had been mucking about with a cricket ball.

'Anyone hungry?' Ani asked. 'Who feels like pineapple fritters?'

She turned left onto Te Atatu Road, driving faster now, in a hurry to get to the fish and chip shop before it closed.

• • •

Uncle Suli's ten-dollar note bought two pineapple fritters from the fish shop, one for each of the boys, and chips to share, with money left over for a loaf of bread from the dairy.

'I'd rather have more chips,' said Henry, standing over the rubbish bin outside the dairy, nibbling the golden rim of his fritter.

'Where's everyone going?' asked Tama, his mouth full. The people in the cars parked either side of the van were hurrying off down Roberts Road.

'Maybe they've got good rubbish there,' said Ani. She locked the van door and walked to the corner. Roberts Road was packed as a car park, groups of people strolling down the street towards a house burning with white lights, lit up like a stadium.

'I know what this is,' said Henry, scampering ahead. 'It's the Christmas house.'

He danced a few steps away and then zig-zagged back to slam against Tama.

'Don't muck about,' said Ani. She pushed them both past stopped cars towards an empty patch of fence.

The house glimmered as though it were studded with diamonds, each architectural feature picked out with a sparkling string of white lights. A gaudy giant Santa perched on the garage roof, his sleigh hanging off the guttering, the reindeers' antlers blinking candy stripes of red and white. Icing-sugar frost sprinkled the grass. The tiny front garden was cluttered with displays – an illuminated snowman, a waving penguin, a model train zipping around an ornamental pond. Even the Norfolk pine was festooned with giant red baubles and drooping lines of lights.

Ani had never seen a house covered in lights, or a street so busy at night. She'd thought that only shops got decorations, holly and snowflakes spray-painted on their windows, artificial greenery swagged across their counters. The rest of the year, this place probably looked like any other suburban house – parched weatherboards and sandy tile roof, tight-lipped venetians closed against the sun. But dressed up for Christmas, it was an illuminated palace.

'Wait till we tell Uncle Suli about this,' said Henry.

'They must be made of money,' growled Tama in Uncle Suli's voice, and they all laughed.

Some people were brazen, opening the gate and walking into the front garden to admire the decorations close up, shuffling around the displays as though they were visiting the zoo. A man carrying a pug dog leaning over the terrace railing to shake someone's hand. The McGregor kids stayed on the other side of the fence, eating the last of the chips. A loudspeaker rigged to the garage door broadcast a tinny-sounding 'White Christmas'.

'In Iceland,' Ani told the boys, 'when it doesn't snow, they call it Red Christmas.'

'Why?' Henry's mouth glistened with fritter grease.

'Not sure,' she said. It was something she'd heard at school, from a geography teacher. He'd been to Iceland to look at their volcanoes and glaciers, because they were different, in some way, from the volcanoes and glaciers here. Ani knew what volcanoes looked like: ordinary green lumps, neutered and serene, lay all over the city. But she'd never seen a glacier. They were all far away, somewhere south of the Bombay Hills.

'Red Christmas,' said Tama. 'We have one of those every year. We don't need to go to Iceland.'

'Come on,' said Ani. She reached out a hand to stroke Tama's hair, but let it fall on his shoulder. 'It's almost ten. We better be getting the van back.'

Tama nodded, but he didn't adjust his grip on the fence or on the ripped piece of newsprint, spotted with grease from the chips, still pinched between his fingers. His gaze followed the miniature train chugging along the circular track around the fish pond, its caboose painted a cheery yellow, a wisp of silver tinsel poking from the funnel.

'Can we stay a bit longer?' asked Henry.

'Two more minutes,' said Ani.

Although Uncle Suli wouldn't be annoyed however late they arrived, she was suddenly eager to go, to pull the van into his driveway, to see the look on his face when they unloaded the shower door. And when they got back to their house, if they were lucky, their mother would be asleep. They could stow everything in the carport until morning. If she was asleep, it wouldn't be like the time they brought home the glass bowl. She wouldn't have the chance to smash it to pieces; she wouldn't slice Henry's fingers, or half-scalp Tama, or slash Ani's clothes – with Ani still in them, thin ribbons of blood lacing her like a corset. The vase could be hidden, maybe even till Christmas. None of the kids would breathe a word. They were good at keeping secrets.

Mon Desir

Eve could see it all from here.

Slime-coloured paint unfurled from each of the back steps, withering off the wood onto the knobbly cobblestones below. High above her head, obscuring the sun, a skimpy banner of washing (two tea towels, a floral housecoat) swelled in the breeze. And there, only inches away from her face, a spider's web bearded the drooping lower lip of the bottom stair.

There was so much to do – the linen cupboards, for example, or the silver – but, lying on the ground, Eve could only think of bigger things, like lawns and walls and floors. The whole house was buckling in the sea air, drying out. The grass needed scouring, and all those trees needed to be hacked back into shape. There was no point in having a house right on the best beach in Auckland if you could only see the water from the upstairs bedrooms.

But it wasn't her house. She just looked after it each

January while the MacPhersons sailed up to the Barrier. Eve had known Tim MacPherson's parents: she'd been bridesmaid at their wedding forty-five years ago. They'd drowned when a terrible storm came up during the Auckland to Fiji race, when Tim was still a Grammar boy.

The way they died didn't put him off yachting. Nothing did. Even after his first wife, Jill, stepped off their boat one night and disappeared forever into the smooth, dark waters off Kawau Island, he hadn't given up sailing. She'd had a drink in her hand that night – the plastic cup was found bobbing nearby in the morning. They'd been arguing; she'd been depressed. It was in the news. Tim never said much to Eve about it, but after that he started asking her to stay in the house, to look after things, while he and the four children went away every January. He'd kept going out in the boat – bigger boats, newer boats – but since Jill died he seemed more wary, worried about things he'd never cared about before. The house grew shabby and Tim didn't seem to mind, but he didn't like it left unattended. Maybe he didn't want to lose anything else.

This was the twelfth January: summer, 1976. Eve was sixty-two now, a widow. Tim was still sailing to the Barrier every summer, but the two older children did their own thing these days. The girl was at university now and had her own friends and plans; the boy, Lance, had fallen out with his father. He didn't like his new stepmother, or she didn't like him. He came and went, staying at the bach on the overgrown adjoining section, because he wasn't welcome in the house anymore. The new stepmother had left strict instructions.

Every year, Eve did a little something to thank the MacPhersons for having her, and this year it was tidying the linen cupboards and polishing the silver. Clearing away cobwebs. She'd make a start as soon as her head stopped hurting, and her hip, and her ankle. As soon as she could lift herself up on a scraped palm, dust off her dress and climb those steep back stairs into the kitchen to find the broom.

'Your mum's fallen again,' Linda told her husband when he arrived home from work. Michael frowned, tugging at his tie. He was Eve's only child, and sometimes he acted, Linda thought, as though it was a responsibility he hadn't wanted and would prefer to delegate. 'When I rang her this afternoon, she told me. I think it happened a day or two ago.'

'That's it,' said Michael, and in response his shiny briefcase tumbled sideways off a chair, spilling the morning's newspaper and an empty plastic lunchbox onto the carpet. The carpet was brown, and the wallpaper was textured, cream and beige: they lived in a milkshake, Linda said once, and he'd told her to do something about it if she wasn't happy.

'What do you mean, that's it?' Linda reached a mitted hand into the oven. Sun seeped through the dandelion-patterned blind above the sink. She hated this time of day in the summer – the heat of the kitchen, the flies buzzing in every time someone opened the ranch-sliders, the clamour of the television news. Michael was always in a mood, complaining about the long drive home, though it had been his idea to move out here.

'I mean, what'll happen next time if she can't get up?' He stood at the counter flicking through the *Star* rather than getting out of his work things. 'She can't stay there by herself anymore.'

'I thought that we could go. Me and Carrie.' Linda's face felt flushed: it was the heat of the oven, or nerves, perhaps. 'We could stay with her until the MacPhersons get back. She's got less than two weeks left – you could come out at the weekends. I'll leave some meals in the freezer.'

'He likes mince. Don't you, Dad?' Carrie had wandered in from the lounge. She wore towelling shorts and a pale blue T-shirt with a glitter palm tree motif. The word CALIFORNIA was spelled out in sparkling letters across the small bumps of her breasts.

'Well,' said Michael. His tie hung from his hand like a dead eel. When a fly landed in one of his wiry sideburns, he didn't seem to notice. Linda resisted the urge to whack at it with the newspaper. 'I don't think the MacPhersons would like all of us staying there, having a free holiday at their place.'

'It's not all of us,' said Carrie. 'It's just me and Mum. And we're looking after Gran, not having a holiday.'

'I suppose you could stay in the bach next door.' Michael didn't like going to the house on the Shore, not even for a day – Linda knew that. His mother had been friends with Tim MacPherson's parents, but he hadn't known Tim: Tim was older, and they'd gone to different sorts of schools, led different sorts of lives. Tim had inherited the house on Takapuna Beach. The only thing Michael had inherited from his father, as he'd pointed out more than once, was a bill for the funeral home.

'It's really just a week and a half,' Linda said again, her breath tight in her chest. She decided not to mention the other thing Eve said, about the MacPhersons' oldest son returning all of a sudden, camping out in the bach, coming up to the house to scrounge food and pick through the booze cupboard and sweet-talk Eve into washing his clothes.

'House is probably falling down by now,' said Michael. 'It gets worse every year. You'd think that the new wife would want to fix things up a bit. I don't want you doing housework over there. We're not their servants.'

'Course not.' Linda shook off her oven glove, pushed hair away from her sticky face. This was the longest conversation they'd had in weeks and it had gone well, she thought. She'd wanted something and asked for it; he'd agreed. This was what normal families did, what she and Michael used to do. 'Carrie can go swimming and sunbathe. I'll make sure Eve is OK.'

'We can leave first thing in the morning,' said Carrie, hopping from foot to foot. She had just turned fourteen. She couldn't wait to go.

They called it 'the bach next door', but really it was a shed by the garden wall with a toilet and sink in the lean-to.

Eve waved down to Lance MacPherson from her kitchen window. He'd propped the surf board he never used against the bleached wall of the bach, stroking it with wax from time to time.

Lance's shirt was unbuttoned to his waist. His shorts tied with a white cord, and he wore a necklace made from small pale shells. Eve remembered him as a sandy-haired little boy, running helter-skelter down the hill to the sea, laughing with his mouth wide open. He was tall and lean now, and his shoulders were broad. She didn't see him run much anymore. He seemed in no hurry to do anything at all.

He'd been over on the Gold Coast, apparently, and Eve wasn't sure why he'd come home. She often saw him sitting on his doorstep, staring out across the beach. Nothing to do, it appeared, but watch the tide wash in and out, and wait for his friends to visit.

She waved again, and he flicked his head up in a half-nod. That meant he'd seen her. The seagulls had seen her, too. They landed on the lawn a few feet away, cawing for crusts. Eve bent over the counter and threw the rest of the bread out the open window. The pain in her ankle was still there, dull and persistent.

Eve was glad that Linda and Carrie were coming; she was surprised when Linda suggested it. Her daughter-in-law was a remote kind of girl, too thin these days, her prettiness drawn tight. Linda used to smile more, say more, but nowadays she seemed unhappy: it was Eve's fault. She hadn't done a good job with Michael. He was souring into an early middle-age, too aware of what he didn't have, what he couldn't get. Too young to be this disappointed, she thought, starting the long walk to the end of driveway: the girls would be arriving soon, and the gate was locked. They thought they were coming to look after her, but Eve thought the opposite was true. Linda, Carrie, Lance MacPherson – in the absence of fathers and mothers, husbands and wives, she'd look after them all.

The house on the beach was Linda's kind of place, rustic and creaking and secret, surrounded by a thick wall of trees. Not rising stark and surprised like their new house, which looked half-naked, picketed by saplings and spindly shrubs. This was the kind of house you could disappear in. It felt as lonely and secure as a castle, mounted on a steep garden strewn with prickles, overlooking the sea. The day surrounded it, still and hot. The sounds were quiet, regular: water rubbing against the sand, and, inside, the ticking of a clock. Linda wandered the hallways, thin rugs bunching under her feet.

'Each of you, choose a bedroom,' Eve told them, 'but remember, it's quieter on one side. The music at that place next door starts up around six. It goes on late at the weekends – I should have warned you.'

'I don't mind,' said Linda. 'Maybe you and I can pop in for a drink one night. Sit by the swimming pool, watch the sun go down. I've never been to the Mon Desir.'

'It's famous, Gran,' said Carrie, peering into a shady bedroom.

'Famous for making a racket,' said Eve. 'Maybe your mum and dad can go on Saturday.'

But when Michael arrived at the weekend, he was tired. He had his Christmas book, the new Peter Benchley, and he wanted to watch the cricket. He shut the curtains to stop the sun reflecting on the television set and spent most of Saturday asleep on the sofa. He told Linda that the drinks at the Mon Desir were too expensive, that the crowd there was a bit rough, but she thought he'd just taken against the place. He wanted the weekend he would have had at home, away from beaches and bars. He even complained about the noise of people's jet boats.

'Better than mowers,' Linda said. They were lying in bed, listening to the faint pumping of a bass, a sprinkling of applause. A woman somewhere in the night shrieked with laughter and Michael turned over, his back to the Mon Desir, to Linda. The night was warm; the cotton sheets felt sticky the way her skin did after she'd been swimming in the sea. In just a few days she'd grown used to having the whole bed to herself.

She pressed a finger against his arm, feeling the bristles of hair, the skin that was always a little dry. Michael's breathing was even and he didn't stir; perhaps he was already asleep. That afternoon Linda had seen Lance MacPherson, lying in the sand on the other side of the stone wall. She'd passed close enough to touch him – she'd almost hit him, in fact, when she swung open the wooden gate leading to the beach. He was asleep too, or pretending to be. His skin was freckled, and the hair on his forearms and legs was a delicate blond. His trunks were untied, the white cords bright and stringy against the gold sheen of his belly. Linda spent longer than she needed to, standing on the stone step, fiddling with the gate latch. Part of her wished he would wake up and say something; she'd caught him looking at her several times this week, though they'd exchanged nothing more than nods. But she didn't want him to open his eyes and find her staring at his stomach, staring at his groin. Wondering if those blond hairs were silky or coarse. Thinking that if she were twenty rather than thirty-five, he would have opened his eyes.

Carrie saw him several times the first week. Glimpsed him, anyway: he was spunky, she decided, and just the right age, twenty-one. She'd met him once before (Gran swore she had) when she was a little girl, but Carrie couldn't remember.

Most summers they just came here for short visits, lunch and a swim on a Saturday. Her father didn't like this beach, or he didn't like this house, or he didn't like the guy who owned this house – it was something like that. But he was wrong: this was a fantastic beach. Rangitoto looked close enough to swim to, and the beach was swarmed, after work and at the weekend, with young people. This was the first summer she been allowed to stay overnight, kept awake by the waves – which always sounded like wind to her, never the sea – and sometimes, especially this weekend, by the muffled throb of music from the hotel next door.

Lance. Lance MacPherson. Hi, Lance. How's it going? That morning, Sunday, Carrie had planned to walk down to the beach, to sashay right past the windows of the bach. She wore her off-the-shoulder, broderie anglaise top and a pair of denim shorts. Just going for a walk, to look for shells, she'd told her mother, but then, all of a sudden, she'd lost her nerve. She felt self-conscious, and decided to change the top; the fabric scratched her skin.

Instead she'd sat on the couch in the dark, panelled lounge, picking at loose threads in the cushion fringe. The trees blocked all the sun from the room, and the furniture – heavy and old-fashioned – all faced away from the windows, turned towards the television. She could hear her grandmother talking to her mother outside in the garden. They'd been stretched out under a sun umbrella since breakfast. Her father had gone out for a walk, to get more milk and the *Sunday News*. There was a dairy down by the jetty, but when Carrie was changing upstairs she'd seen him stalking up the driveway, headed in the wrong direction. Once upon a time she would have chased after him, to tag along or tell him to go through the garden and cut across the beach. It wasn't that she was too lazy – that was only a small part of it, anyway. Maybe he wanted to take his time. Maybe he wanted to take the long way. She understood these things now: they all wanted to be left alone.

Carrie leaned back, and something hard poked her: she pulled out her father's book, *Jaws*, an empty envelope marking his place. Her eyes skimmed the first page and flicked to the second:

pulling the woman down with him. They fumbled with each other's clothing, twined limbs around limbs, and thrashed with urgent ardor on the cold sand.

Someone was calling her: Linda, shouting for more suntan lotion. Carrie cuffed the book under a cushion and stomped down the hall to the bathroom. She dropped the bottle out the back window with a bad grace, the only grace she'd been able to master so far, and it slithered out of her mother's hands.

She wondered if Lance MacPherson ever went to the Mon Desir.

Linda preferred the beach during the week when it wasn't crowded. She tried to keep Eve off her feet, but it wasn't easy. After dinner, she ran water in the kitchen sink for the dishes, taking turns with Carrie to wash and dry.

'Don't forget the birds,' said Eve. 'They're used to regular mealtimes too.'

Carrie raised her eyebrows and tossed a slice of bread onto the grass. 'I don't think you're supposed to give them bread, Gran. It's not good for them, you know.'

Before she dipped her hands into the hot water, Linda took off her engagement ring and lay it on the flaking sill of the open window. The diamonds were small and sharp, winking in the light. The emeralds looked as lurid as Palmolive liquid against the dense green of the garden.

Michael had left early on Sunday afternoon, saying he'd had too much sun and that he needed to iron some shirts for work. This wasn't true – Linda had ironed ten days' worth before she left – but she said nothing. He was playing the martyr for his mother, not noticing that his mother didn't seem to mind whether he stayed or left: Eve was busy that afternoon, teaching Carrie how to make proper coleslaw.

Even though he'd said very little all weekend, the house felt quiet after he was gone. It was the same when they were at home, in the new house in Pakuranga. Michael brought noise with him, she'd always thought, even though she knew that was unfair. The noise was in her own head, buzzing like an out-of-tune radio station, whenever he was near. Every small sound associated with him – the rustle of a newspaper, the mumble of a cricket commentator – scratched at her nerves.

Only when they were in bed, in the dark, in the quiet, could she bring herself to be close to him, and then it was always tentative, a furtive touch, as though she were petting a bad-tempered cat. Linda turned her back to him during the day; he turned his back to her at night. This was their stalemate, and she didn't know a way out of it without talking in some new and frightening way. She was afraid of what she would say, of what she would hear. That's why staying on Takapuna Beach was a relief. During the week their conversations were limited to clipped nightly phone calls, and at the weekend the house and the garden and the harbour were big. They could keep their distance, get lost. There were plenty of places to hide.

In the neat square of lawn beneath the kitchen windows, Eve sat under the shade of a striped beach umbrella, the still-aching ankle propped on a footstool. In her lap, she cradled three pieces of silver, a bottle of polish and a yellow cloth.

'Wouldn't you rather have the paper,' Linda asked. 'Or a book?'

But Eve was happy with the radio – Carrie's transistor tuned, for the first time in its short life, to the Concert Programme – and the silver. Linda and Carrie wandered off down the beach for a languid trip to the dairy.

Eve hadn't spotted Lance much over the weekend. She hoped he might stroll up to the house this afternoon, because she'd like to talk to him about the old days. Tell him about his father, about his mother, Jill. He'd still remember her clearly, even if the younger ones didn't. Nobody mentioned Jill anymore. You'd think she'd done something wrong, something much worse than dying.

Eve imagined him walking up, flopping down on the grass next to her chair. You're like your mother around the eyes, she'd tell him. Jill's eyes always narrowed and crinkled when she smiled. Just like you, she'd say. Eve pictured him grinning at this, though he didn't seem to smile much anymore. His face was blank and set, as though it was held in place by clothes pegs, and there was a hardness to his eyes that she didn't remember from before.

She could hear voices coming up the slope from the beach, but it wasn't Lance, of course. Lance never came up unless he wanted something. It was Linda and Carrie back from their walk, their lips stained Popsicle-orange, complaining about prickles in their feet. Beverly was about to arrive, they reminded her – Linda's new friend from their new street. She and Linda had met at a Tupperware party, where Linda had won all the games – they were silly quizzes, she'd told Eve; a child could have won them – and had followed Beverly's lead when Beverly refused to buy a single piece of Tupperware, even though that meant the hostess wouldn't get her free gift.

Beverly was a tall blonde, her hair teased high, her eyebrows plucked into startled arches. Within ten minutes of click-clacking into the front hall in high-heeled sandals, she'd stripped down to a bikini and a skimpy sarong, and was rummaging through the kitchen cupboards for a tin opener.

'So this is how the other half lives,' she said, peering out the kitchen window. 'Oh my God, Linda. We're not in Pakuranga anymore, darling. You never told me you had family money.'

'It's not our family.' Linda poured a tin of coconut cream into a plastic jug. 'And this looks like Tupperware, I'm afraid.'

'God! We're the only women of taste in Auckland. Add the rum, and then the pineapple juice.'

'I look after the house every January,' Eve told her. 'The owners are away on their boat.'

'How very Upstairs, Downstairs.' Beverly mixed the drinks with a spoon and glugged equal amounts into four tumblers.

153

Carrie looked warily at her mother. 'Go on, let her have a glass – it won't kill her. And you too, Eve. They're tropical. Who's that spunk wandering in the garden? The pool boy?'

'The young master of the house,' said Linda, scratching at a mosquito bite on her arm. 'He's not supposed to be here.'

'I'll hide him for you,' said Beverly. 'Right under my sarong.'

They sat in the garden, the sun frying their ear lobes and elbows and toes, and after two drinks Linda and Beverly and Carrie set off to walk the length of the beach before the tide came in. Shaded by the brim of her hat, Eve felt her eyes closing, the milky dregs of her drink still sloshing in the glass nestled in her lap. She dozed off into a fitful sleep and woke to find Lance standing in front of her, a golden, smiling mirage. When she blinked he'd disappeared, and Eve chided herself for fancying things, but the glass she'd been holding was set on the ground.

Something about this creeping around unsettled her, though she wanted to talk to him, wanted him to seek her out. Getting down to the bach was difficult; Eve didn't want to intrude. She just wanted to sit down with him face-to-face for a while. When he was a boy, Lance had been easy to read, easy to love. The person he'd become – watchful, lurking, unfathomable – was a stranger.

Eve struggled out of her chair and stood, hands on hips, looking for the girls. They were on the sand, opening the garden gate, about to climb up the prickly lawn. But that brazen Beverly was walking in another direction, sashaying over to the bach next door. And suddenly there was Lance, standing talking to her. Eve squinted: his T-shirt was a dirty brown, streaked with white paint marks, and he wore the frayed jeans she'd washed for him the day before. Linda and Carrie seemed to be hanging back, not joining in the conversation.

She felt an intense surge of irritation, a twisting in her stomach. Lance's mouth was moving; he was talking away to that Beverly, someone who'd just breezed in for the afternoon, when all Eve could get out of him were grunts and nods and muttered requests. For a moment she considered waddling down the hill to join them, but it was too steep and bumpy a descent for her unsteady legs. Her eyes pricked with tears – foolish tears, she thought, annoyed with herself now. Until today she'd told herself that tending Lance with small, quiet services – folding his clean T-shirts, preparing a plate of sandwiches – was enough, but perhaps it was enough only for him. Eve was hungry for the sound of his voice.

The conversation was over. The three girls clambered up the hill, a red-cheeked Linda leading the way.

'He's a cheeky young monkey, that one,' Beverly said, bending over and exhaling: all three were out of breath. 'I don't think you should let him stay down there, Eve. He's a bad influence.'

'What was he saying?' Eve asked, almost breathless herself. The words rushed out, half-swallowed.

'That we could come for a moonlight stroll with him,' said Beverly. 'That he'd be waiting tonight on the beach. Can you believe it? Young enough to be my . . .'

She shook her head.

'He was probably joking,' Eve said.

'Didn't smile once,' Beverly told her. 'Even when he winked!'

Carrie giggled, tugging on her shorts. Beverly turned around to give a mock-glare in the direction of the bach. Lance had disappeared. Eve had seen him wander off already down the beach without a backward glance.

'He winked at you?' Eve repeated. The sun drilled into her eyes.

'Winked at Linda here, I do believe.'

'Don't be silly,' said Linda. Her voice was sharp. 'You were the one doing all the talking.'

'I don't think he's interested in talking.'

This conversation, Eve decided, wasn't suitable for Carrie. She asked her granddaughter to help her inside, blinking as they stepped through the back door, adjusting her eyes to the dim light of the kitchen. Beverly said she had to go because Grant, her husband, liked his tea on the table at six. Eve was relieved. Sometimes the summer days were too long, the beach and garden too exposed. She'd be glad to get back to the peace and order of her own small home, where few visitors disrupted her routine. The only men's voices she ever expected to hear were on the radio, reading the news, or Michael's when he rang to tell her they were just going through the motions, he and Linda, and he wasn't sure how much longer he could stand it.

After Beverly was gone, nobody felt like doing much of anything.

'We've got heat stroke,' said Eve, and Carrie complained that her arms and legs felt heavy. Linda scrambled some eggs: they ate their meals off trays in front of the television.

It was still light outside when Linda stacked the plates

and pan in the sink, but she didn't wash up until later, after Michael had rung to check on them, and Eve had decided to have an early night. She and Carrie sat around watching police shows – one English, one American – on television until Carrie was half-asleep as well and needed to be prodded to go to bed.

Through the kitchen window, small slices of beach, the colour of brown sugar, were visible between the trees. The sea drew in and out in slow breaths. Linda turned on the taps and burped the bottle of Palmolive into the water. The plastic jug was still awash with piña colada: the ants hadn't got to it yet. Linda poured in more rum until the creamy mixture separated, whizzing it together with her finger. Then she drained it in surreptitious gulps, drinking straight from the jug and wincing at the curdled sickliness. She wiped away the creamy residue on her mouth with the back of her hand. Michael would be appalled at all this – the swilling from the jug, the dirty finger, the extra rum. Beverly's influence, he'd say. He didn't want her to have friends. He wanted her to have Tupperware.

When the sink was full, she took off her engagement ring and placed it on the sill. And then, irritable with the routine of cooking, dishes, tides, she slipped off her wedding ring as well. It always felt heavy on her finger, but in her hand it seemed as insubstantial as the shells Lance wore strung around his neck. She held it in the air like an unusual specimen and then set it back on the sill. The white tan mark on her ring finger looked drawn-on, a shaky piña colada-coloured line.

The lapping water was silky and insinuating, an invitation

to slip away. She couldn't see Rangitoto from here and, even if she was on the beach, it would be disappearing into the darkness by now. She wondered how long it would take to get there. She could kneel on Lance's surfboard and slide through the waves, paddling it like a canoe. Linda had never been on a surfboard. It didn't interest her, usually; surfing was a child's game – all that waiting around just to come back. Striking out beyond the breaking surf: that was far more appealing. Passing the lumpy grey of Rangitoto, humming with its night noises, and heading out through the Gulf.

Was that what Lance was thinking about, day after day, sitting on the steps of the bach – running away to sea? He didn't have a home any more, after all. He was free of things and places, free of chores and bills and appointments. Untethered. He could drift wherever he liked.

'I was waiting for you.' The voice startled Linda: she yelped like a puppy who'd been stood on, and dropped the plastic jug, the last thing to be washed, into the water. Lance MacPherson was standing below the kitchen window, gazing up at her. He kept his voice low, and there was no break in it, nothing to suggest nerves, uncertainty. Michael was this age, twenty-one, when he first asked Linda out: he'd sounded as though he was in pain.

'Come on,' said Lance, almost whispering. His hair was pale, and his narrowed eyes looked sea-green. The rest of him she couldn't see clearly. 'It's just a walk.'

'I . . . I can't.'

'They're all asleep,' he said, and Linda wondered how he knew. 'Waste of a nice night, stuck inside doing the dishes.'

She hesitated, drying her hands on a tea towel.

'Just five minutes then,' she heard herself say, and then she was opening the back door and taking quick, quiet steps down the back stairs before there was time to think. They walked down the slope together – but not really together, Linda thought, aware of the distance between them, of the silence. She didn't trust herself to speak, anyway; she was burning inside, as though the rum had gone down the wrong way. There was nothing wrong in this, she told herself, trying to ignore the prickling threads of tension pulled taut beneath her skin. There was nothing wrong in a grown woman going for a walk on the beach in the evening: if she lived here, she'd do it all the time.

But when they reached the garden gate it was darker and emptier on the sand than Linda had anticipated. The sounds of Lance lifting the latch, and of the gate squeaking open, were louder than the sea. He reached out to help her down the stone steps, and when her palm brushed his it felt as though she was holding her hand above a flame.

Even her legs couldn't be trusted: she stumbled on the steps, her feet sinking into the cool sand on the other side of the wall.

'Steady,' said Lance, no laughter in his voice, and his hands were on her, holding her up, turning her away from the sea. His face, cold as the sand, pressed into hers and Linda closed her eyes, dizzy with all the sensations – the scrape of his lips, the damp intrusion of his tongue, the unfamiliar planes of his face knocking against hers. Even when she opened her eyes, she couldn't see him or anything else. He'd kept his distance since they arrived, but now Lance seemed to surround her, one hand holding back her hair, the other pressed into the small of her back. She didn't know how he had the idea, the courage, for any of this, or why she had allowed herself to be led down the lawn to the shadows of the wall. Beverly was the one who talked to him. He'd winked at Beverly.

'Mmm,' Linda said, trying to wriggle away. She'd meant to say no, but she felt incapable of coherence. Again she was misread: Lance seemed to think she wanted to lie down. He lowered her to the ground, dipping her like a ballroom dancer, and then he was clamped on top, pinning her hands above her head. Sand was in her eyes, in her mouth, scratching like stubble. The more she twisted to get away, the harder Lance pressed himself into her. One of his hands gripped her wrists; with the other he was tugging at her clothes, pushing up her sundress.

She thrashed her legs, trying to buck him off, but every turn pushed her into his hardness. His free hand chiselled a path between her thighs and his mouth sucked at hers like a vacuum. It was hard to breathe, let alone speak. He jabbed between her legs. The crotch of her underwear was wrenched aside, and when he plunged one finger into her, it felt as rough as a stick.

Lance moved to one side, and Linda was able to pull her head free.

'Stop,' she said. Her voice, choked and deep, didn't sound like her own. 'You're hurting me!'

The grip on her wrists relaxed. Linda pushed at his shoulders as hard as she could, trying to shove him away. It was easier now, as though her strange, mangled voice had broken a spell. Lance pulled his hand from between her thighs and rolled off her; Linda clutched at her clothes, pulling everything back into place. She was shivering with cold.

'I didn't want this,' she said, trying not to cry. They were sitting side by side now, facing the water. The grin of the moon disappeared behind a drift of cloud.

'That's exactly what she said.' Lance sounded amused, and Linda turned to him, enraged at his mockery. He raised his finger in his mouth and sucked it, drawing it slowly from his mouth as though it were an ice block. 'And she was lying as well.'

A searing panic seized her.

'Who?' she demanded, her voice cracking. Either she was going to cry or be sick: she felt like doing both.

Lance didn't even turn his head.

'You taste the same, too,' he said. Linda clambered to her feet, swallowing back a wave of rum-flavoured bile. Not Carrie, she thought. Not Carrie.

'Who are you talking about?' The clouds peeled away from the moon, and she could see Lance's face again. He was staring out towards the invisible sea, the offending fingertip resting against his thin bottom lip. Linda wanted to smack his hand away from his face, but when he stood up, she flinched.

'My stepmother,' he said. He looked at her for one long, frozen moment, and then ambled off towards the water. Linda backed away, stubbing her heels on the stone wall. The gate hung open, and she hurried through without closing it, striding up the hill. Back in the house she moved from room to room, turning off every light downstairs, feeling her way to the stairs. In bed, with her eyes closed, her face stinging with shame, she could see that look on Lance's face. There was no happiness in it, no triumph, no satisfaction. But it was the first time, Linda realised, that she'd ever seen him smile.

This wasn't really a surprise, not to Eve. Lance had to disappear sooner or later, before his father and stepmother got home and threw him off the premises.

And it wasn't really a surprise that he'd taken the silver candlesticks and the box with the fish knives and the box with the cake forks and the punch bowl and his silver christening mug. What remained of the housekeeping money, forty dollars, that Tim had left for Eve in an envelope in the cutlery drawer. And, worst of all, Linda's engagement and wedding rings, forgotten on the kitchen windowsill the night before and only remembered in the morning, when Eve noticed that other things were missing. Linda had leaned over the sink, sobbing, distraught at losing her rings. She couldn't be consoled. Eve felt sorry for her, and relieved, as well, that Linda was so sentimental about them. Perhaps everything would be all right with her and Michael after all.

But by the time Michael arrived to rage and thunder through the house, Linda had recovered her usual cool. She told him to keep his voice down: she didn't want Carrie to hear, not yet.

'She *should* hear,' he said. 'I don't want her to grow up as bloody gullible as some other people around here.'

'It's my fault,' said Eve. 'I shouldn't have let the boy hang around. I knew he wasn't allowed in the house, but I didn't think he would do this.'

Linda stroked Eve's sleeve, shook her head.

'Nobody knew this would happen,' she said. Her eyes were still red from all the crying. 'Tim won't blame you.'

Eve didn't know what Tim would say. She wondered if she'd be asked back next year, after all this. She didn't really mind the noise from the hotel, not really. It was noisy in Mt Roskill too, where her home unit faced the busy main road. None of the family liked visiting her there.

'Your rings,' she said to Linda. 'I'll tell Tim when he gets back. He'll put things right.'

'You're not staying in this house another night,' said Michael, and it wasn't clear to Eve, or to Linda, which of them he was addressing. 'I'm serious. You're not staying here again.'

And he was right, as it turned out: the next January was wet and cold, and the MacPhersons didn't go away, and then Eve had a stroke, couldn't get around so well anymore. Six years later, Linda saw someone who might have been Tim MacPherson at Eve's funeral, but she didn't approach him. She didn't talk to many people that day: she and Michael were recently divorced, and some things – former daughter-in-law, ex-wife – were still hard for her to say.

Once, driving along Hurstmere Road, Linda noticed the old gate across the driveway had been replaced with something more formidable that opened by remote control. And then one day it was all gone – the house, the garden, the bach, the wall, the Mon Desir. A big apartment complex, with balconies and below-ground garages, went up in its place. Every inch of the land looked concreted over, unrecognisable. When Linda visited Takapuna Beach again, she couldn't remember exactly where the section began and ended, or where the gate used to hang. It looked like an entirely different place, free of all its associations, all its histories.

That last day at the house, Carrie didn't hear about Lance and the silver and the rings until late in the afternoon. When her father arrived, she was at the bottom of the garden, lying prone on her beach towel as near the bach as she dared. All she could hear was the song on her transistor, the voice of a hovering seagull and an outboard motor humming in the shallows.

Rank with Coppertone, eyes shut against the sun, she pictured Lance walking over. She imagined him dropping onto the brown grass beside her and asking, in a cool, off-hand manner, if she'd go for a drink with him tonight at the Mon Desir.

They'd go right after dinner, she decided, and sit together by the pool listening to a band, watching the sun set. He'd order her a tequila sunrise. Afterwards, they'd dawdle back along the quiet beach, kicking the sand heaped against the stone wall at the bottom of the garden. They'd look out at the moon, low on the horizon and hazy through the clouds. There, under the drooping pohutukawas, he'd reach for her.

Her mouth would touch his thin, sandy lips. He'd taste of salt and beer, perhaps, or maybe he'd be sweet and soft, like jelly. His hand would skim her arm. They'd press together, gently at first, shoulders and knees.

Lance would whisper her name softly so it sounded like the trees rustling in the wind. Carrie, he'd say. The trees would whisper it back: Carrie, Carrie, Carrie. Lance would kiss her again and then, perhaps, they'd fumble with each other's clothing. She'd hear nothing but the breeze in the trees and the sound of his breath and the water lapping, soft and steady. The moon would disappear behind the blackness of Rangitoto. They'd drop to the ground and twine limbs around limbs and then thrash, thrash, thrash with urgent ardour on the cold sand.

Many Mansions

Although Barbara Mackenzie's funeral was not till three, they started filling stainless steel trays with peanuts at nine in the morning.

Catherine, her daughter-in-law, arrived on the overnight flight from Boston, flying into Heathrow when it was still dark. Her flight was early, but Peter Mackenzie was waiting for her in the melee of Arrivals, leaning against a pillar with the morning paper folded in his coat pocket. He wore a sweater Catherine had never seen before; his dark hair was long and untidy, and his face looked pale and tired. He reached a hand out to take her bag and they walked to the car park without speaking.

On the way to his father's house, Catherine asked what the hospital had said, exactly, when he went to collect his mother's belongings, and Peter asked about the girls. It was almost a month since he'd moved out of the house in

Somerville. He'd spent the last two weeks back in England.

'It's just as well you didn't bring them,' he said, glancing at her. 'There's not much room in the house.'

'They didn't really know her that well anyway,' Catherine said. It sounded harsher than she intended – more untrue – and he flinched, as though she'd flicked him in the eye. The girls, Tilda and Hazel, were hers, not Peter's; the way she always reminded him was one of the things they'd fought about. He was a second husband, a stepfather, much younger than her. The marriage, less than a year ago, had been a mistake: on this they agreed.

She tried to stifle a yawn, aware that this might annoy him even more. Leaving Boston was a scramble – persuading her ex-husband in New Haven to take the girls midweek, cancelling her classes, finding a flight. Barbara had died four days ago, but Peter hadn't called to tell her until it was almost too late to make it to the funeral.

'They don't really know *me*,' said Peter, suddenly fierce, and he would only give terse answers to her questions for the rest of the journey.

Peter's two sisters, who had driven down together from London the day before, were still in bed. Catherine set to work laying out cups and saucers on the table in the breakfast room. By the time his younger sister, Jennie, wafted downstairs, wet hair pinned high on her head, asking in a half-whisper if there was anything that she could do, it had already been established that they were short of everything – cups, plates, forks, teapots. Catherine surveyed the many wine glasses and tumblers, hired yesterday in the village, arranged in orderly regiments on the glass-topped coffee table. Peter was looking for the other bottle opener.

'One won't be enough,' he said, rifling through the dresser drawers, spilling napkins and tea towels onto the floor. Jennie sat drinking coffee, watching them fall. Catherine stooped to gather them up.

'You can have my mug when I'm finished,' Jennie offered, talking to Peter. She'd nodded at Catherine when she came downstairs, but they hadn't spoken at all. 'If you need more cups.'

She drained her coffee and held out the empty mug, looking away when Catherine took it from her hand.

Peter's older sister, Rachel, descended in time to answer the door to the third flower delivery of the day, a canoe of yellow carnations. She carried it mutely into the kitchen and balanced it on top of the microwave.

'There's toast if you want it,' Catherine said, standing at the sink, washing the mug and a jam-smeared plate. Rachel – dark and tall, like Peter, dressed in the same satiny purple blouse she'd worn on Christmas Day – sniffed in response. Peter's sisters were indignant on his behalf: Catherine understood that. They were indignant and outraged, because the woman at the sink this morning was not their mother: in their mother's place was the woman who had dragged their boyish, handsome brother off to be a glorified nanny in another country. The woman who had infiltrated their mother's last Christmas with her unknown daughters and forced them all to eat at one when they'd always eaten at three, the woman who'd whisked their brother away from the happy family table, puddles of hot custard still congealing in the pudding bowls, so they could spend the rest of their short visit home with *her* odd, fractious family in the wilds of Yorkshire. The woman who'd driven their sweet-natured, long-suffering brother out so he was homeless, between countries, left to deal with his mother's last illness alone.

None of this was wrong, exactly; Catherine knew that. Peter's sisters were indignant, and they were bereaved. They'd done nothing but cry for days – Jennie, on her mobile in the breakfast room, was saying just that.

Peter's Aunt Anne appeared at the end of the drive, dropped off by one of her sons in his new snub-nosed executive car, and began a slow walk towards the house clutching a wooden canteen of cutlery and a tired-looking black hat. She'd want a cup of tea, Catherine suspected, switching the kettle on. Jennie, her phone call finished, slithered into the kitchen.

'Why is everyone arriving so bloody early?' Rachel muttered, her mouth full of toast.

'God knows,' replied Jennie, stretching her arms above her head. 'Get the first go at Mum's things, perhaps.'

Both sisters arched their eyebrows. Barbara had always widened her eyes in the same way when she was telling stories. Catherine had never noticed this resemblance before. Peter's sisters had never seemed like their mother in any way.

The doorbell squawked, as though Aunt Anne had nudged it with one shoulder, but neither sister moved. So Catherine opened the door to Peter's aunt – already flustered about who was coming, and when they needed to get to the church – and stood back when his father charged down the stairs, demanding Anne's opinion on whether the occasion warranted releasing the Royal Doulton from the dust-free depths of the china cabinet. Peter appeared again: it was a family conference. They didn't need her in the kitchen, Catherine decided. She was wary of expressing any interest in the Royal Doulton. Nobody seemed to want any more tea.

The garden was long and narrow. Frost still gilded the lawn and the early morning sun illuminated skeletal rosebushes and the dull green of the hedge. At the living room window, Catherine stood pressing her shins against the low sill, squinting beyond the garden shed at the rhododendron at the end of the garden. It never flowered. She remembered Barbara pointing this out to her the first time they walked around the garden together. The Mackenzies had the wrong kind of soil.

The pond in the middle of the garden was covered with wire net for the winter. Barbara had warned her not to step on the paving stones. Peter had laid them one summer holiday when he was at college. He had meant well, Barbara told her, but they were constantly collapsing into the pond.

'Because I'm not really happy about using them,' Peter's father was saying in his loud, deliberate voice. There was a flurry – agreement or disagreement – in the kitchen. The doorbell rang again: more flowers.

'I mean, would you use your Wedgwood?' he continued, walking into the living room with an empty plastic bag in his hand, speaking to Catherine's back. 'I suppose you would. You don't need to worry if someone breaks something. But I'm on a strict budget. This is all very expensive.'

He stepped out the back door into the garden, still talking.

'I mean, I have to put my hand in my pocket every day.'

Peter's sisters had gone upstairs again: they were getting ready to go out. Aunt Anne was on the telephone to the other aunts, asking them to bring more teacups.

'Not mugs,' she said firmly. 'Barbara would not be happy with mugs.'

Catherine placed a peanut tray on each side table and sat down on a footstool to rest. She felt hot, as though she were standing too close to a radiator. Peter came into the room and told her to have a lie down on Rachel's bed; his sisters were driving out to the funeral home one last time.

As soon as they left, Catherine collected her overnight bag from the hall cupboard and climbed the stairs to the front room. This was where she and Peter had slept on Christmas Eve, the girls on cots at the foot of the bed. It looked the same – sprigged apricot wallpaper, short, cream curtains at the window, the room belted with a narrow, pasted-on dado rail. Like every room upstairs, it smelled of the peach-scented liquid soap Barbara bought for the bathroom.

Catherine had to step over Rachel's suitcase to draw the curtains. Rachel always stayed there, Peter told her, because she was the oldest, and it was the biggest room; Christmas was an exception. Tonight the usual order would be restored: Rachel in the big room, Jennie in the study, Peter in his small boyhood bedroom. His father alone now in the room at the back of the house. Catherine no longer had a claim to a bed here; she'd stay in a hotel in Guildford and fly back tomorrow. There was no point in hanging around in England – her parents were away at their place on the Costa Brava, and she didn't feel like paying social calls to friends.

Nobody even knew she was in the country.

Although she was exhausted, it took Catherine some time to get to sleep. Was Aunt Anne right? Would Barbara have been unhappy with mugs at her funeral? This was one of the many things they could have asked her at Christmas but did not. Catherine wouldn't have thought to ask this, anyway. She'd wanted to ask Barbara how she made such a rich, dense Christmas pudding, but there was too much noise, not enough time. As soon as lunch was over, they had to race off to the M25 for the long drive north.

It was their first – and only – Christmas together as the new, extended Mackenzie family; the year before, with the wedding coming up, they'd stayed in Boston. The year before that, Catherine and Peter were still a secret. He flew over to Boston for the new year, when the girls were away skiing with their father. He loved her, he loved the States. He couldn't stay there with her unless they got married.

'My father's a pain in the neck,' he'd told her, 'but you'll love my mother.'

And he was right: Catherine loved Barbara. At Christmas, Catherine brought her a jar of brandy butter from Taylors of Harrogate.

'We don't eat anything shop-bought,' Jennie had said, stuffing the carry bag into the pantry. 'Mum makes everything from scratch.'

But after lunch, Barbara heated up the brandy butter and served it in a Royal Doulton dish, a tiny silver ladle resting on the saucer. When everyone else poured custard over their pudding – even Catherine's girls, instant converts – Barbara slid a primrose-coloured spoonful of butter onto hers.

'This is a treat,' she said, smiling at Catherine. She looked tired. 'Something different. And not having to think of it myself.'

They didn't know she was ill then. The cancer had waited until the first twinges of spring to pounce, just a handful of weeks ago. There'd been no time at all for questions.

By the time Catherine woke up, more people had arrived, uncles and cousins and old friends who lived far away and had given themselves too much time to get there, just in case. She shook out her black jacket, rummaging in her bag for the pearl earrings that Barbara gave her before their wedding, and went downstairs.

Now everyone wanted tea, if it wasn't too much trouble. Catherine stood in the kitchen boiling water and filling the dishwasher with dirty cups, carrying out fresh trays every fifteen minutes. People asked her what her girls were called, and told her that she and Peter should think about living in England for a while, especially after this, especially now, and said how miraculous it was that the weather had cleared; you couldn't wish for a better day. Aunt Anne was peevish, because one of her sons had arrived wearing jeans and a short-sleeved shirt. Jennie and Rachel were smoking outside on the patio, shivering without their coats on. Upstairs, Catherine had seen Peter's father, dressed in a navy blue suit and sitting on the edge of his bed. He probably meant to stay there until the car arrived.

Peter walked up to her – she was tapping tea leaves into the sink – and asked her shyly, sullenly, if his tie was straight. She turned to look at him, her face flushed with the steam from the kettle. The sun poured in through the kitchen window and she began sneezing helplessly, stung by the bright light and stultified by the overwhelming scent of cellophane-wrapped flowers cluttering the counter.

When the car arrived, there was not enough room. Catherine locked up the house and rode to the church with one of the neighbours, arriving just in time to slip into an aisle seat near the back. Four undertakers in grey coats carried in the coffin, with the family, hunch-shouldered, filing behind. Peter's face was taut, holding everything back. One summer, long ago, on a day trip to Scarborough, she hurried into a church during a rainstorm; there was a wedding going on, and she'd slid into the back pew, sitting for a while, listening to the flat-vowelled promises. She was an interloper then and she felt like one now, waiting to be spotted, to be turfed out.

The vicar – young, plump and entirely unknown to the family – read the introduction. Catherine had been here once before, on Christmas Eve, when everyone tumbled off to midnight mass after a night at the pub. Barbara, who said that it was too hot in the pub and too cold in church, had stayed home with the girls, letting them help her make stuffing and bread sauce. She told them they could call her Granny Barbara, but Hazel, Catherine's little one, always called her the Bread Lady.

Barbara's was the only service that day, so the building was chilly. Everyone sat in their coats, standing and kneeling and singing and praying as instructed, dragging on the hymns, stumbling on the Psalms. Lines of Technicolor apostles crowded the windows like spectators. Beneath them, medieval stone heads jutted from the walls, strange gaping faces of men with sunken cheeks and worker's hats, the builders of the church captured ugly and ordinary below the feet of the stained-glass saints. These heads, their pumiced skin the colour of sand, gazed wild and astonished at each other across the ranks of pews, stranded in an eternity of commemoration.

As instructed, Catherine sang and stood and knelt on the dusty prayer cushion. The stone heads had witnessed centuries of vows, processions and ceremonies, countless sung evensongs and holy communions, the monotonous ebb and flow of christenings, confirmations, weddings, funerals. How many times had the litany echoed off the walls and resounded around their frigid ears? Tears sluiced the sides of her nose, running into the corners of her mouth, and she wondered how their shouts would sound – the anguish, the joy, the deliverance – if suddenly, after hundred of years of masonic torpor, these petrified labourers could come to life.

In the cemetery, the sun was setting beyond the ragged outline of yew trees in the next field. People stood scattered around the grave, waiting for the vicar to begin talking again. The gang of undertakers lowered the coffin into the ground, then doubled in an ostentatious synchronised bow. Catherine walked over to Peter and placed her arm loosely around his waist. He didn't shrug her off. His head was bowed and his heavy winter coat hung perfectly still. The vicar spoke, his words carried away by the breeze. When he turned away, setting off along the path towards the church, the four undertakers each gathered up a handful of pale soil and in turn let it fall gently into the grave. Everyone else stood watchful and motionless.

'You should throw some soil,' Catherine whispered to Peter. Without looking at her, he bent down and scooped a little in his hand. His father tried to follow his example, but there was barely enough to fill his fingernails; the mound of earth next to the grave was sealed with a thin coverlet sheet of artificial grass.

'I don't want to do that,' Jennie hissed. Her hair still looked wet. Rachel was crying, clinging to her sister.

An undertaker had lain his black silk top hat on the ground a few feet away, beside a pyramid of waxy white lilies. The flower arrangements were placed in a long line, like entries in a competition, their cards peeping out. Mourners shuffled past, admiring and awkward, bending over for a closer view.

Catherine could hear voices asking who was Peter's wife.

'No, not me,' said the cousin who had been sitting next to him in church. 'That's Catherine over there.'

A wiry woman came over and grabbed Catherine's arm.

'Two soup plates,' she said, her eyes teary. 'We were the two soup plates.'

Catherine watched the woman walk away before she realised she was talking about the wedding.

'Thank you,' she called. She had to say something. 'Thank you very much.'

They'd been given twelve soup plates, and Peter had told her that, as far as he was concerned, she could keep all of them.

• • •

Back at the house, people were sitting outside in their cars waiting for someone to let them in. Catherine ran down the driveway and unlocked the door, leaving it ajar behind her. In the kitchen she switched on the kettle and then the oven, tugging open packages of food and tipping the contents onto baking trays. Soon every room was humming with mourners, drinking tea and sherry and wine. Old ladies crept up to Catherine, wanting a little more hot water or diffidently offering to help. Some asked if she were Peter's American wife, as if he had several of different nationalities: they sounded disappointed when she told them she only lived in Boston, that she was from North Yorkshire. Some looked surprised when they found out she was the one Peter had married, perhaps because she was thirteen years older than Peter, and only twelve years younger than Barbara.

The aunts ferried platters in and out of the living room and, although she hadn't asked him to, Peter brought her a glass of wine. Rachel leaned her head in, and, without looking Catherine in the eye, asked why the potato salad hadn't been put out. The smoke alarm went off twice because the kitchen door was open, and one of Peter's old school friends – who hadn't come over for the wedding – whacked it silent with the back of a wooden spoon. When at last nobody seemed to want any more tea, Catherine ventured out to collect dishes. Although it was generally agreed that nobody knew what to say at a time like this, everyone in the living room was talking very loudly.

'The weather held,' someone said.

'I didn't think much of that vicar.'

'Did you get the sausage rolls at Marks?'

'I think so,' said Catherine, though she couldn't remember what it said on the packet; she'd torn it open without looking.

'A lovely day for Barbara,' someone told her. 'She would have been out in the garden on a day like this.'

'More in the summer, though,' said another woman, and Catherine nodded. She'd never seen this garden in the summer. 'She'd be out every day then.'

By seven o'clock most people had left. Aunt Anne was lurking, frazzled, in the kitchen, because her forks were still trapped inside the dishwasher. Peter jerked open the door and rescued them, steaming hot, cramming them into their plastic-covered canteen. A cousin reversed down the driveway, and Catherine carried one of the flower arrangements out to his car, laying it carefully on the back seat.

'They managed to get through eight bottles of wine as well,' said Peter's father, clutching the empties to his chest on his way out to the garage. 'I suppose I shouldn't complain. This isn't something that happens every day.'

It wasn't every day, either, that Catherine got a message on her home number like the one Peter's father had left ten days ago, telling her she was a selfish bitch, that she'd caused his son nothing but unhappiness, that she'd taken him away from his family when they needed him most, and that there was nothing wrong with Barbara – not one thing – until the day Peter told them his marriage was over. That was how Catherine found out Barbara was ill. Peter had told her nothing. When he called, it was to speak to the girls.

When the last of the mourners had gone home, and

Peter's sisters had taken their father to the pub, Peter offered to pick Catherine up the next day from her hotel and drive her back to the airport.

'Thanks for coming,' he said in a small, tight voice. They were sitting at the table in the breakfast room, drinking coffee and picking at some leftover ham. Catherine sat looking up Barbara's cookbooks – covers torn, spines broken, scraps of paper sticking out – lined along the countertop. Peter silently passed one down, a notebook with handwritten recipes and menus ripped from magazines.

'This is the one,' he said. 'The Christmas pudding.'

Catherine thought of Barbara's face, flushed and happy, on the other side of the dining table, dolloping servings into the Royal Doulton bowls, laughing when it fell onto the cloth, annoyed when it dripped onto her new silk blouse. The girls had helped Catherine choose that blouse; they bought it at Hobbs in Guildford the day before.

The recipe was listed under 'G'.

'Why G?' Catherine asked, frowning at the page.

'It was Granny's,' Peter replied, pouring some more coffee. 'She gave Mum the recipe.'

Catherine shrugged her shoes off. There were peanuts ground into the carpet under her toes. This was the last time she'd feel this carpet, she thought; today was the last time she'd come to this house and smell its sweet peachy scent, look out on the rhododendrons that never flowered. She had to squint to read Barbara's handwriting through the stains, and the smudges; the ink had been dripped on.

'What does this say, do you think?' she asked Peter.

'You should take it,' he said.

'What?'

'Take the recipe.'

'Your sisters'll want it,' she told him.

'They never cook anything. Tilda and Hazel have done more cooking than those two. Mum would . . . look, just take it. Tell the girls it's a present from the Bread Lady.'

'I don't even know if I can make sense of it.' This was untrue, just another one of the untruths Catherine had told today, another pretence. She wasn't expecting kindness from Peter right now. It was hard to look at him, so she held the book up instead. 'Can this be right?'

'Seems like an awful lot of suet,' he agreed, and they smiled at each other for the first time that day.

The Argyle

At seven o'clock, Jason Vale pulls his Jeep into the half-moon driveway of the Argyle Hotel. He's here to collect a woman called Kelly Susskind, to take her out to dinner. They had a meeting late that afternoon at his office in Century City, an appointment he had to move from earlier in the day. She couldn't get on a flight back to Chicago this evening, so he felt obliged to make the offer. This is her first time in Los Angeles.

The valets at the Argyle wear boxy grey uniforms that look like over-washed costumes from a thirties musical. One swings open the car door, waiting for Jason to climb out, but when he says he's just picking someone up, the valet stops smiling and closes the door again. Kelly appears in a blur of revolving doors and clatters down the bleached stairs: her heels are higher than the ones she wore this afternoon.

She's around thirty, around his age. Today at the meeting,

she wore a sombre suit, her fair hair leaking from the knot behind her head. Now she's dressed in black pants and a gauzy blouse. Her hair is loose, splayed over her shoulders. She climbs into the car in a breathless rush, thanking the valet who opened the passenger door, giving Jason the quick half-smile of a stranger. He feels like a taxi driver.

Sunset Boulevard is striped red and white with car lights, and it's several minutes before he can edge into the lanes of traffic travelling east. Jason asks her if she prefers Italian or Mexican, and Kelly says that it's really good of him to give up his Friday evening, the same thing she said in his office that afternoon. The light turns green and the Jeep stutters forward, too close to the car in front. Kelly snickers, pointing up at a billboard for a television show; he's not sure if she's laughing at the billboard or Los Angeles or the way he drives, distracted and hesitant, as though he's never driven a car before this evening.

Kelly felt out of place at Jason's office today, pale and overdressed, but at dinner, after gulping down a drink, she relaxes. Her blouse and shoes are new, bought late this afternoon on Melrose as a reward for being stranded, for having time to herself.

Jason isn't wearing a jacket: he untidies the table with his phone and pager, and she teases him about this when the waiter can't find room on the table for their appetizers. The stunted candle flickering inside a smeared Mason jar keeps puttering out, so Kelly produces a box of matches, pilfered from the Argyle's clubby dining room; they take turns at reviving the flame until the waiter snatches the jar away and replaces it, without speaking, with a more co-operative candle from another table.

They talk about the meeting today, Jason's Japanese colleague, Kelly's irritable boss, her room at the Argyle. Her bed is shaped like a scallop shell, she tells him, and the room is small, and breaking into the pristine canister of cashews in the louvered closet costs eleven dollars. She has to cut the place some slack, Jason tells her. When it was called the Sunset Tower, Errol Flynn and Marilyn Monroe lived in apartments there. Bugsy Siegel had a place on the ground floor.

The Argyle is not like other hotels in other cities that she's invaded for a night or two with her wheelie bag and laptop. Her room is a shadowy grey – the headboard, the carpet, the stiff paper wrapped around the soap, even the light seeping through the taut corrugations of the net curtains. It's permanently early evening, easy to feel suspended in a fading photographic still, posed on the shell-shaped bed like a starlet from another era. It's not a place for watching TV and checking emails, as she usually does, filling in time until she goes home to her husband and little boy.

Perhaps it's for this reason that tonight she's not talking about her husband or son. She and Jason brush the topic of partners – he's married; no children – but the conversation doesn't settle there. They drink wine and talk about places they've been on vacation, places they went to college. When the cheque comes, Kelly realises that they're discussing the lives they had before they were married or, when the talk ricochets back to work, the lives they have independent of their families. This she likes – being free of routine and expectation. Tonight she will not have to pay bills online, or tip a net bag of brightly coloured rubber letters into the bath; she will not have to spoon Thai take-out, the usual Friday night meal, into cold bowls and eat it sitting on the sofa, watching *Six Feet Under* on DVD.

Tonight, after Jason slips his credit card into the black vinyl folder, he fishes in his wallet for the valet ticket and pulls out a pass for a club in Hollywood. Kelly says she'd love to go.

Jason has never been here before, though he's driven past it many times. The club is in an old movie theatre that's been stripped of its seats and screen, a dance floor looped around a giant horseshoe of a bar. The line outside is sparse, but inside is a sloshing sea of teenagers, dancing in fluid, ever-changing configurations. Jason and Kelly lean against the bar, sucking on bottles of beer, laughing over the thud of the music at the comic extremities of fashion on display: the girls are squeezed into undersized tops and skirts, while the boys swim in baggy T-shirts, pants drooping from their hipbones and puddling over bulbous sneakers. The more confident are up on stage, turned to face the crowd below. One girl, her soft midriff pouching over a stiff denim mini, stretches her arms into the air and arches her back like a novice stripper; her friends, ranged around her in a chorus line, copy each of her moves, glancing at each other for reassurance as though they're looking in a mirror.

Now they're here, Jason doesn't know what to do. He's too old for clubs. He got the pass at the office from one of the younger guys, whose girlfriend works at a radio station. The last time he danced was at his wedding. But he didn't bring Kelly here so they could stand at the bar: he wants to touch her. He could barely think of anything else all through dinner.

So when she finishes her beer, he grabs her hand, pulling her into the crowd. They dance like the teenagers nearby, eddying around each other, avoiding eye contact. Jason reverts to the self-conscious moves of high school, something between an amble and a shuffle, occasionally swaying into a semi-crouch as though he's doing the limbo. Kelly dances in tight circles, flicking her hair each time she turns. When he catches her eye, she grins at him. He feels excited, conspiratorial: although everyone around them is almost certainly underage, he and Kelly are the interlopers. The crowd presses in and washes them towards the stairs. He takes Kelly's soft, cool hand again, leading her through a perfumed blast of dry ice up onto the stage.

Unlike the girls posturing in the footlights, Kelly seems reluctant to be an exhibitionist. She pulls free of his grip and moves – half-walking, half-dancing – towards the back of the stage; Jason follows. Here the kids move in a trance, receding from one group and forming new couples and trios, grinding in slow-motion. Two short, heavy-set boys sandwich a girl, obscuring all but her pony-tailed head. Other girls inch together, dragging hands over each other's arms and hips, their gestures a dumb show for the circling boys. In the wings, hidden from the dance floor below the stage by a barricade of speakers, several couples writhe in unison, faces grimacing in concentration – they're a little too close, dancing a little too slowly. Jason brushes Kelly's sleeve, tilting her towards the darkened recesses of the stage, and soon, like him, she's just pretending to dance, watching the kids retreat into the wings, observing their joyless coupling, the way they drift back onto the stage to be swallowed by the crowd.

Kelly looks back at him, but she doesn't roll her eyes or raise her eyebrows or smile. She dances a little closer, brushes against him more. When the spotlight starts picking out dancers for instant prizes, Jason suggests they leave. The night is cool. On the way back to the Argyle, they listen to the radio, Kelly restlessly scanning the stations: she says she's looking for the song they were just dancing to, up on the stage.

Back at the Argyle, Jason leaves his car keys with the valet and walks with Kelly through the lobby and into the elevator. They don't kiss until they're in her room, standing on the fingernail of carpet between the curving bed and grey wall of closets, grinding together like the kids in the club. Kelly tugs him onto the bed, but it doesn't seem big enough for two people, or long enough for someone as tall as Jason: he manoeuvres Kelly around as though she's the needle of a compass, trying to find a position that works. Twists of sheet ensnare Jason's legs; his fingers catch in Kelly's hair. Crunched together on this uncomfortable folly of a bed, they don't fit together easily. Kelly is dry, inhospitable. She's frowning, absorbed in the mechanics of the act. Neither of them speak. They're strangers making use of the darkness, rutting in the wings.

Kelly is awakened by the drone of the dehumidifier above the sink. She lies still with her eyes closed, listening to Jason click open the bathroom door and scrabble around the bed for his clothes. When he scoops up his cell phone from the bedside table, she pretends to stir. He leans over her, whispering that he has to go, brushing a dry kiss on her forehead. His skin looks as grey as the carpet.

After Jason leaves, Kelly dangles a foot off the scalloped edge of the bed. Her face tingles, irritated by his stubble, and she can still taste the sourness of his tongue. She gets up to bolt the door and drops back into bed, slipping in and out of sleep until the reproachful squeak of the maid's cart in the hallway reminds her of the time. The hotel is expecting her to go: her bill is already printed, pushed underneath her door. A new shift of valets will be milling around outside. When Kelly emerges through the revolving doors, one will have her rental car waiting: he'll hold the door open, run around the back of the car to lift her bag into the trunk, his hand ready to receive the tip.

She runs herself a bath, stroking the water to sting her fingertips awake. Even though she's been rebooked on an early flight, it'll be late afternoon before she arrives in Chicago, already dark, a frigid wind gusting off the lake. The snow that closed the airport yesterday will be banked outside her house, frozen solid.

When their son was a baby, before she went back to work, her husband used to be the one who went on business trips. Each time he walked in to their messy house – under-furnished, strewn with plastic baby rubble – after one of these trips, everything he did would slice at her: the way he glanced around the place, disapproving and unsurprised; the way he always managed to arrive after the baby was asleep in bed; and the way he'd complain about how tired he was, how drained, how grubby. He would shove his clothes into the washing machine and then stand for almost half an hour under the shower's sharp jets. Kelly used to think all the complaints were a pretence, that he enjoyed the escape of his trips away. She suspected he sometimes stayed away longer than necessary; she suspected him of sleeping with strangers.

Part of her had wondered what that would be like: now she knows. And now she understands, too, how her husband used to feel when he arrived home. When she gets back to Chicago, nothing will have changed. Her life will be ordinary, the same. Even though they pay someone to clean the place these days, there will be clothes in the dryer to fold, toys to trip over on the stairs. Her husband will notice the new shoes and blouse, and make some wry comment about how hard she must have been working in Los Angeles. But he won't press her on anything, and she'll make no confessions. Los Angeles was a place she got to pretend for a night, and it's a relief, in a way, that the sex was so leaden. It was sexier, more exciting, when they were in the club.

She zips up her bag and pulls the bedcover straight, wishing she was home already. Beyond the disorienting twilight of this hotel, Los Angeles is an over-lit stage set surrounded by sprawling, untidy back lots. Everyone plays a part – the hotel maids, the teenagers humping each other last night, the valets. Kelly longs to rinse herself clean, to sleep in her own square bed again. Now she understands why, after the intrusions of all those other places, all those strange bodies and mouths, her husband wanted to be alone.

• • •

Jason turns off Sunset, heading towards the freeway. He's taken this route, driving home through the city's mottled canyons, thousands of times. The hills are parched and colourless in the weak early morning light. It won't take him long to get back to the house in the Valley. His wife might be sleeping on the sofa, draped in a crocheted blanket, one hand still curled around the television remote. Maybe she'll be sitting at the kitchen table, her back stiff with fury, reading the paper. When she hears the Jeep braking on the driveway, she'll shuffle the sections together, push the paper away, so it looks like she's been doing nothing all night but staring up at the clock.

When he opens the door, they'll look into each other's drained faces and the only sounds will be the click of the closing door, the metallic splash of his keys on the kitchen counter. She'll be waiting for him to say something. She'll be waiting for him to explain himself, to announce an excuse, to apologise. But he doesn't have anything to say. He never does. All the way home, he wonders if maybe this time will be different, if maybe this time he's done enough. Maybe he'll arrive home this morning and find she's already gone.

The City God

He told her that he caught a taxi to work every day. He told her that he caught a taxi home. Taxis in Shanghai were cheap and fast. Nobody had a car, he told her, but everywhere Sylvia went there were thousands of cars, roaring down avenues and around corners, intent on mowing her down. The lights at pedestrian crossings beeped, flashing numbers at her, counting down seconds. If she didn't make it across the road in time, she would be killed. At one intersection, a motorcycle drove onto the footpath and almost ran over her foot. She stepped out of the way, into the path of someone spitting. Everyone spits here, he told her. That's why she had to take her shoes off and leave them just inside the front door. He told her she wasn't to track China into the apartment.

Her son had a lot to tell her. He worked in some sheer gleaming tower in Pudong, the other side of the big river, where just a few years ago it was all rice paddies and hovels.

Now everyone lined up on this side of the river to gaze across at this shiny new city. Crowds of gawkers, Chinese and foreign, stood with their backs to the grand old British banks and trading companies lining the Bund. These buildings were restaurants and bars and shops selling luxury goods now. Big business had crossed the river, he told her.

'You'll have to come over and see my office,' he said. 'I'm on the fifty-sixth floor. You can catch the train that goes under the river if you like – it goes through this psychedelic tunnel. Maybe Ros can bring you over one day.'

But her daughter-in-law said she never went to Justin's office.

'Never invited,' she told Sylvia. 'If he really wanted you over there, he'd take you himself.'

Ros's idea of a day out was a trip to the huge IKEA or a shopping expedition to the City Market near the Portman Ritz, in search of crème fraiche or organic coffee. She was as tall and polished as the office towers across the river – slender, hard-edged, platinum. When she and Sylvia went out shopping, they always dropped into a Starbuck's for a latte and a slice of dry cake. They always caught a taxi home.

Sylvia preferred going out alone, despite the perils of walking. On her first day out in Shanghai, she learned to respond to noises – the whistles of the crossing guards, the horn of a car turning right on red, the urgent trill of bicycle bells. In a market, she flattened herself against a display of small, snowy cauliflowers at the sound of a moped purring past down the narrow aisle. Walking home in the late afternoon darkness, she listened for bicycles and their bells because none of them, she discovered, had lights.

• • •

After a week in Shanghai, Sylvia was missing Roy, her husband; since his heart operation, he didn't like travelling such long distances. She wished Justin would come home more often, but she didn't like to say anything to him about it. He was very busy at work, she knew, and when he travelled it was for business. Last weekend, just before Sylvia arrived, he'd been in Hong Kong. Ros hadn't gone with him, though she talked about the shops in Hong Kong as though they were some kind of paradise.

Sylvia spent the day wandering, then returned, feet aching, to the sparsely furnished white apartment. Ros wanted to know what she'd seen, so Sylvia listed a few landmarks. Most clear in her memory were people – the girl in a fur shrug walking her beagle, the dog pulling at its Burberry leash; the tiny woman in rough clothes, prostrating herself on the footpath, her forehead hitting the concrete over and over. And some of the English signs she'd seen were perplexing as well, so she'd written them down. Outside the market, a banner read: 'Construct a consumer environment of rest assured is a common duty of whole society.' On the boards of photographs depicting the history of the Nanjing Road, she'd learned that 'the street is strongly characterized with the fresh concept of a combinational fascination'. The caption for a photograph of the Nanjing Road at night, illuminated and multicoloured, read simply: 'Splendid and Gorgeous'. Splendid and gorgeous, she'd been repeating silently all day.

None of this she told Ros. Instead Sylvia produced the things she'd bought that day: a book of postcards, a small pink tin filled with inedible sweets, a blue-and-white porcelain dish from the bird market, a bag of mandarins. Ros frowned at all these foreign objects and told her the things she should be buying, like fabric and knock-off designer bags.

When Justin got home, later than expected, they sat down for dinner. His job was very, very demanding, he said.

'You seem to have plenty of time for karaoke bars,' Ros said.

'You know that's business.'

'Your mother's barely seen you. She's out wandering the streets while you're drinking whiskey and singing "Born to be Wild" with some teenage hostess.'

'It's a business thing,' Justin told Sylvia. 'I'm taking Friday afternoon off so we can go around the Old Town together.'

'A half day! You should be honoured, Sylvia.'

Sylvia didn't like the way they spoke to each other. She didn't remember this from Auckland, but she never stayed with them in Auckland. Ros was serving dinner now; Justin was talking about expanding markets. Sylvia's wine glass was empty already, and when Justin leaned over to fill it he kept talking, looking her straight in the eye. She was amazed he didn't spill any.

Ros had made pasta for dinner, with a sauce of olives and tomatoes and anchovies. For most of the meal, Justin talked about his Chinese employees and what a problem they were. At school they learned everything by rote and now they couldn't use their initiative. In Chinese companies, the general manager was like a god, and everyone was expected to follow his instructions. They didn't know how to question things, how to innovate. They were too reactive.

'You two don't seem very happy here,' Sylvia suggested. She'd had two glasses of wine. It was the first time all week that she'd expressed a definite opinion.

'What are you talking about, Mum?' Justin seemed angry. He was broad-shouldered like Roy, but otherwise he didn't resemble either of his parents much. Justin looked like her grandfather, stern and dissatisfied. 'We love it here. We love the lifestyle.'

'I've never seen the stars at night,' Ros said, taking another long slug of wine. 'It's smoggy all the time.'

'You can see the stars tonight,' Justin told her. 'Just look out the bloody window!'

'All I can see is scaffolding and cranes.'

'The smog used to be bad,' Justin said to Sylvia. 'But a lot of the factories were pushed out of the city. In Beijing it's much worse. And everyone's really aggressive up there.'

'Because they can't see the sky,' said Ros. 'And they don't know what grass is.'

Sylvia was still wondering about the word 'lifestyle'. In New Zealand, people talked about owning lifestyle blocks, and this seemed to mean having a few acres of land in the country where you could grow some carrots or keep a horse. But Sylvia never gave much thought to her own lifestyle. It involved driving to the supermarket, she supposed, and Sky TV.

'What *is* your lifestyle?' she asked Justin. He gave her a hard look. 'Do you mean catching taxis?'

'I'm here to make my fortune,' he told her quietly. 'We're riding the crest here. Shanghai is the number two port in the world – did you know that? Bigger than Rotterdam and knocking on Singapore's door. Lots of opportunities. Very open-minded, of course.'

'I thought we'd go to Yin for dinner tomorrow night,' said Ros, collecting their bowls and carrying them to the small kitchen. It all looked very flash, but there wasn't an oven, and the stove only had two elements. Ros would leave the dishes piled in the sink for the *ayi* to wash tomorrow morning. 'They have live jazz there. Unless you'd prefer Indian or Thai or something.'

Sylvia told them she was easy – whatever they wanted. Later, in her little bedroom on the street-side of the apartment, she raised the blind and looked out the window. Ros was right. She couldn't see a single star in the sky.

He told her not to give money to beggars. He told her that if someone approached her saying they'd lost all their money, it was a scam. He told her that the scruffy men on bicycles who clanged heavy school bells were collecting rubbish. They were migrant men, he said, and not to be trusted, though Shanghai was a safe city for foreigners.

For all its crowds, the city did feel safe, and perhaps that was why Sylvia let the girl walk into the building with her. She'd caught a taxi back from the museum, as instructed. Ros had given her a piece of paper with the address written in Chinese characters, and this she'd presented to the taxi driver. He'd understood it, and driven her home quickly through lurching traffic, but getting out of the cab Sylvia felt flustered, as though she was late. This was her last full day here: she and Ros had been out yesterday to the fabric market, and today Justin was coming home early from work to take her around the bazaar in the Old Town. She dropped her package from the museum shop – more postcard books, a T-shirt for her nephew – onto the ground. The girl stepped forward to help her. And then they were walking up the steps together; the security guard was opening the door and they were both inside the marble-floored lobby.

'You live here?' Sylvia asked the girl. She didn't want to be rude, but she hadn't seen any Chinese people in here at all, apart from the guards.

'I'm visiting friend,' said the girl, smiling. She spoke American-inflected English to Sylvia. To the guard she spoke swift sing-song Chinese, pointing at Sylvia and towards the lift. 'Ros Fullerton.'

'You know Ros?' Sylvia was pleased. Ros seemed to have very few friends here, apart from a group of American expatriates she met up with for lunch in Xintiandi once a month. Ros referred to them as The Wives. She told Sylvia that they all sat around complaining about Shanghai.

The girl nodded. She was a pretty thing, slight and rosy cheeked. She wore her long hair loose, the way Ros used to do years ago. Her skirt was very short and the bag hiked onto one shoulder was very large. The spiky heels of her boots clicked across the floor. At the lift she hesitated.

'You Ros's mother?' she asked.

'Mother-in-law,' Sylvia explained.

'Ah!' The girl smiled again, nodding with approval when Sylvia pressed the button for the sixth floor. 'I am Emily.'

'It's nice to meet you, Emily.' Ros hadn't mentioned that a friend was coming to visit her this afternoon. Inside the apartment, while Sylvia slid her shoes off, Ros didn't get up from the dining table, where she sat flicking through the *Shanghai Daily*. She looked over at Emily, and Emily – bag still shouldered, boots still on – looked at her. That was when Sylvia realized they didn't know each other at all.

'Ros,' said Emily. She wasn't smiling now. Her voice shook. 'I am Emily Chin. I am lover of your husband, Justin. We went Hong Kong together last weekend. This not first time.'

Sylvia was still standing on the doormat, its stubby bristles prickling through her stockings. She didn't dare move. Ros was still holding a page of the newspaper, about to turn it. There was no expression on her face – not surprise, not anger. She was looking at Emily the way Sylvia looked at paintings in a gallery, pausing to take everything in, half-conscious of her own reflection.

'I am his girlfriend,' Emily went on, her voice a little louder. 'For six months. He loves me, and wants to tell you, but the time is not right.'

Ros said nothing. Sylvia didn't know what to do. She should never have let Emily walk in with her. She should have asked the security guard to call Ros from reception, except the guard didn't seem to speak English, and maybe Emily would have made her little speech anyway, over the phone.

The front door opened, cracking Sylvia on the elbow. She stepped off the mat, making way for Justin. Now there were four of them in the room, and nobody was speaking. Everyone was expressionless. If this were a soap opera, Sylvia thought, Emily would be trembling and defiant. Ros would be distraught, possibly enraged, clutching the newspaper to her. She, Sylvia, would be aghast, clasping her bosom, or maybe suffering palpitations. Justin would be looking perturbed at the very least, glancing from his wife to his mistress and back. In real life, they were all frozen. It was awkward. Justin looked a little shifty and uncomfortable, the way he looked when he was a child when he'd eaten too many plums, but he didn't move. Ros was still sitting down; everyone else faced her. Nobody knew what to do, Sylvia thought. All the soap operas in the world couldn't prepare you for this.

'I think you should go home,' Justin said quietly and for a moment Sylvia thought he was talking to her. Then Emily's mouth quivered, and she started to cry. He reached out a hand to touch her sleeve. It was a gentle gesture, out of character for Justin – or out of character, at least, for the person he'd become. He cared about this girl.

'You bought me the same bag.' Ros was speaking at last. She didn't sound bitter. She sounded sad, though her face was still neutral, almost dreamy.

'Really,' Justin said to Emily. 'Take a taxi. Have you got enough money for a cab?'

Emily, whimpering, shook her head. Sylvia still had the change from her taxi ride, strange notes stuffed into the pocket of her coat. She reached for the messy bundle and held it out.

'Here,' she said. Justin took the wad of money and handed it to Emily. Ros snorted, half under her breath. Swallowing a sob, Emily clicked out of the apartment and closed the door behind her. The three of them were left, still in place, Sylvia and Justin still in their coats. Sylvia shook her head, trying to waken herself out of the stupor: she had to leave as well. She bent down to pick up her shoes, and the movement seemed loud and theatrical, even though it wasn't; the moment was broken.

'It's your mother's last day,' Ros told Justin. 'You have to take her to the Old Town.'

'No, no,' said Sylvia, struggling to slide on her shoes. 'I'll go out. You two stay here and . . . and talk.'

'I've got nothing to say,' said Ros. She closed the newspaper. 'Have you?'

'Ros,' said Justin. He was an immoveable lump, in the way like a discarded bag of groceries. 'Don't . . . don't *do* anything.'

'Like what?' Ros was brisk, standing up, pushing back her chair. 'Like don't book myself a ticket home on Sylvia's flight tomorrow? Wouldn't that make it easier for you?'

Justin shook his head slowly. He looked as though someone had slapped him across the face.

'Don't go,' he said, so softly Sylvia could barely hear him.

'Take him to the Old Town, please,' Ros said to Sylvia. 'Get him out of here. And one other thing.'

She marched into the big bedroom. Sylvia waited, breath held, listening to sounds of scuffling through the closet. When Ros returned, she was holding a brown shoulder bag, the twin of the bag Emily had carried. She emptied it upside down over the table. The only thing that fell out was half a torn packet of throat lozenges, followed by a fluttering of receipts.

'Throw this out, will you?' Ros thrust the bag at Sylvia. 'Just chuck it out in the street.'

Sylvia took the bag, and told her that she would.

● ● ●

He'd told her that Beijing was the place to go for historic buildings and temples, but there was one place in the middle of the bazaar, the Temple of the City God, that sounded promising in the guide book.

They crossed the outer courtyard, hurrying through the smoke of the burning braziers, passing tables piled with packets of incense, and islands of discarded shopping bags and wrapping paper. The stone-flagged corridor linking the temple's courtyards was walled with glass cases housing dozens of small statues. A gaggle of old women, all dressed in bright blue tunics, all so miniscule they made Sylvia feel Amazonian, kowtowed before these cases.

Each ceiling panel depicted a green-winged heron, and Sylvia wanted to ask Justin lots of questions – the significance of the heron, the names of the mini gods, the meaning of the piles of fruit interspersed with the statues. But he'd said almost nothing on the taxi ride here or while they were walking through the thronged cobbled streets of the bazaar. She'd told him again in the taxi that he didn't have to come out with her, but he'd just shaken his head and looked stricken. Sylvia wasn't sure what she was meant to do in a situation like this – commiserate with him or chastise him. Perhaps Ros would leave him; perhaps she wouldn't. Perhaps Justin wanted her to leave him; perhaps he didn't. Perhaps he loved this young girl, Emily; perhaps not. Other people's marriages were their business, too untidy and complicated for anyone else to navigate. All Sylvia really wanted to do was to go home, where things were easier to understand.

It was quiet here in the temple – that is, quiet until the tiny women crowded into the inner courtyard and began to sing, accompanying their discordant song with small percussive instruments. Sylvia drifted from one English sign to another, trying to make sense of the place, wishing she'd remembered to bring the guide book: she'd left the apartment carrying Ros's unwanted bag, but not her own. From the signs she learned that one room was the Hall of the God of Wealth and that the one opposite was the Hall of the Goddess of Mercy with her delicate blue headdress, platters of brown apples at her feet. A man sat at a rickety desk, playing the flute, a sheaf of music spread out next to his plastic cup. The cup had a lid; it was like something a baby would drink from.

Justin had wandered on to the room of the City God himself, and Sylvia followed him. The City God was small, much smaller than she'd expected. Compared with the giant statue of a general they'd come across in the first room, the City God was almost a disappointment. Everything was red – the fake candles in tall stands, the letters in the 'No Fire in the Hall' signs, the boxes for offerings by each altar, and the broad lacquered face of the City God himself. He sat glowering behind his gold curtains like a performer in a puppet show. A young couple kowtowed before him, asking his advice, no doubt. This was why he sat here, she remembered from the guide book: to hear questions on business or personal matters, and dispense some kind of mute advice.

Sylvia stood near the doorway, not wanting to disturb their prayers. In the courtyard, the tiny women in blue had finished singing. Now they were arguing, clutching each other's wrists, pointing in different directions. One of them started singing again in a thin, wavering voice, until the others talked over her, making her stop. They sounded so passionate and so conflicted that Sylvia couldn't help herself: she tapped Justin on the shoulder and asked him, in a whisper, what he thought they were arguing about. He glanced down at her, red-eyed and surprised, as though he'd forgotten that she was there, and told her he didn't know.

Rangatira
Little Barrier Island, 1895

The girl wants to know everything.

She follows me around, a notebook poking from the pocket of her skirt. At first I thought she was waiting for me to die. Perhaps she'd been sent to raise the alarm, in case I tumble headfirst from the rocks at the end of the point, or slump forward one afternoon into the fire. She's the wife of my nephew's second son, and she has no children yet to chase after.

She creeps around behind me, the hem of her skirt brushing the pebbles like a broom.

'The men from Auckland will be here again soon,' she says.

'I hope they bring some tar paper with them. There's damp in the back wall of my house.'

But the Pākehā never bring anything useful with them:

we both know that. The men come here to argue with my nephew and the only paper they carry is smudged with writing.

The last two visits, they brought along the man with the red-tipped ears. He's a different sort of Pākehā, snuffling and curious. He doesn't pay attention to the talk around the fire, but sits at a distance, making drawings of the gardens, or peering up at the pātaka as though a rat's run off with his watch.

'He says none of this'll be here much longer,' says the girl. She's a young thing, with fuzzy hair and big feet. Her husband found her up at the Great Barrier, near my old place. 'He's an historian, koro. He wants to make a record.'

I've seen the Pākehā's sketches: they're not much of a record. The Bohemian painter should come up here, stop hiding in that dark room in Auckland. The Bohemian is too pale, too nervous. His hands shake when he picks up a saucer of tea, and he shuffles his feet across the carpet. He needs to sail into the gulf, visit us on Hauturu, fill his lungs with cool sea air.

But instead, the men from Auckland bring Red Ears with them. He wants to know, the girl says, about my exploits and adventures, about military campaigns.

'He says you're the last of the warriors,' the girl tells me, trying to flatter me into sitting down and talking to her notebook. I've heard him say this. When the Pākehā visits, he says everything in a loud voice, looking at the girl, because he thinks I can't understand English. One day I'll speak up and surprise him. I'll tell him that my nephew has ten children and expects many grandchildren. Everyone says that our race is dying, and that may be true. But nobody's dying right now here on Hauturu, except for me.

'Whenever you're ready,' says the girl. She has to write them down, every word, exactly as I say them. That's what the Pākehā says. He's given her the notebook.

I'll tell her the stories, I suppose, because I like to talk, and at least when she's listening, she's not rustling around behind me. But she's heard most of the stories already, and can read the rest in my face. The Pākehā's waiting for this notebook full of words, but he could walk down Queen Street to the Bohemian painter's room and look at my picture hanging on the wall. He'll see everything he needs to know.

It's all there in my moko. I don't need a pen and paper to tell people who I am.

This island has a new name, Little Barrier, but to those of us who live here, it's Hauturu, the place the wind rests. When Taramainuku threw his seine across the waters of the gulf, Hauturu was its centrepost, ensuring the net didn't drift away or sink to the bottom of the sea. The first people to live here were the descendants of Toi-te-huatahi himself. They sailed out to the island, cut their way through thickets and vines, and made their homes under the mānuka. Our Ngāti Wai ancestors fought the Tainui people for the right to live here. We drove them away and took possession of the beach. For as long as I can remember, my family have lived along the shore, the smoke from our fires drifting up to meet the clouds encircling the mountain.

There were fourteen of us with a claim to this place. Eleven have gone. They were given money to buy new land somewhere else. That's the way it's done now, they tell me. People are driven away by a different kind of might, the kind written down on a piece of paper. They pretend to be happy to go, but they look ashamed, taking down their whare, burning rubbish. Their wives scuff through the ashes, carrying pots and boxes and picture frames to their boats.

Three of us are left – me, my nephew, and his wife, Te Kiri's daughter, living here with our fruit trees and pigs. My nephew's children come and go: they're young enough to spread their lives thin across many places. They sell kauri gum and kūmara and firewood, across on the mainland, for money.

'Tell me about the battles you fought, koro,' says the girl. Sometimes I forget that she's there, waiting to catch my words and slam them shut in her book. She sits down next to me, her black skirt spread out over the shingle like a dogskin left to dry in the sun, and I try to recall for her each of my campaigns.

'I am an old man now, a very old man,' I say. I'm as old as the century, though I usually tell people I'm one hundred: nobody knows the difference. The girl bends her head, starts her scribbling. 'It is a great many years since I first went forth to fight in battles after the fashion of the Māori.'

I talk until I'm tired, and then rest for a while, looking out at the sea. It's dull green today, like the bush. The stones are warm in the sun, but it's going to be hard standing up later.

The girl asks me some questions about years, but I don't know about such things. I know my first fight was at Tāmaki, at the Ngāti Paoa pā; that my second fight was at the Tōtara, near the mouth of the Thames River, and so on. I remember how my arms ached with the days of paddling, and how much of our time was spent setting up camps and preparing for battle. I remember how it felt to leap over the side of the waka into the shallows, desperate for the fight to begin.

'We came in sight of our enemies,' I tell her, 'and then, how I jumped in the haka! Unrolling my tongue, eyes pūkana . . .'

'We might have to explain pūkana to him,' says the girl.

'He's an historian, not a fool.'

She grins at me, tapping her pencil against a pebble.

'I'll say that you made your eyes big,' she says, 'so the whiteness blinded your enemies, and then you rolled them to make your face horrible.'

I wave my hand at her. She can write what she likes to make the Pākehā see the story. He'll want to know where we fought and how we fared, and that I can give him. There's more to it than this, of course, but I can't go into all the details now. It's too late in the afternoon.

When I set off on my eight war expeditions, I knew I would be away from my home for months at a time. Each fight had its losses and slaughters and captives, and also its days of monotony, of waiting. Sometimes there were meetings and negotiations, too, and they could go on for more than a week. I saw things I never want to see again: beaches rusting with blood, seagulls picking at the exposed meat of dead bodies, skewered joints of human flesh roasting over our fires. I've seen the heads of the dead piled in a pyramid, like stones, or spiked on a long pole, held high and carried away from battle the way I'm told the British wave their standard – except we meant to ridicule our enemies, to snatch their moko away. If there were families left to grieve, of course: we made slaves of hundreds of them, and others fled inland, away from the sounds of the guns.

And I expect the Pākehā will want to know about Hongi, who led us on so many of these campaigns, who brought us the muskets. When Hongi took a ball through the tip of his English helmet, his foreign armour winking and flashing like the sun, I was there, fighting alongside him – I was barely a man, then, the moko still fresh on my face. That was the first time I saw other warriors hanging crucified on palisades, their screams of rage and pain louder than the blasting of the muskets. Hongi, trying to climb, had caught his foot in a vine. The English helmet saved him.

They tell me I was gifted, then, in the art of war. With the muskets, we could fell a beach crowded with our enemies quicker than clearing bush. We always carried the weapons of our ancestors, too, the greenstone mere, the stone patu, the whalebone pouwhenua. We used these to finish the job, to chase down the ones running away from the musket fire. I could slice away the tip of a man's head with one sweep of the patu, or smash his nose deep into his face; I could flick his eyes out with a twist of the taiaha. Any fool is a great warrior with a musket in his hand. The real warrior fights face-to-face, close enough to see a man's teeth drip from his mouth like fish bones, to see the ridges of another chief's moko turn from green to bloody red.

This is the point of the pūkana. One man can kill more people than the greatest war party, if he knows how to instil fear. My bulging eyes transformed me into a demon, transfixing my enemy, preparing him to die. By unfurling my tongue, I reminded him of the tip of my taiaha, about to stab at his shins, and let him peer into the mouth that would be gobbling his seared flesh later that day.

Back then, even after many days rowing in rough seas, I was eager to kill, desperate to attack, and I knew how to show it in my face. We would leap into the shallows, yelling out our threats, widening and rolling our eyes, contorting our features into monstrous masks. I could see fear, but I never felt it. After the fight, we would drag away the bodies of our enemies to cook over hot stones. With every mouthful, we celebrated their defeat and degradation.

But then the missionary baptised me, almost seventy years ago, and put an end to all that. Nobody even talks of these things anymore. I tell the girl to write down 'the customary scenes that followed a battle'. That's good enough for the Pākehā historian. He doesn't have to be told everything.

The men from Auckland are back on the island again. Their coats and whiskers are ash-grey, and when they speak to us, they stare down at the dust on their boots. I look at it too, because it's hard for me to stand up straight these days. They call themselves officers of the Crown, but I doubt that the Queen would think much of the way they look.

This is their fourth visit, and they've brought a piece of blue paper with them this time. The Pākehā who speaks through his nose steps forward.

'Paratene Te Manu,' he says, thrusting the paper towards me. 'This is your summons.'

The blue paper quivers in front of me.

'Tell them I'm not going to court,' I say to my nephew. I'm too old to speak English anymore.

'You must quit the Little Barrier by the end of this month,' says the Pākehā.

'Tell them I'm not leaving the island.'

My nephew talks to the men, and the one with whiskers like a stoat grows red in the face.

'The island has been declared a reserve for the preservation of native fauna,' says Whiskers, looking at my nephew. 'By Act of Parliament, it is now the property of the Crown.'

The one with the voice like a nose flute stabs the paper towards me, but I have no intention of taking it in my hand. He can see that, I suppose, because he places the piece of paper on the ground, inches from my toes.

I pick up a mānuka stick lying on the ground, and swing it over the paper. With small, careful steps, I dance around the paper, jabbing the stick down at it, as though the paper is the prone body of an enemy, waiting for the lethal blow. I hop on my left foot, and then my right. It's not easy for an old man, and I wish my trousers weren't so long, but I make my point. Even the wind agrees with me: a breeze lifts the paper, blowing it towards the water. One of the Pākehā has to chase after it.

'This is my island, and I'm going to die here,' I say. My nephew can tell them what I'm saying if he wants to. I don't care. I brandish my stick, wishing it really was a taiaha: I'd like to slice the ears off every one of them.

The Pākehā have to leave quickly, before the wind changes. My nephew says he'll go back to the courts and talk some more. He likes to sail down to Auckland, to race his boat and go to the courts and argue about where we can or can't live. Sometimes he's away for weeks at a time, catching the train to Wellington, where he can find even more Pākehā to argue with at Parliament House.

It's a long time since I made my promise to the missionary, to live in peace for the rest of my life. The word was spoken, and it was heard: this is how we made our agreement. Now the Pākehā come here, tickling my toes with a piece of paper. The wind can blow a piece of paper into the sea; the waves can rinse away its words.

Since the day I made my promise, I've left the island a few times. But now I can't stand up straight anymore. The next time I leave, my body will lie still on a pallet. Perhaps they'll leave me there until the flesh peels off the carcass, and then hide my bones in one of the caves higher up Hauturu. Or perhaps they'll bury me in the ground, in the Pākehā way. It won't matter to me: my wairua will have ascended to heaven by then. Or perhaps it will have soared to the tip of the mountain and begun the long journey home over the ocean; I don't mind either way.

In the days I spent surrounded by dying and killing, death was the point of everything. I confronted it every day. Now I'm reminded of it all the time by other people. I can see it in their faces. It feels like everyone's waiting for me to die, so other things can end, too.

Maybe I'm imagining this. There are things I see, and things I dream, and things I remember. Sometimes I'm not sure which is which. Every day it's harder to climb from my sleeping mat, to pull on my trousers. I walk in smaller circles, and the beach feels as broad and endless as the Hauraki Plains. And the mainland seems to get closer, as though Hauturu is a raft, washing in on the tide: one night, we'll hit the rocks of the peninsula.

I'll come back to visit them all here, though, after I'm dead. Whenever I see the Pākehā sailing up from Auckland, scribbling on bits of paper, I'll take the form of a fantail, peep-peeping at everyone on the island from the stock fence, lighting on their hoes, warning them of trouble approaching. Even the smallest of birds can make more noise than a piece of paper.

'Talk about the time you went to England,' says the girl. She still has pages to fill, I see. War exploits are not enough for her friend the historian.

Now, this is a story I like to tell. I can even remember the dates.

Fourteen of us were invited on the trip, all of us rangatira people. We sailed away to England on the first day of February, 1863. The voyage was longer than any I had undertaken. We didn't arrive in England until May. None of us fell ill during the journey, although it was often very cold out at sea, and we spent a lot of time in cramped quarters below deck, listening to the ship creak.

London is a vast city, like many different Aucklands stitched together, and even in the summertime it's smoky with fog. The skies were so grey and the Pākehā so pale, it seemed as though we'd sailed into the underworld. The first night, we stayed in a brick house that looked like a giant chimney. When I looked out the windows, which were as grimy as the streets, I could see ghoulish white faces on everyone walking by. Young Hariata, the wife of Hare Pomare, whispered to me that we couldn't stay there too long, because the people of London would kill us. Some of our group began to worry that the visit was an ambush, that we would never return home. I wasn't afraid, but I don't like feeling outnumbered.

The next morning, Mr Jenkins, who brought us from New Zealand, escorted us to the railway station. I'd never climbed inside a train before, and when it flew towards us, spouting steam like a volcano, clattering and whistling and sighing, we stood bunched together, in case we were swept away by its strong wind. The train rushed off with us, travelling south to the coast. There we stayed in a smaller house, and everyone was happy, because fewer Pākehā swarmed around us, and we knew we could easily escape out to sea.

The Prince of Wales lived nearby, and we were taken to meet him. The Prince was short, with sideburns thick as fur. His servants brought us tiny twinkling glasses of green cordial: Te Hapimana joked later that it looked like sea water. Mr Jenkins bowed every time the Prince looked at him. We exchanged greetings, and told the Prince 'hariru', after the Pākehā fashion, but we were all eager to be off to see the Queen.

Like me, the Queen lives on an island, so she sent a steamer to collect us. The island didn't look like Hauturu at all: there's no mountain or forest. Mr Jenkins pointed out the lilac bushes to the women in our party, and they all nodded and exclaimed, as he seemed to expect.

The Queen's house was long, with many stairs and doors and hallways, urns like great stone goblets lining the terrace wall to catch the rain. We were given rooms in which to change before meeting with the Queen. She didn't want to see her Māori subjects wearing their suits and gold watches:

217

she wanted to see the clothing of our ancestors. So we draped feather cloaks over our shoulders, and the women tied piupiu around their waists. In our hands we carried the old carved weapons. I held a heavy greenstone mere, warm to the touch, to present to her later.

In a sunny room with a carpet of many colours, we waited for the Queen and her courtiers. She was even smaller than her son and round as a teapot, but she radiated great mana. We made our salutations in Māori, and then went up to her, one by one, to say 'hariru', Ngahuia was the first. She said 'hariru', and then kissed the Queen's extended hand, so we all did the same thing. I, Paratene Te Manu, was the last to say 'hariru' to the Queen.

'Salutations to you,' the Queen said, in a voice as clear as a bellbird's, 'the Māori people of New Zealand.'

Hare Pomare told her we were afraid to stay in London, because we'd been told the Pākehā there would kill us. Mr Jenkins fell over his words trying to explain this to the Queen.

'I will not be pleased if my Māori people are killed,' she replied. 'I am not willing that New Zealand should be destroyed.'

We were all happy with this. After a few more exchanges, the Queen looked at me.

'Are you not going to say anything?' she asked.

'I am,' I replied, and Mr Jenkins leaned forward to hear my words and tell them to the Queen. 'Be generous to the Māori people.'

The Queen nodded her head.

'Yes,' she said. She looked at me with her bird eyes. 'I am kindly disposed to the Māori race.'

Then the Queen invited us to eat some food before returning to the steamer, and our audience with her was at an end. Before she left the room, we presented her with our native garments. Ngahuia took the greenstone hei tiki from around her neck, and handed it to the great lady. The Queen looked very pleased. She unpinned the diamond brooch from her dress, and gave it to Ngahuia. There were other gifts waiting for us, in the room where food was laid out on a table as long as a tree trunk.

Years ago, when Hongi went to visit King George, he too was given fine jewels and clothing. The old King was very pleased with his Māori chief, and presented him with many valuable gifts. Hongi kept the English armour, but, on his way home, he traded all the other gifts in Sydney for muskets, powder and shot. Without all those gifts from the King, we wouldn't have been such a mighty force. On this visit, however, we brought our gifts home to New Zealand. Wharepapa even brought back an English wife. Times had changed. Every tribe owned guns, and the only people still engaged in battle were fighting the British.

There's one other thing, I tell the girl. One other thing from that trip to England that I will never forget. When we returned to London, we were taken to see the Queen's lions, because none of us had ever seen lions before.

The lions were huge creatures, wearing beards of feathered toetoe. They paced in their iron cages, fierce and angry, shouting at us with wide, hungry mouths. They shouted so loud, I suggested that they be brought out before us, so we might fight them.

This made Mr Jenkins shake his head and flap his hands.

The Queen would not be pleased, he said, if the lions were killed by us.

We didn't want to displease the Queen, so we walked away without fighting them. Their shouts followed us through the park. I dreamed about them pacing in their cages on my first night back on Hauturu, after the long voyage back to New Zealand.

I went to Auckland one last time about ten years ago, to visit the painter from Bohemia. I should tell the girl about this, next time she's on the island.

Auckland stinks. The wharves are cloudy with black smoke and Queen Street is puddled with animal dirt. A foul river of human muck runs behind it, dancing with flies. But I used to go down there regularly, to meet with people, or buy a suit, or make a trade with some of the merchants. Once my nephew's wife wanted a pianoforte, so I sailed down with my nephew to pick it up. Eventually I grew too old to be bothered with all Auckland's noise and machines. But my old friend, Te Hau Takiri Wharepapa, visited me on the island, full of stories about this Bohemian chap. A lot of rangatira wanted a picture of themselves and they paid the Bohemian money to get one. But sometimes the painter was interested in particular people – because they were handsome, said Wharepapa, who has always been very conceited, or because of their moko – and asked to paint them for his own collection. This painter wanted to meet me.

The Bohemian had a short beard shaped like a tongue, and wore a woollen cap to keep his ideas from escaping. He boiled me up some tea in his studio, which was a big, dark room up the stairs from a haberdasher's shop, and asked to take my likeness. So I stayed in Auckland for almost two weeks, visiting the Bohemian every day or two. It took longer to paint the moko than to chisel it into my face. He sat me in front of a blanket hanging from the ceiling, and wrapped me in a woven cloak. Like the Queen, painters don't want to see their Māori subjects in a suit! I must remember that one, to tell the girl.

All the time he drew or painted, I watched him. You can see that in the finished picture: my eyes looking straight at him. I had to hold my face very still, so he could paint in every whisker. All around me, covering the red wallpaper, were paintings the Bohemian had done. I could recognise a number of the faces, especially the men from the Northern tribes.

Perhaps it was more than ten years ago; perhaps it was twenty. Perhaps the Bohemian is dead. Maybe he got tired of painting strangers, because he had no pictures of his own family on the wall. All those faces staring down at him, but none of them his own tūpuna. I would have talked to him about it, but neither of us liked to speak English much. Once, after he had stopped for the day and we were toasting pieces of bread, I asked him to tell me something from the newspaper sitting folded on his table. He told me that he didn't like to read, either, and only bought the paper if he needed something to start the fire.

He could read faces, though. This wasn't something he said to me, of course. I could see it by looking around the room. I could see it in the painting he made of my face, every line and ray in my moko, every curve and hook, precise. At one time, a stranger could look at me and know everything in that one glance – that I am a descendant of the first line on both sides, an eldest son, a warrior, a rangatira. Even the shadows the Bohemian painted didn't hide the anchor on my chin, the mark that tells people I was a teacher of weapons.

My nephew and his sons, they don't wear a moko. Their faces are smooth, like babies'. When my nephew goes to court, nobody knows who he is. Here on my face is my ancestry, my rank, my occupation, my signature. If I were to stand up in court, the judge would know he was dealing with a rangatira. All these Māori nowadays, they look the same. No wonder the judge has no respect.

When the Bohemian showed me the painting, it wasn't quite finished. The sight of it startled me: my hair and whiskers were so white, my expression so grave. The moko on my face looked like it was carved into the canvas. Without thinking, I reached out a hand to touch the painting, because I know the grooves of my moko through my fingertips. The Bohemian shook his head, pulling at my sleeve, lifting my arm away. Then he smiled at me, and I smiled at him. We were both pleased with the painting.

After I came back to Hauturu, everyone was full of questions. One of my nephew's sons asked me: is it like staring into a looking-glass, koro? – as though I have time to be gazing at myself every day. It's strange to think of someone sketching the shape of it with such care, for the first time since the tohunga drew the design onto my face with a piece of charcoal, just before the days of chiselling began.

Sometimes I think that I'd like to see that painting again, see it hanging there for all the ladies and gentlemen to look at on the Bohemian's wall. Maybe I should have tried to pay him, so I could have carried the painting home with me, but I knew he wanted it for his wall. The Bohemian was very proud of that picture.

The girl shakes me awake and tells me we have to go.

For a moment, I think I'm still asleep and the girl has come to me in a dream: she wants me to travel to Auckland to see the painter or to see the Queen, and the waka is waiting; it will take too many days to row, I want to tell her, and my arms are too feeble now to pull an oar or swing a taiaha. My days of expeditions and voyages are over.

'Wake up, koro,' she says. I open my eyes and see her round face, not smiling, inches away from mine. 'You have to get dressed. Men are here to take you away.'

Perhaps I'm not dreaming: perhaps I'm dead. This wasn't what I was expecting, but maybe the men are here to escort me to the underworld. Hine-nui-te-pō, the great woman of the night, is drawing me close at last.

'The commissioner's here,' the girl whispers. 'And soldiers. You have to come now.'

So I'm not dead. Hine-nui-te-pō would never send Pākehā.

'We're being evicted,' says the girl, and she helps me to my feet. The light outside the open door is dim; it's still very early in the morning. The trees glisten with dew. The commissioner, the one who speaks through his nose, stands outside my nephew's house. He's rubbing his hands together, because it's always cold and damp here just after dawn.

The girl hands me my jacket and gathers a few of my

things into a bag. The beach is crowded with Pākehā, soldiers in red and policemen in blue, every one of them with a gun. I haven't seen so much weaponry since my last war expedition to the Mahia Peninsula, where my uncle, Tau-ko-kupu, fell, and we slew great numbers of men in retribution. I'm surprised the noise of their boots crunching across the rocks didn't wake me. Now chickens are squawking, and seagulls screech above our heads. My nephew's voice is raised in argument. The soldiers pace the beach, agitated. A steamer sits waiting, not far from shore.

'Koro,' says the girl. She takes my arm and leads me to the water's edge, where two boy-faced soldiers are waiting to row me to the steamer. It's hard for me to climb into the boat: my trousers are wet to the knee, weighing down my creaking legs. But I refuse the hands held out by the Pākehā. The girl steadies the boat with both hands, waves darkening her dress. Her husband, my nephew's son, lifts me in and slides my bag between my feet. He's a strong boy, tall the way I was, once. A policeman pushes the boat off, clambering in behind me. I'm passed onto the steamer like a sack of kūmara, and stand on the deck, looking back towards my home. My nephew arrives next, with one of his sons, and then his wife is brought out to the steamer. Two of the blue uniforms have to carry her from her house down to the boat, because she refuses to leave the island.

The commissioner climbs on board, snapping at one of the soldiers for taking so long to row. He orders the men to watch my nephew's wife for the first part of the journey, in case she dives overboard and swims back to shore. She's an old bird now, but she can still swim farther than a man.

The girl isn't on the steamer. I heard the commissioner talking, saying that some of the others could leave in their own boats. I thought he said he was only interested in the rangatiras, but perhaps the word he used was ringleaders. The girl and her husband have already skimmed away across the water, headed for the pā near Omaha. My nephew called out to them, to remember to milk the cows. We can come back for our livestock and other belongings another time, the commissioner tells him, under Crown supervision. Now we have to travel to Auckland, to get dumped in Devonport like passengers who can't afford the full price of a ticket, and make our own way back up the coast.

The steamer puffs around in a circle until it's facing south. My nephew stands with his back to the island. There's a defiant look on his face, and he tells the commissioner that he's going back to Parliament House in a month's time to argue some more. He has a new lawyer, a famous man who lives in a room with a big desk and many, many books. My nephew can read English as well as any lawyer, but he doesn't have all those books.

My nephew's wife says nothing. She has a rage in her eyes. She's Te Kiri's daughter, after all. When she was a child, all this land was his. She grew up on his beach, keeping watch for waka approaching from the south, the bleached bones of his enemies poking the soles of her feet through the sand dunes.

The place we leave behind is thick with trees, loud with birdcall, but the mainland has been skinned bare. Tongues of wind curl around us, as though Hauturu is lashing us, whipping us around and around. The island already looks dark and far away, its shape obscured by the forest. The wind in my face is loud and angry. I can hear the lions in their cages: the sky fills with the sound of their shouts. I roll out my tongue. I raise my stick in the air, so the lions can see I'm ready to fight. I show them the whites of my eyes.

Spanish Around the Home

¿Cuáles son sus apellidos?
What are your names?

They will have more than one last name. This may be confusing at first. Just use their first names. This is what you're used to; this is what they expect.

They may try to call you Mrs. You will have to explain the custom of using Miss and your first name. They will get used to it.

Your name will not sound the way it should sound. You will get used to it.

¿De qué país es usted?
What country are you from?

The Spanish ruled this city once. They brought us all those shady courtyards in the Quarter, and red beans and rice.

None of these people are from Spain.

They may be from Mexico; they may not be from Mexico. For example, there are a lot of people from Honduras here in New Orleans. Before the storm, more than a hundred thousand Hondurans lived in the greater New Orleans area. Some of them had been here for ten years, since Hurricane Mitch tore up Central America.

This doesn't mean they speak English well. This does not mean they have a work permit.

¿Tiene permiso de trabajo?
Do you have a work permit?

Ask to see it. Ask for a copy. Ask for references. Ask for a social security number. You cannot be too careful.

¿Cuánto tiempo hace que está en los Estados Unidos?
How long have you been in the United States?

A new employee might say he or she is a citizen of this country. This is possible. Millions of people become new citizens every year. New Orleans has shrunk, but the United States is growing and growing.

Not enough of these new citizens go to the empty parts of the country: they want to live the same places everyone else wants to live, like Miami and Los Angeles and Dallas. You should be pleased that some of them want to come to New Orleans. You should be happy that there are workers willing to dust your parlour and trim the hedges.

Please note: sometimes people seem foreign when they're actually American. Sometimes they might just be from Texas. Sometimes they might just be from New Orleans. Not everyone speaks English these days. French isn't the second language around here anymore.

¿Cuántas horas puede trabajar?
How many hours can you work?

Your new employees may not live a few blocks away. They may live out in New Orleans East or on the West Bank. They may have large families who make demands on them. Your old employees often had large families, but that was different. They understood.

¿Puede quedarse a dormir?
Can you stay overnight?

Watch a prospective employee carefully when you ask this. If they flinch, interview someone else. You need someone you can rely on. You need someone you can call any time. You need someone who is a part of your family.

¿Lee inglés?
Do you read English?

Some things need to be read to you. Maybe you can't find your reading glasses and you want to hear what Chris Rose has to say in the *Times-Picayune*. Maybe you can't make out the label on a bottle of pills. Maybe you need someone to read aloud from the *TV Guide* or an email from your son: the type is so very small. You're used to someone being with you, everywhere except the voting booth and the examination room at the doctor's. You're used to someone telling you things, doing things for you.

¿Sabe conducir?
Do you drive a car?

This is crucial. Ask to see a driver's licence. Ask for a copy. Make sure the state that issued it isn't Nuevo Léon.

Yo sé manejar pero no sé estacionar el coche.
I know how to drive, but I don't know how to park the car.

You prefer it when someone else does the driving. It's easier and nicer when someone can come to the drugstore and hair salon with you. At Amy's, they can get their nails done as well. At the doctor's, they can read magazines. At Langenstein's, they can find the Better Cheddar for you: the type is so very small.

No me gusta llegar tarde.
I don't like to arrive late.

You know all about doing things *mañana*. New Orleans has always moved slowly. Carnival floats get stuck rounding the corner at Napoleon and St Charles. The city council and the school board hold public meetings where everyone gives speeches and shouts at one another, and nothing gets done. Cars stolen in Mississippi sit for weeks gathering leaves near the CCs on Jefferson, and nobody thinks to have them towed away. The post office on Carrolton runs out of holiday stamps a week before Christmas and doesn't bother ordering more. The only thing moving fast around here are the pick-ups going through red lights.

With new employees, you have the chance to take your stand.

Haga el favor de limpiar la cocina. Haga el favor de lavar la ropa. Haga el favor de llenar el tanque de gasolina. Haga el favor de cambiar el aceite.
Please clean the kitchen. Please wash the clothes. Please fill the gas tank. Please change the oil.

Don't be afraid to ask for what you want. Set the bar high. You may be pleasantly surprised: your new employees will be quite hardworking and diligent. They have the immigrant mentality. In recent years, there's been too little of the immigrant mentality around here. The post office on Carrolton could do with more of the immigrant mentality. The cashiers at Walgreens could do with more of the immigrant mentality.

Tiene que separar la ropa de color de la blanca.
You have to separate the colours from the white.

Make yourself perfectly clear.

La sopa está fría.
The soup is cold.

Some things will not be the way you want them. They will not taste the way they used to taste. They will be off in some way. You won't be able to put your finger on it.

Estoy ansioso. Tengo dolor de cabeza.
I am anxious. I have a headache.

Tell your new employees how you feel. This is a very stressful time. You don't have anyone to talk to anymore. Your old employees knew you. They knew your children. They made crab cakes the way you liked them. They knew how to bank the white poinsettias in the front yard every December. They would watch a story on television with you and discuss the characters as though the actors and actresses lived on your street. They made you a cake on your birthday.

Estoy deprimido.
I am depressed.

This is understandable: don't be ashamed. They are gone. The houses they rented still stink of the flood, or else the houses have been gutted and fixed up. The landlords want bigger rents and tenants from Alabama who work in construction.

They live in Houston now. They live in Atlanta. They live in Philadelphia, where they don't have to work because their grown-up children have middle-class jobs. They live in Eugene, Oregon, where their grandchildren go to schools that don't have metal detectors. They are not coming back.

This is why you need to learn Spanish.

Estoy cansado.
I am tired.

We are all tired. The city looks like a construction site but still, whole neighbourhoods are grassy and derelict. No matter how many teams of willing high school seniors and cheerful Mennonites come down to help rebuild, the process is slow. The country has moved on. Louisiana is not a rich state. It's not a swing state. New Orleans can lie in pieces for years. Nobody will notice.

¿Cuánto tiempo necesita usted para arreglar el problema?
How long will it take to fix the problem?

If your new employees are taking your car to have its brakes tested or transmission replaced, this is a useful question to ask them. If you are talking about the city, this question is pointless. Try not to focus on problems. Think about LSU's winning season. Think about Carnival next year. Think about Brad Pitt and Angelina Jolie spending the holidays at their place in the Quarter.

Llame al médico.
Please call the doctor.

The doctor cannot help you. In the last two years, he's prescribed too many sleeping pills, too much Xanax. Soon he'll be moving away as well. Walking home from Newman after a soccer game, his kids were robbed of their cell phones and iPods. He would have left months ago, but the house on Nashville is still on the market.

Ha habido un accidente.
There has been an accident.

Hurricanes and floods are accidents of Nature. They'll all understand this – the Mexicans, the Guatemalans, the Costa Ricans, the Hondurans, the El Salvadorians, the Panamanians. The Belizeans will understand it as well, but they will understand it in English. They all know about hurricanes and floods.

Hizo mal tiempo. Hizo mucho viento.
The weather was bad. It was very windy.

They don't know, perhaps, about the US Army Corps of Engineers and how their faulty work and negligent maintenance resulted in breaches of the levees and canals. They don't understand, perhaps, that human error caused the flood. There is no word in the glossary for 'breach'. There are no words in the glossary for 'dysfunctional' and 'catastrophic failure'.

Do not attempt to explain any of this. These people come to the United States to get away from environmental danger, political dysfunction, social breakdown, and crumbling infrastructures. They do not expect to find the same things here in the greatest country in the world.

¡Qué desastre!
What a disaster!

Do not use the word 'disaster'. You do not want your new employees to take flight. You do not want them to look for jobs in Denver, where it never floods. Who will drive you to the post office? Who will drop off your prescriptions? Who will read you the list of new iced teas at CCs? The type is so very small.

Estoy muy agradecida.
I'm very grateful.

Don't forget to thank your new employees. Treat them well. Make them feel welcome in the United States. Pay them a fair wage. Give them things you don't want anymore to take home to their families. Hope you don't live to see another hurricane and flood.

But if you're unlucky – because accidents do happen – and another hurricane hits the city, you'll need to rely on your new employees. They will board up your house and fill up your car and pack your suitcases and drive you to safety. You may be stuck in a car together for many, many hours.

Practise your Spanish. Soon you'll speak it every day. You will get used to it.

Chain Bridge

Eva calls me at Christmas, as usual, because she can't be bothered writing cards or sending letters.

'Anna my dear, come at Easter, because I will have some free days,' she urges. 'Easter is early, but it won't be cold here. It is never cold in Budapest.'

Eva has been asking me to visit for several years, ever since she finished her journalism course in New York and returned to Hungary. She has a new apartment, she tells me, and a new job, and a boyfriend who is not new at all.

'He is quite boring,' she says. 'You don't have to meet him if you don't want. Maybe I will get rid of him this winter, before you come.'

At Christmas any time off seems impossible, but by late winter I've lost my job: I have all the time in the world. When I arrive in Budapest on a grey March afternoon, the city is still scrappy with snow, and it's already dark when the cab drops me off at the corner of her street. Eva lives at the foot of the Hill of Roses, on a stunted lane illuminated only by one dim streetlight. The narrow street ends in a broad flight of stairs carved into the hillside, barely visible in the darkness.

The lobby and stairwell of Eva's building are shabby and neglected; the walls crumble like dry cake onto the floor. She had told me that the building once housed grand apartments. Now it's carved up into small flats four times the original number. I walk up the stairs, not trusting the elevator, and ring the bell of the third-floor balcony. Through the glazed glass, I see Eva scampering from her front door in slippers, arms folded against the cold.

'Miss Anna!' she says, fumbling with the lock. She gives me a brisk hug. 'Come quick – I am *freezing*.'

I haven't seen Eva for several years. Although she looks exactly the same, she seems more preoccupied than ever with her appearance, perhaps because of her new job as a local television news reporter. During a desultory tour of the apartment, Eva pauses under the bathroom's fluorescent light to point out newly acquired grey hairs and the beginnings of some fine lines around her eyes.

'You can see I am finished,' she says, twisting her moth-brown hair out of the way with one hand so I can more closely observe her thin, pointed face. 'You are lucky to be fair. The grey doesn't show.'

'You look as pretty as ever,' I say, and Eva pouts at her reflection, feigning indifference to the compliment, deliberating if it's compliment enough.

We sit in her white, orderly kitchen and Eva makes us tea, mine a clear pale brown, her own awash in lemon pith.

'So you are still living in the same place,' she says. 'And still at the same bank.'

'Same apartment, different bank,' I tell her. When Eva first knew me, I was an analyst at Morgan Stanley. She was a grad student at NYU, subletting the den – pretty much a closet – in an apartment owned by one of the other analysts on my floor. Eva went back to Hungary; I enrolled in the MBA program at Stern because I thought it would fast-track me to a better job and better pay. For the past year and a half – until a few weeks ago, in fact – I'd been an associate at Gorman Parker.

These were the things I shouldn't have done: stayed in the city to go to grad school; racked up another hundred grand in student loans; gone to work at Gorman Parker. I could tell Eva all this; I could tell her that I'd lost my job. But I don't want to talk about it with anyone. Not even my parents know. They just think I'm in Europe on business again, adding on a quick vacation. This is one good thing about not being allowed to send personal emails from my work account. Everyone I know has been too scared to contact me at work, ever since I told them about the analyst I worked with in my first year out of school: he forwarded a joke, sent by his brother, to a few other analysts. The Morgan Stanley secret police found out about it and he was fired the same day.

Eva is talking again. The moment to tell her about my lost job, my failed life, has passed.

'I miss it, you know. *America*. Your apartment was nice, I remember. Here things are very . . . I mean, in not such a good condition.'

'Dilapidated?'

She leans across the table and clasps my arm. 'What is that? What is that you said?'

I repeat it, surprised that the word is new to her. Eva has always spoken English well, in a clipped British inflection. For a moment she looks a little annoyed, as though I've set her a trap. Then she relaxes her grip and stops frowning.

'My English has gone to hell,' she confides and takes me through to the living room, where I'll be sleeping. 'Tomorrow you can meet Peter. He says he wants to show you around,' and at this she rolls her eyes, 'if you can bear it.'

'So you haven't got rid of him after all,' I say, laughing at her. She gives me a stage pout.

'And tomorrow night I will interrogate you about your love life, because you tell me nothing.'

'Nothing much to tell,' I say. This is another lie.

Eva gets up to return her cup to the kitchen. 'Nothing to tell, when you could never come to Budapest until now, even though you were always travelling here and there?' Walking by, she gives my hair a soft, swift stroke. 'And I must tell you that I love your coat, and your shoes too. You are so New York, black, black, black. Maybe that's why you look so pale. I want to see all your things, you know. And I want to hear *everything*.'

After Eva goes to bed in her small room off the kitchen, I lie awake and wonder what to tell her. I've come to Budapest for a few weeks not simply because I have no job, and to be without a job in New York is to not exist, to not belong, but because I'm tired of stewing in sadness, and I'm hoping visiting Eva will distract me. There's something appealing in the city's grim, wintry face, as well; while Eva's at work, I'm free to spend my days unsmiling, glum as the sky and the sidewalks.

I have nothing to tell Eva but the most banal of tales, anyway: that I was in love with a married man, and that our relationship is over. I don't want to sob over it, or have the affair dissected. I don't want to conjure him up again out of the past. I certainly don't want sympathy – which is, perhaps, the reason I've chosen to visit Eva, of all my friends.

And in this unfamiliar place, where everything is strange and new, perhaps the memory of him – his face, his voice, his promises – will disappear. I don't want to conjure him up again out of the past for Eva. I don't want to remember him at all.

The morning after I arrive, Peter calls for me. We're going to catch the bus along the river to the Chain Bridge.

I'm very curious to meet him. Peter is an old friend of Eva's. She's known him for more than ten years, and they were lovers on a casual basis – casual, at any rate, to Eva – before she went to America.

Eva had several boyfriends while she was in New York, including another of my colleagues who, it turned out, was attractive to her only because he was American and slightly taller than she was. Later on, there was an Hungarian photographer with whom she squabbled constantly, and a real estate agent who thought she was a countess and took her skiing. This particular relationship ended for mysterious reasons one weekend when he tried to teach her how to roller-blade. She referred to him from that point on as Mr Money, 'because that is all he's interested in, darling – money, and stupid things that strap to your feet.'

Peter arrives that morning wearing a sweater with a

ragged neck, brown corduroy trousers, and a pair of flimsy spectacles, which he keeps removing in order to fiddle with them, or clean them, or to emphasise a particular point. Peter is of average height and build, with thinning brown hair and a very genial expression. He doesn't appear to notice Eva's dismissive manner, and spends ten minutes trying to persuade her to come with us.

'Some people don't understand about jobs and careers, you see,' she tells me, as if he were not in the room. 'Some people are *supposed* to be architects. But instead, they are tourists, with plenty of time to run around Budapest, looking at this and that.'

'Please don't let me keep you from work,' I say at once. Peter wipes his glasses on the hem of his sweater and does not appear to be listening. 'Really, Peter, I can look around by myself; it's no problem.'

'I don't have to work today,' he says. Eva snorts, pouring the remainder of the coffee down the sink without offering him a cup. He smiles at me. 'It's not too cold for you?'

The day is windy and only intermittently clear, and there's no warmth in the sun at all. In the funicular climbing Castle Hill we stand at the window, watching the receding river and the flat plain of the city on its far banks. There are very few people in the streets at the top of the hill. Peter points out everything old or picturesque or unusual, vast wooden doors that open into a broad courtyard, an apricot-coloured house. At the corner of a quiet street we look up at lions' heads and garlands of flowers carved into the wall until the chill of the wind moves us on. There's a closed-down quiet to the place, the feeling of still being slightly out of season.

From a cold alcove in the lookout near the church we stop to watch a thin, grey cloud spurt hail down the Danube. It passes along the river in a matter of minutes like a trail of steam, obscuring the rooftops and flat-fronted buildings on the Pest side. Some half-hearted hail drifts onto the hillside, and we retreat to the subterranean interior of the church. Every other tourist in the city seems to be huddling in there, waiting for the sky to clear. People sit in small groups, reading foreign newspapers and guidebooks, or they pace the aisles, peering up at the dark windows. Peter and I huddle near the back, and he tells me stories of kings and saints and composers in a low whisper.

'But of course the church has been rebuilt many times,' he says. 'Like all of this area. The city was conquered and destroyed and rebuilt, and then destroyed again. All the oldest parts of Budapest are really only fragments. But this is what Americans always want to see – I'm sorry, I meant American tourists, or tourists generally.'

'That's OK,' I tell him. I've travelled in Europe enough to know that Americans are scorned. I'm past caring. 'Do you mean everything was destroyed during the war?'

'Many wars. Turks, Austrians, Germans, Russians,' he says, glancing surreptitiously at a Japanese couple sitting behind us. 'Not so much is original after this many centuries and this many armies. There is much destruction, and then rebuilding, but nothing is the way it was before. It just has the appearance. You will see it all over the city – covering up the marks on the houses. Things look better here than they did just a few years ago. Really, this is true.'

A tour group arrives, and Peter suggests we go somewhere

for a coffee. He wants to talk about Eva, so we find a small café and take a seat in the window.

'I love her,' he says, looking me in the eye, daring me to contradict him. I don't know what to say. Eva hasn't told me much about their relationship, apart from the broad hints that she's on the perpetual brink of ending it.

'You are thinking that she talks of finishing with me.' Peter's reading my mind. He smiles and lies his glasses alongside his cup; crystals of spilled sugar stick to the lenses. 'But Eva is always talking. She talks about leaving me, leaving her job, leaving Hungary. Sometimes she goes, but she always comes back.'

'Perhaps she's more settled now,' I say, thinking that this is unlikely to be true. She's a restless person, Eva. I was the one who stayed put.

'I don't know,' he says, smiling again. His face is understated, serene. 'Do you think so?'

I start to say something else but stop myself. I don't really know Eva anymore, not well. She could have a vast, hidden, secret life that I know nothing about. Maybe she's a liar, like me.

'Tell me more about the city,' I ask him, and we talk of other things while he drains his coffee, pressing cake crumbs onto his forefinger, and then begin our walk back down the hill.

'One thing you must see that is real,' he says with a mischievous laugh, 'is in the Basilica. Nothing has been done to this thing – no rebuilding, no renovation, no *preservation*. It belongs to someone. To Saint Stephen – you know him?'

It begins to drizzle, and Peter trots ahead of me.

'It is his hand,' he calls back over his shoulder. 'The right hand of Saint Stephen. You can see it before you leave.'

Later, Eva tells me that Peter wasn't joking.

'I haven't seen it since I was in school, and that was a *long* time ago, darling. But I don't think it will have changed. It's been sitting there in a glass box for a thousand years. Trust Peter to tell you about stupid things, and make you walk around that hill all day when it is practically snowing. Did you take photos?'

There are no photographs of Will and me. We took no photos of ourselves together, although we spent hundreds of hours in each other's company, in many different places. There are just the pictures that I carry inside my head. Every few weeks during our relationship, I would mentally gather them together for review, leafing through, lingering over them – especially when we were apart.

The trouble with committing all these scenes to memory is that, unlike pictures in a photo album, they can't be put away. I took so much care to preserve them in my mind that it's impossible now to get them out of my head. They're as vivid in Budapest as they are in New York.

The telephone by Eva's bed reminds me of my own bedside table stained with dust and coffee, piled with books and magazines and unfolded letters, the telephone poised and waiting. Will travelled on business more than I did, calling me – often in the middle of the night – from Moscow, Buenos Aires, Guangzhou. I always pictured him stretched out flat on a big hotel bed or slouched on a hard-backed chair, the light of the television flashing behind his head.

And wherever I went, I called him – or rather, I checked my voicemail obsessively for his messages, tapping the password with quivering fingers as though I was on some espionage mission. I called him from a shopping mall in New Jersey, and from a booming London department store, surrounded by washing machines and electric teakettles. I called from departure lounges, from identical hotel rooms in the cities I flew to with the rest of a particular client team. One morning, at my parents' house in Houston, while they ate their breakfast and read the paper, I took my phone outside, wandering around on the damp patio, night dress tucked into a pair of shorts, so I could listen, over and over, to the message he'd left.

Once he called from his own parents' garden in Rosedale in western Massachusetts, his voice faint and urgent. It was early in the day and he had stolen away from the house before anyone else was awake. I pictured him there in the shy morning light, the long fields beyond, looking back towards the place where his family were sleeping.

This is what I remember most clearly: my ear pressed to a phone – at work, at home, outside the entrance to the subway, in a town car driving to the airport – punching in the numbers that would transport me to him, wherever he was. Sometimes, when we actually got to speak to each other, we didn't have that much to say. I just wanted to hear the sound of his voice.

The following evening Peter collects us in his car, and Eva insists that I sit in the front seat. She takes the opportunity to reorganise my hairstyle, pulling out the elastic band that's holding it in place. Peter drives across the river, glancing at her in the rear-view mirror as though she's about to escape through the back door at any minute. We're going to a bar on a street that was once named after the Rosenbergs.

'But now it's called Moon Street, Anna, so Americans can go there again,' Eva teases, leaning forward. 'To meet European men.'

'Anna isn't American,' Peter tells her. 'She's a Texan.' Eva snaps at him in Hungarian.

'She wants me to drive quickly,' he says. 'She thinks she still lives in New York and everything is a big hurry.'

An old friend of Peter's with the improbably genie-like name of Zoltan is meeting us at the bar and Eva is anxious not to keep him waiting. She drums her fingers on the back of Peter's seat. It seems as if he's driving more slowly now than before, although there's hardly any traffic. The car creeps along the street.

'Always the big hurry,' Peter mutters. Changing down a gear, he slows the car until it stutters with the strain. The engine sounds like it's about to cut out. Peter is laughing to himself. Eva gives a loud, impatient sigh and flings herself back in her seat.

Zoltan is already at the bar when we arrive, halfway through a glass of beer. When he stands up to shake my hand, he towers over me. He's darker than Peter, and even more unkempt. He seems to be wearing several layers of sweaters, peeling them off throughout the evening to reveal, eventually, an over-washed T-shirt with its pocket ripped off.

'Anna is a top banker,' Eva declares. 'Very clever as well as very beautiful, like all my friends. Darling, Zoltan is a sculptor, which is why he wears rags and says nothing that makes any sense.'

Zoltan looks sheepish at this introduction.

'I am not a sculptor,' he says in a thick, rolling accent. He offers me a cigarette, and I shake my head. 'I make nothing.'

'He makes these men who walk like this,' Eva tells me, swinging her arms and mimicking, I presume, the figures' ferocious scowls. 'Big, giant, striding men. But they stand in one place. I'm not explaining this well.'

'The figures do not move,' says Zoltan. 'That's the problem. They are . . .'

'Static?' Eva suggests, exhaling smoke.

He frowns. 'I cannot make them move.'

'But nothing made of stone can move,' says Eva. She sounds both consoling and bored, as though she's making a hospital visit. Zoltan holds up his hand to interrupt her. The gesture, bold and almost rude, transfixes me, but Eva is scuffling in her bag for something, and doesn't seem to notice.

'It can appear to move, even if it does not,' he says, lowering his hand.

'Obviously.' Eva reaches up to the tray of drinks that Peter has carried over; he and Zoltan begin talking to each other in Hungarian.

Eva leans towards me to whisper about Zoltan. I've never met a sculptor before, and I ask her what else he does to earn money.

'Nothing much,' she mutters, wrinkling her nose. 'Once he was something else – I don't remember what.' Zoltan has set himself the remedial task of sketching the city's statues, she tells me, and spends most days outside, drawing in the cold. 'He is too obsessed with this so-called artist's block. He wastes his time walking around drawing other people's statues. You should go out with him one day.'

'So he can waste his time with me?'

'He will think about you instead of his problem.'

'And what will I think about?' I tease, bending to pick my scarf off the floor.

'Him, of course,' said Eva, as if this is a very stupid question. 'You are on vacation, darling. What else do you have to think about?'

Peter adjusts his chair with a scrape, in order to face Zoltan directly. This appears to annoy Eva.

'American men are not like Hungarian men,' she tells me. 'Hungarians are very polite to women. But they are really old-fashioned, and quite boring. Americans like to go out at night, to the theatre or to the movies or to dinner.'

'And what do Hungarians like to do?'

Eva raises her voice to nearly a shout.

'They get drunk and go home and beat their wives.'

Peter stops talking to Zoltan and gives Eva his full attention.

Two days later, Zoltan calls me at Eva's and asks me to meet him at a restaurant on the Inner Ring road, a wide avenue of shops and businesses that encircles the central part of town. The road is confusing, with a different name for each of its five segments, but I'm only a little late. The restaurant is almost empty. Zoltan is sitting at a pink-clothed table in the centre of the room, glaring at the resident gypsy band, who start playing 'Over the Rainbow' when I walk in.

Clearly Zoltan has made an effort to dress more respectably. He's wearing a faded denim shirt haphazardly tucked into his pants, and only one sweater. I notice that his nose splays slightly to the left, as though it was broken at some point. The deep lines around his mouth make his face look like a puppet's. His hair is flecked with grey, and he seems older than Peter, even though Eva says they're the same age. I like the way his voice sounds.

'I hear music – not *this* music,' he says, gesturing towards the gypsy band with a dismissive wave. I'm picking at the appetiser we're sharing, a goose liver risotto with a surplus of peas. 'And I want to show the idea of the music. The memory of it.' He looks uncertain. 'You understand? In the stone.'

'So people can see the movement?'

'No. Feel the movement. But this is impossible for me.'

I'm used to a different sort of dinner conversation – tax-advantaged derivative securities, say – and my grasp of sculpture-related topics is slight. But I've been reading my guidebook, the only book I brought with me, so I ask him why most of the statues in the city pay tribute to failed heroes or poets who committed suicide, men who were exiled or executed. He shrugs, as though the answer is self-evident.

'There's a park I read about,' I tell him. 'With all the old socialist statues.'

'We can go there,' he says. What's left of our appetiser is taken away and replaced with plates of catfish in a congealed caviar sauce. 'Tomorrow or the next day. I'll take you.'

It's drizzling when we leave the restaurant, so we run to the side street where his car is parked. He has to climb in through the passenger side because the driver's door is jammed. The car looks too small for him and, when he wriggles over the stick shift, his knees crack against the steering wheel. I lower myself into the car after him and twist in the dark for my seatbelt.

'Here,' he says, reaching over. His face nudges mine, and I lift my arms up around his neck to get them out of his way. He stops fidgeting with the belt and, still stretched across me, kisses me hard on the mouth.

Will and I spent a lot of time kissing in his car. Cobbled streets in SoHo, outside a restaurant on the East Side, in the alley leading from his parking garage, at cross-town stoplights. On some nights it was reckless and fierce; on others it was tender, sometimes almost chaste. I loved being close to his face, of seeing the way he looked at me, of his wistful, hungry look when I closed the car door behind me. That part of the picture was always the same.

Will's car was even smaller than Zoltan's. It was a black convertible, bought when he turned forty – just another predictable thing that made us seem the same as all the other illicit couples furtively groping in cars before one of them drove home to the suburbs. I stifle a laugh at the thought of it, which Zoltan interprets it as a gasp. He slides a hand down onto one of my breasts and pinches the nipple between the tips of his fingers.

'Ouch,' I say.

Zoltan stops kissing me and settles into his seat to start the car. I reach out to caress his knee. His knee feels strange to me, thick and bony at the same time. Zoltan cups my hand with his, and we drive all the way back to Eva's like this, not speaking. He has to change gears with his left hand.

Most of my days are spent alone, riding around the city in trams and buses. I buy a clutch of lavender-coloured tickets at a newspaper stand. The first time I catch a tram, I have trouble operating the ticket validation machine, and have to appeal for help to a sullen youth slouched against it. He stares at me, ramming the black lever down without speaking. Soon I notice that on any given tram, bus or metro ride, I'm the only person stamping a ticket. Eva tells me that this is at least the fourth system introduced in order to persuade the people of Budapest to buy tickets, and it is proving as unsuccessful as all those preceding it. My quick transaction with the validation machine inevitably results in long looks from my fellow passengers, who then extend their gazes to dispassionate appraisals of my coat, bag and shoes.

Travelling the city, learning the numbers of buses and the twisting parameters of their routes, waiting in a cluster of people for a tram rounding a bend, its bell ringing – these small adventures in a foreign place give me a childlike sense of accomplishment. Every so often I disembark and spend an hour wandering, drifting past market booths and shops and banks. I venture through open doorways into expansive Viennese courtyards or dusky lobbies, tripping over pigeons and empty beer bottles. In the afternoons I sit in the window at Gérbeaud's or some other grand café, reading whatever English-language newspaper I can find that day at a street kiosk. I try not to read the business news, something I've done assiduously every day since I was an undergraduate. The best newspapers are the English ones, with their outraged headlines and unknown celebrities.

Wherever I ride or walk in the city, I am watched. The buildings of Budapest are peopled with stone figures, surmounting windows, holding up sills, raised high on pedestals. Most of these are mythical creatures or angels. Sometimes they simply take the form of a heroic torso. Composers stare down at me from the Opera House. Lorelei-like women pass elaborate wreaths to each other across a doorway. Creamy arms strain to support pediments, or cradle babies, or point toward the sky. The past has settled like a fine dust into their curves and fissures. They've seen the Austrians come and the Germans come and the Russians come; now they're watching me. I walk the streets of Budapest under their constant stony surveillance.

Peter asks me to meet him at the Café Astoria, near his office. On the phone, he says that he'd like me to try their special coffee, but, as usual, he just wants to discuss Eva. He is much more disheartened than usual, frowning down into his drink. He hasn't seen Eva since the night we all went out to the bar.

'Perhaps it's because I'm here, and she doesn't want to leave me alone,' I say.

'You're alone every day,' Peter objects. 'And you have Zoltan. That's why I introduced you.'

I take a quick swig of coffee, trying not to feel irritated. I don't need Zoltan to babysit me, and anyway, I don't 'have' him. He's just a weird foreign guy who pinched my nipple and offered to take me for a tour of Soviet-era statues: it's hardly an exciting romance.

Peter removes his glasses and rubs his eyes.

'Anna, now you are my friend, too,' he says, his voice almost a whine. 'Tell me. I have been following her, waiting for her – there is someone else, I know. You must tell me.'

'There's nothing to tell. I really don't think so.'

'I saw her go into a house this week, a house I don't know, near Déak Tér. Do you know who lives there? Do you know who she's seeing?'

'I don't know anything.'

'So you must help me find out,' he says, reaching for my hand across the table. I let him take it and try to look sympathetic. His hand is clammy, squeezing mine too tightly. 'Will you help me?'

His face is so pathetic that it's almost childlike. I want to get out of the café, go for a long walk somewhere, get lost. I swallow the last of my coffee and tell him that I have to leave. It's too cold to walk, so I climb onto a jolting tram without checking to see where it's going; before long all I can see is my own blurred reflection in the glass.

Will took me to his house in Westchester just once, when he came home a day early from his family's summer vacation. He made me wriggle down in the car, in case any of the neighbours spotted me. I could only sit up when we were safely enclosed in the garage, parked next to the other car – a blue Volvo, expansive enough for dogs and hockey sticks and bags of groceries. Unstable shelves and children's bicycles hung on the walls. The house was big and open, and Will stalked around the kitchen and the sunken living room, yanking curtains shut. I sat still, legs outstretched. The floor was cool beneath my bare shins, and I focused on the framed picture above the fireplace, an old map of Massachusetts.

'Keep away from the windows,' he said, turning off the light in the dining room. He chose some wine from his cellar in the basement, and then left me sitting on a sagging L-shaped couch in the living room while he carried his bags upstairs. I sat holding my drink, feeling small in the cavernous room, swallowed whole.

Once it was dark, Will gave me a tour of the house. He was at once shy and proud, like a child bringing a friend home from school for the first time, pointing out blinds due to be replaced, a bench bought in Indonesia, the walk-in closet larger than his daughter's room. I drifted through the rooms like a trespassing ghost. I was used to a small one-bedroom apartment: this was the first real house I'd been to in months. It felt bigger than a city, and far away from anywhere I recognised or could navigate without a map. I had no idea how to get anywhere from here – certainly no idea how to find my way home.

He swung open the door to the bedroom where we would sleep that night. The bed was high, with an embroidered white spread. On the bureau, a pair of his wife's earrings lay discarded in a dish, next to a framed photograph. His wife – angular, thin-lipped, her dark hair bobbed – was laughing, holding the hand of their oldest son. In the photo Will was heavier, and his hair was still black.

'It's the first time I've brought anyone home,' he said, and I knew he meant it as a compliment, not as a reminder that I wasn't his first mistress.

The next morning, while Will was shaving, I lay in bed with my eyes closed, trying to imagine myself living in that house, even though it was the most unlikely of all possible outcomes. I'd never imagined myself as a suburban wife, but that day I wanted it more than anything. I wanted to swaddle myself in that life, to pull it on like a well-cut coat. The guise of mistress didn't suit me: it was too much like my job, where associates and analysts were supposed to be uncomplaining and enthusiastic, never making demands, always available. Everything was about the MDs and VPs, making them sound smart and look good. However late I worked or early I started, at work I had to appear poised and industrious and keen. All the associates were good at hiding what they truly thought: showing dread or uncertainty would only reveal weakness. When Will and I were out together, we laughed all the time. I never let him see how I'd made myself miserable with hope.

He came out of the bathroom, towelling his hair dry.

'We have to go now, sweetie,' he said. His eyes were shining, bright blue flecked with gold. I tumbled out of bed and pulled on my clothes, and Will wandered into the walk-in closet, whistling.

I bent over his wife's side of the bed to smooth the sheets. The elastic band in my hair had wriggled free during the night and lay half obscured under a pillow. I poked at it with one finger, pushing it a little further under the pillow. I could leave it there, I thought: one small trace of myself in that perfect white house. This evening, his wife would pull back the covers and find it, a thin circlet woolly with blonde hair. She would know that I existed. She would know that I had slept in her bed.

Will walked back into the room, looking at me in a tender

and slightly anxious way, like I was a sick child.

'Don't forget me,' he said, as if I was about to embark on a long journey somewhere foreign and dangerous that day rather than just return to my place in Brooklyn Heights. 'Will you?'

I shook my head.

'Are you sure you have everything?' He glanced at his reflection in the mirror, jingling his pocketed car keys. He was impatient to leave, to drive me home and get back to his own real life again. His family would be here this afternoon. 'Don't leave anything, will you?'

He walked away down the hallway, whistling again.

I picked up the elastic band, twisted it into my hair and followed him downstairs to the garage.

A few days after our dinner, Zoltan drives me deep into the patchy, grey hills of Buda to find the socialist statues. Because I'm spending so much time alone, it's good to be out with someone, and – though I'd never admit it to Peter and Eva – Zoltan is the ideal person to hang out with right now. He asks me very few questions. He shows little interest in where I live, or where I'm from, or what I do. He even seems to have forgotten our kiss in the car.

The city peters out some time before we arrive at the park, a small treeless stretch of gravel on top of a low hill. It's bordered on one side by the main road, which backs onto a field of pylons, and on the other by a scattering of houses. We are the only visitors there.

Zoltan has several dozen statues to choose from and fixes on one at the end of the path. It's a running man wearing worker's clothes, one fist clenched, the other dragging a bronze flag.

'It's a Republic of Councils monument,' I read from the English guide provided at the main entrance. 'It used to stand in the City Park, across from the statue of Lenin.'

Zoltan crouches on the gravel to draw. The statue is huge, five time his height, with immense thighs and disproportionately long arms. It looks like Marlon Brando.

'It was placed on the site of a church that was destroyed in the '50s to build Parade Square,' I tell him. 'Is that Heroes Square now?'

Zoltan grunted.

'And after the statue was moved here, a cross was erected where the church stood. This is very confusing.' I put the book away and, for the next half hour, wander around the other statues while Zoltan works. The most striking is a statue of a Soviet Soldier holding a flagstaff, his rifle across his chest. The top of my head just reaches the hem of his coat. His face is lifted to the sun, eyes closed, and the flag hangs lank behind him. From the plaque nearby I learn that he once stood on Gellert Hill overlooking the Danube, a memorial to the Red Army that once towered over the other monuments on the hill – one to Saint Gellert and one to some long-ago victory over Austria. Most of the Red Army memorial was still standing on the hill. The soldier, massive and splendid, was its only exile, now guarding a telephone box, a wire fence and a few barking dogs.

'Not even the flag moves,' says Zoltan, walking up behind me. He shakes his head at me, laughing. 'You have found the most still of all the statues.'

'You don't have to draw this. I'm just looking at it.'

'We should go now. Maybe you would you like to see Saint Stephen's hand?'

At the Basilica, a German tour group follows us into the side chapel housing the relic. The room is cluttered with wooden chairs, the kind you sit on at school plays; handmade displays about the church's renovations line the walls. A miniature gold cathedral sits at the end of the room, surrounded by people.

A tour guide feeds change into a meter to illuminate the display. I push up through the crowd, many of whom are laughing, the quiet, nervous laugh of people uncertain about what they're seeing. No one stays long to gaze at it. Zoltan doesn't bother to look at all, waiting for me on one of the wooden chairs at the back.

Inside its gilt palace, the shrivelled hand lies sealed inside a glass canister, like Snow White in her transparent coffin, except the hand is a deep chocolate brown, the colour of excrement and almost the same shape. From the side of the case, it looks like an infant's clenched fist, a small thumb clearly visible. I try to imagine the act of amputation, the men gathering around the dead king to slice off his right hand and preserve it for centuries of subjects, patriots, and believers.

Zoltan is amused by my fascination with this tiny, sodden package of decayed flesh.

'If you like hands, Anna,' he says, 'you should see the big hand of Stalin.'

That hand, he tells me, is the only remnant of a giant statue destroyed a few weeks before the Russian invasion began in 1956.

'The statue was very big,' he says, fingering his car keys in his pocket. 'The hand is the only part left. The rest they smashed up. People took pieces of it, like the Berlin Wall.'

'Did anything happen to your family then – in 1956, I mean?' I ask him, but Zoltan is already on his way back down the stairs and doesn't appear to hear the question.

I sit outside the American Embassy on a lopsided bench, waiting for Eva to finish work. The Embassy is the colour and texture of lemon peel, shuttered against the weak, late-afternoon sun. I can't find a comfortable position on the grubby, warped planks of the bench. Beyond the pointed gold star on top of some memorial is the spire of the Parliament building. The drab Hungarian Television block where Eva works lies across the Square.

I'm used to waiting. For a long time it felt like a permanent state. Standing on the steps of my building, watching for Will's car. In hotel rooms, flicking through a magazine, waiting for his footstep in the passageway. Outside a parking lot, cold searing through the soles of my shoes, humming to myself to pass the time. Will waited for me at corners, wearing sunglasses and a foolish expression, or at bars, where my drink was bought for me before I arrived, or in restaurants, where he was always impatient to order. I could recognise at a glance the shape his face took as he waited to cross the street, or looked for me through the window of his car. I knew the way he would see me and then look away, without smiling, without recognition, as if we had not been waiting for that moment all week. Even after we stopped seeing each other, I couldn't stop looking for him, expecting

– hoping – to see him everywhere.

Eva is walking towards me, wearing a long brown coat. She looks exactly as she did when I first met her, the same slim, haughty face, her mischievous smile. She waves to me and lengthens her stride.

'You have been waiting long? We can cross the Chain Bridge if you are not too cold.' We start walking, arms linked. 'You know, I had to buy this coat in Vienna, which meant I was practically bankrupt. But the clothes here are terrible.'

She continues in this vein as we walk home, pointing out fashion atrocities in shop windows.

'Maybe you can do some shopping while you're here,' she suggests in her most derisive voice, the one she usually reserves for Peter.

Apart from her coat, Eva's clothes are mostly American. Her bag is a Prada knock-off, which another friend bought for her in Chinatown. She wouldn't dream of carrying it in New York, she tells me, because people there would know it wasn't the real thing.

We stop to photograph each other on a traffic island by the river. Eva poses in her sunglasses and doesn't smile. The sky is broad and blue behind her head. She makes two attempts to reciprocate, but is too impatient for the shutter to click, upturning the camera twice to check just as the camera flashes at her face.

'So it will either be sky or my chin, I'm sorry,' she says, handing the camera back to me. 'But you have only taken six photographs? Not all of Peter, I hope.'

We walk to a brightly lit Mexican bar, where the American bartender makes me a succession of real martinis. Eva complains about Hungary and Peter interchangeably. She has decided that they're both holding her back.

'Ever since I returned, I am an outsider. That's how my mother and her boyfriend see me. They are always asking me when I'm getting married. They say, you are nearly thirty now, and everyone in Hungary is married. I can't bear it.'

'*They're* not married, right?'

'She's still married to my father. She says terrible things about him always. I can't bear it.'

'Will you ever marry Peter?'

Eva looks pensive, swirling her drink around in its glass.

'Actually,' she says, 'I had my fortune told – my palm, you know? And the fortune-teller said that my future was here, in Hungary, and that I could go, but I would always return. Should always return,' she corrects herself. 'Because this is where my life will be lived.'

'I've never had my palm read,' I tell her. Eva reaches for my hand across the table.

'Let me see. You will probably have one child. No, two. Have you ever had an abortion?'

'No. I don't think I believe this.'

'And this is your love line. I'm not sure what that means.' She jabs her finger into my palm. 'And this bit here,' she says, prodding the haunch of my thumb, 'this means you like sex, a lot. But I already knew that about you. That's why I wanted you to meet Zoltan.'

I pull my hand away. 'You still haven't answered my question about Peter.'

Eva pouts her lips and rolls her eyes, a fantastic trick that gives her the appearance of an elongated gargoyle.

'I don't know. We are very different. But I can't imagine him not *being* here.'

This is the kindest thing I have ever heard her say about him, and she immediately seems to regret it. Her face hardens.

'But he is jealous of my job and very suspicious of all the people I meet. He thinks I will become a celebrity, reading the news, meeting politicians, and then I will be bored with him.'

'I'm not sure how you could be more bored with him than you are already.'

Eva grins. 'I like to make him suspicious. For no reason, you understand – there is no one else. I don't have the time.'

'Well, it's working. I'd ask you why you like tormenting him so much, but I don't think I want to know.'

Eva looks very pleased at this.

'My dear Anna, of course not!' she chortles. 'You certainly do not want to know all the horrible things that go on inside other people's heads. But now you must tell me if you are in love with Zoltan. He is not bad at all, for a Hungarian.'

Zoltan positions himself against the bridge's railing, halfway between the first arch and the stone lion's pedestal.

'Walk – from there,' he points to the lion, 'to there.'

Light rain is falling, but I walk up and down, up and down, swinging my arms, my head high in the air. Zoltan doesn't seem to notice the rain, even though it's smudging his drawings. I'm walking at a stilted, unnatural pace, almost in slow motion, thinking it's easier for Zoltan to draw that way. He says nothing, giving me no other directions. His pencil sweeps the page, and he turns the leaves of his pad briskly, drawing me from left to right, and then in reverse after I pivot at the base of the lion.

We're here on the Chain Bridge because Zoltan wants to try drawing a moving figure again. He's tired of statues. I've abandoned Eva, who is meeting Peter at an exhibition and demanded that I act as a human shield. Going out with Zoltan was the only excuse she'd accept, though I didn't tell her the assignation was work-related, for him at least. Even though it's raining I don't mind walking back and forth along the bridge. It's a relief to be free of the Eva-and-Peter drama for a few hours.

Zoltan stops me and points out a man, standing under one of the arches, who's begun playing the violin.

'He taps his foot out of time,' he says. We listen to the man play for a while until Zoltan asks me to start walking again.

At first I just concentrate on the movement, avoiding the gaze of other pedestrians. I fix my eyes on my two targets and begin walking more quickly, waiting for Zoltan to say something. Soon I'm striding back and forth, as fast as I can without running. He doesn't ask me to slow down. After a while I no longer notice people, not even Zoltan, who changes his position at some point. Before long I can't see the lions, or the stone pediments, or the four lamps I have to traverse on my way to the arch.

When heavy rain begins dousing the bridge, Zoltan calls to me to stop; we run to his car and he drives me to his apartment. In its small, drab living room, we look through the sheaf of sketches.

'Maybe there is something,' he says. He points to a drawing of my arm swinging in its long black sleeve. The arm looks ready to float free from my shoulder.

I want to turn on the television to see if Eva is on the early news, but Zoltan's set isn't working. He drops the papers onto the floor.

'Take off your clothes,' he says, in the same tone he used on the bridge when he asked me to walk. I do what he asks, slowly, folding each item and laying it on the chair. He stands in the doorway leading to the bedroom, looking at me. I begin to move towards him.

'Stay,' he says, abruptly raising his hand the way he did in the bar the night we met. The distance between us makes me uncomfortable. I feel self-conscious, tired of being looked at.

'I don't want to stand anymore,' I say, walking past him into the bedroom. The bed is unmade and narrow. I perch at the end. Zoltan follows me in and sits down next to me, pulling his sweater over his head.

'Eva says that the Chain Bridge was blown up by the Germans at the end of the war,' I tell him. 'She says the lions were damaged. One of them's in a museum, falling to pieces.'

Zoltan says nothing, bending to pull his socks off.

'So the lions on the bridge now are replicas of the old lions.'

'It's a long time since that war.' He stands up to shuffle out of his jeans. 'The new lions are not so young. They have no tongues, did you see?'

'No.' I feel very cold without my clothes on. 'I didn't notice. All the time we spent on the bridge.'

'Nearly fifty years,' Zoltan says, smiling, and I'm not sure if he's teasing me. He's naked now too, leaning against my thighs, pressing me backwards against the bed. His body, thick and hairy, seems immensely strong. When his mouth rubs the side of my face and neck, my skin feels tingling and sticky in its wake. He swings on top of me, and I ripple my body against his. We lick at each other's faces, suddenly greedy, the way dogs drink water.

He pulls my hair back, wrenching it upward from the roots, and the motion jerks my head back. His fists, full of my hair, knock against the flimsy headboard. I dig my fingernails into his earlobes till he winces and we breathe tight into each other's faces. His eyes are so close to mine I can't see them both clearly: they merge with his eyebrows into one thick, dark line.

Zoltan's mouth gapes open and I look straight into it, at his uneven teeth, the pulleys of saliva and the thicket of white veins beneath his tongue. I want to put my head inside his mouth, to be swallowed. He lets go of my hair and moves my legs further apart; I stretch them taut, waiting for him to push into me. He's holding his breath, but I'm panting in a way that lifts my chest, as though I've been running, When he slides in and out of me, I tighten my thighs, watching the way he twists his head back each time. I wish I were inside him. I wish I could crawl into him and disappear – creep into his brambles of arteries and bones and sinew, slither past each pulsing organ on my way, leak like sweat into his eyes and ears and nose.

I imagine curling up inside him, spinning head over heels, and feel his body moving, counting time. I close my eyes to listen for the music in his head. It's there, distant and off-key. A fiddler is playing the same phrase over and over and taps his foot on the cobblestone, not quite in time.

There's the sound of footsteps, the sharp click of heels. A woman walks along the bridge, her arms swinging. She passes by so quickly that she's just a blur of movement, arms, fair hair, a long black coat. She walks up and down, but I can't quite see her face. It's getting dark, and there's a light rain falling. It's too hard to make out her features. She could be anyone.

I open my eyes and look at Zoltan. His expression is fixed, intensifying into a slight grimace when he comes, though he still doesn't make a sound. His eyes glaze over, and he flinches, then shudders, as if he's been hit on the back of the head. We lie face to face but his eyes are like dirty windows, reflecting nothing.

The last evening Will and I spent together was not long after the New Year. It had been a mild, cloudy day, and rain was falling by the time I left work. He picked me up a few blocks from the office: we were driving to my place, to eat dinner nearby. Sometimes we had sex in my apartment before we ate, in case the service was slow and we ran out of time. Sometimes one or both of us worked so late there was no time for anything but sex.

The rain grew heavier as we crossed the Brooklyn Bridge.

'This is very difficult,' he said, speaking quickly, his face red. I stared straight ahead out the windscreen and listened to him make his rehearsed speech.

He said all the things that people say in movies. He talked

in a cold, high-pitched voice, his right hand closed like a fist over the stick shift. I looked out my window through the taut lines of the bridge to the water below.

'She and I, we have too much history.' His knuckles were pale, and his hands appeared much smaller than usual. He looked like a child in a toy car, dwarfed by the grandeur of the bridge. He spoke in short, nervous bursts. The moment seemed familiar, mundane.

I squinted out the window at the dark water, the dark sky. The car turned off the bridge, and we sat waiting for the lights to change.

'Of course, I trust you to be discreet,' Will said, as if he were concluding a meeting. I turned to get a side view of his handsome face, its ruddiness and stray eyebrow hair, its familiar furrows and grey bristles. He was saying the same thing again, and this time it was a question. He didn't really trust me at all. The words quivered not with the emotion of leaving me, but because he was anxious I'd make trouble for him.

Without meaning to, without thinking about it, I got out of the car and closed the door. Skirting the other cars, I climbed up a bank of scruffy bushes, scratching my shins. The heel of one of my shoes caught on the railings of the low fence. I clambered up onto the sidewalk and walked as fast as I could to the bridge's stairs.

My coat was still in the car, so my jacket and skirt and hose were soon soaked through, stuck to my skin. I kept pushing my hair back out of my face because my bangs were dripping into my eyes; rain ran down the back of my neck and into my shoes and bag.

The boardwalk runs along the centre of the bridge, high above the traffic. That night it was nearly deserted because of the rain, except for a cyclist or two and some determined joggers, their faces shrouded in rain hoods. I marched over the planks, following the painted dividing line towards the lights of the city. My feet sloshed in shoes that felt too big now; my skirt clung to my legs, rubbing them like damp cardboard every time I took a step. A man in a blue raincoat approached and passed me on the other side of the boardwalk, muttering something vaguely obscene. The bridge seemed to go on forever. When I got to the other side of the river, I couldn't find a cab and had to ride home, soaked and shivering, on the subway. Will had left my coat in the entryway to my house, bundled under the mailboxes, but there was no note, no phone message.

I don't know why I walked all that way in the rain, the wrong direction from home. Running back to Manhattan wouldn't change anything; it wouldn't reverse the things said in the car on the drive across the bridge. Maybe I expected him to park the car and follow me up onto the bridge, running after me, shouting my name. At any minute, I would hear his footsteps, quick and firm, behind me on the boardwalk. He would come for me. He wouldn't let me go.

Although some part of me that was still rational knew that none of this would happen, I was still hoping he'd change his mind and come looking for me when I reached the stoplights near City Hall. I hoped all the way home on the subway, every time my phone rang, every time I saw a car like his. I hoped it every day when I walked into the building where I worked and saw him getting into an elevator, or walking into a conference room. I hoped for week after week, until

I couldn't tell the difference between hope and delusion anymore, until I was assigned to his team again for a big pitch in Zurich, in part because I could speak German and some French, and I could tell by the way he talked to me and looked at me in our first meeting – cold, impatient – that everything was over.

A few days before I'm due to leave Budapest, Eva takes me to the Gellert Baths. We swim in circles for a while in the big indoor pool, past thick marble columns and lions' heads that dribble water onto us. The baths are crowded with hotel guests in white towelling robes and shower caps, waddling old ladies with pointed cups in their bathing suits, young men in goggles and tight nylon shorts. In the women's Turkish baths we strip in cubicles that reek of chlorine and walk to a dark tiled pool. Eva is tired, her head resting on the ledge, thin arms outstretched.

'And what are you thinking now, Anna?' she says, closing her eyes.

'Nothing much,' I say. 'Just that I'm sitting around naked in Eastern Europe.'

Eva's laugh is raucous, and several of the other women look over at us.

'But,' she says, in a quieter voice, 'this must make you feel very skinny indeed.'

We sit giggling like teenagers.

'I will miss you when you go,' she says. 'Even though I have seen absolutely nothing of you, because you are so very besotted with Zoltan, and statues, and hands that have been cut off, and trams that go nowhere.'

'Maybe you'll come visit me in New York soon.'

'Hmmm. Maybe.' Eva dismisses this idea, splashing the water with the flat of her hand. 'Could you ever live in Hungary, do you think?'

'Perhaps,' I say. 'I wouldn't mind, really.'

'No, no,' she says, shaking her head. 'You wouldn't *mind*? It's like a punishment living here.' She starts laughing. 'Of course you would mind. You would *abhor* it here. You could never get an amazing job like yours over here.'

'I should have told you this.' The steam flushes my face. 'I mean, I should have told you before. I got fired from my job last month.'

Though I've grown so used to holding everything in, it's a relief to tell Eva this at last.

'No!' She's horrified. 'But why? You are a star. It makes no sense.'

'I wasn't really a star,' I tell her. 'But it was over small things, really.'

I explained it to her as best I could, knowing how ridiculous it would sound to someone outside the industry. When we worked after eight pm, we were allowed to order food as long as the bill per person was under thirty dollars. Associates and analysts often spent more than that, writing names of co-workers who'd already gone home on their receipts and expense reports to justify the cost. At the start of the Zurich airport project, the analyst and I worked late every night for a week. On the Friday night, I let him go before eight – it was his anniversary; his girlfriend had made reservations at Jean-Georges – and ordered forty-five dollars worth of Thai food for myself, so I'd have leftovers to eat at home that weekend.

'They fired you over take-out food?' Eva is aghast.

'That, plus a few weeks earlier I'd been in San Francisco for some meetings, and I kept the rental car on Saturday instead of returning it right away. Investment banks are really strict about this kind of thing.' I tell her about the guy at Morgan Stanley sacked for forwarding a personal email; I explain how email is monitored all the time. She shakes her head in disbelief. 'Someone went through my expense reports pretty thoroughly and found a few discrepancies. That's all they need. Every so often, they have crackdowns when they think staff are getting too complacent.'

This is true, but I don't think it was true in my case. I wasn't the worst offender by any means in my pool of junior bankers. The guy who was fired back at Morgan Stanley was one of the weakest of the new analysts; everyone saw it as an excuse to get rid of him. My work record wasn't the problem. The managing director on the last pitch I was working on told me that in another year, I could make assistant vice president.

'It's like this country under the communists,' says Eva. 'You poor thing! What will you do?'

'Look for another job,' I reply. Between this trip and my rent, my savings are already dwindling. 'Maybe in another city. I have so much debt from school – living somewhere cheaper wouldn't be a bad thing.'

'Maybe over here – why not?'

'Europe's expensive these days,' I tell her. In the year and a half I was at the company, I'd gone on three European work trips with Will: Paris, London, Munich. These were the best of times for us. We could eat dinner together every night, albeit with clients and other colleagues present; we could sleep together every night in his hotel room – always his, in case his wife called the hotel instead of his cell phone. We never had to call each other. He made sure to build unnecessary extra time into each trip, so we could stay over a Saturday and have time to wander around, another night to spend in one bed.

The thought of going back to these places now made me feel sick. Any of the cities we explored together, any of the cities he visited when I stayed at home – looking up the time difference, waiting for his call, looking forward to the gifts he brought back for me – were items on a list I couldn't bear to read. Forbidden cities, I think of them now. Places I associate with my own stupidity, my own hubris.

Eva is chattering about how, some day, Zoltan's work will be selected for the Venice Biennale, and his rich patrons will shower him with money.

'He will buy a big house in Budapest and you will live in it,' she declares. She stands up abruptly, a slender, sultry Venus, her skin a little pink from the hot water. Some of the other women are frowning at her. 'Look at all these pigs wallowing in the mud!'

I follow her out of the pool, swishing through the water.

'You must insist on a maid,' she advises, 'because I think Zoltan is very dirty. And he can beat her whenever he must prove his Hungarian manhood.'

We both start laughing. Back in the changing rooms, I can hear Eva chuckling through the walls of her cubicle while we get dressed. There's a thud as she falls against the wall, trying to put on her shoes, and this makes us laugh even harder. The locker attendant gives us a stern look, as though we're drunk, and we stagger into the lobby with our arms linked.

Leaning over the mezzanine balcony is Peter, waiting for us to come out. His head looks tiny against the high vaults of the ceiling, but I can just make out his expression, a mixture of disappointment and relief. He shouts something and the sound, harsh and choked, echoes away through the lobby.

'It's Peter,' I tell her, though I'm sure she's seen him as well.

'Ignore him,' Eva tells me, screwing up her face. We walk out into the street towards the river, towards the bridge, heads held high.

'Do you think we've lost him?'

'No. Don't look back,' she says. Her arm tenses; she's excited. 'Pretend he's not there.'

'What if he catches us?' I say, and she giggles, as though we're playing a child's game. Eva starts to run, pulling me along at first, then dropping my arm so she can run faster.

'Run, Anna, run!' she shouts, sprinting ahead of me. I slow to a walk and then stop, watching her bound along the pavement towards the other side of the river. Her coat flaps behind her; her bag bounces against her hip.

There are other things about the day I was fired, things I can't tell her. We were due to leave for Zurich that night: an analyst, a vice-president, Will – who was the project's MD, the person the Swiss office had particularly requested – and me. He called me into his office and told me, in one breathless sentence, that I wouldn't be flying to Europe with them after all, that I had to be replaced. Down in HR, they'd explain everything, he said, picking up a stack of papers, not looking me in the eye. Someone was waiting in the doorway, poised to lead me away.

And yes, down in HR everything was explained. I had broken small but significant rules: I had to hand over my ID and leave the building under escort. My purse, suitcase, and coat had been retrieved from my cubicle, so there was no reason for me to return to my floor. This was the coat I'd abandoned in Will's car, the one he'd left for me in the vestibule of my building. The next day at work, the day after he ended our relationship, I'd sent him an email. It read: Thanks for returning my coat.

These were the things I shouldn't have done: stayed in the city to go to grad school; racked up another hundred grand in student loans; gone to work at Gorman Parker; embarked on an affair with a managing director; imagined that the relationship might have a future; sent him an email that other people might see, that might make other people ask questions; broken the rules.

Eva is out of sight, somewhere on the other side of the river. I turn around. A number of people are walking along the bridge, heads bent against the wind, but I can't see Peter anywhere. He must have given up, or not realised we were crossing the river. Perhaps it wasn't Peter in the baths at all, and I just imagined him calling Eva's name. I stand there staring, scanning the unsmiling faces for one that I recognise, but there's no one.

No one looking for me. No one following me, no one calling my name. Nobody's running after me to say he's changed his mind. There's no point in standing here, waiting. I have to keep walking across the river, across the bridge.

Acknowledgements

Creative New Zealand; The Michael King Writers' Centre; Bill Manhire, Glenn Schaeffer, and the International Institute of Modern Letters; Tulane University's Georges Lurcy Faculty Research Fund, Research Enhancement Fund, and Committee on Research Summer Fellowship; Geoff Walker and Harriet Elworthy at Penguin; John Huria; James Alan McPherson, the late Frank Conroy, Marilynne Robinson, Ethan Canin, and Elizabeth McCracken; Sarah Rogers, Rebecca Johns, Michelle Falkoff, Bjorn Nordfjord, and Leeann and Steve Paterson; Ginger Strand, John Authers, Susan Aasen; Matthew Hill, Martha Carillo, Lynn-Elisabeth Hill, and Tom Moody.